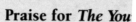

S. J. Short is an Australian author residing in Canada.

After a decade writing the lighter side of fiction, she woke up one day with a need to go to the dark side. Her first thriller, *The Young Widows*, was plotted over a single dinner with her husband, who was nervous that after ten years of writing happily ever afters she suddenly wanted to write about murder.

Now she writes twisty, female-centric mysteries and can often be found pondering the perfect way to kill someone. She lives in Toronto with her husband, where she writes with a glorious view of Lake Ontario and her coffee machine at arm's reach.

THE YOUNG WIDOWS

S. J. SHORT

avon.

Published by AVON
A division of HarperCollins*Publishers*
1 London Bridge Street
London SE1 9GF

www.harpercollins.co.uk

HarperCollins*Publishers*
Macken House
39/40 Mayor Street Upper
Dublin 1
D01 C9W8

A Paperback Original 2024
1
First published in Great Britain by HarperCollins*Publishers* 2024

A catalogue copy of this book is available from the British Library.

ISBN: 978-0-00-867286-7

Typeset by Palimpsest Book Production Ltd, Falkirk, Stirlingshire

Printed and bound in the UK using
100% Renewable Electricity by CPI Group (UK) Ltd

MIX
Paper | Supporting
responsible forestry
FSC™ C007454

This book contains FSC™ certified paper and other controlled
sources to ensure responsible forest management.

For more information visit: www.harpercollins.co.uk/green

To my husband, thank goodness you didn't inspire this one.

Prologue

Now

He thinks he should feel something. Anything.

But for the moment, he's numb. A woman stands in front of him, like a goddess with electric eyes and a smile fuelled by fury. Her teeth are bared. She is ready for battle. Overhead, rain pelts down from a charred sky, relentlessly soaking them through. Her body is rendered near-naked as wet fabric clings to every line and curve, becoming more translucent by the second, and yet she doesn't move to shield herself.

She is going to kill him.

Cold droplets slide down the back of his neck into his shirt collar and the wind drills into his bones. His tie is a noose. He trusted her. Appreciated her. Told her things about himself that he would never tell another living soul.

Was he perfect? Far from it.

But he never expected her to fight back. Not like this. What happened to the pliable, manageable modelling-clay woman she was yesterday? How did she surprise him like this? How did she best him?

1

He looks over the edge of the balcony. There's a pool below and the water ripples in the wind, splashing over the edge like waves on a beach. The air howls. Taunting him. Condemning him. Beckoning him. The floor tilts beneath his feet. There's a deep churning sensation in his stomach and he's sure that he will throw up the meal he ate a few hours ago. The sensation swells. There's acid in his throat.

But he can't move.

Shock has turned him to petrified wood. He is a statue of a man realising that the tables have been permanently turned. He's a fool. A loser. A fly in a spider's web.

'You . . . you drugged me.' His words are slurred, his tongue dense and thick as a plank of wood. Yet his mind races.

'Yes,' she replies. It feels as though she can look inside him, all his fears and regrets flickering in his brain like a slide show. 'I did drug you.'

'Why?' His voice is a whine.

In front of him, she sways, but she hasn't moved an inch. He blinks. The image is all wrong. Things aren't moving the way they should. It's like the world has become liquid, without structure. Everything is slipping through his fingers.

'Because you deserve it.' She takes a step forward, the length of her dress clinging to her legs in the rain. Water runs in rivulets over her shoulders and arms and cheeks. At first he thought she might be crying, but there is nothing but victory in her eyes. 'This is for everyone you've hurt. For all of us.'

Then she pushes him.

His body tumbles, graceless and forceful, over the balcony and towards the ground. It all happens so fast. One minute he's standing, and the next he's flying. The world comes in flashes of colour – terracotta tile, blue water, lush green grass, charcoal clouds. He doesn't even have a moment to scream because his mind and body aren't connected anymore. The drugs have addled him.

He lands with a great thud on the edge of the pool, the impact to his head so bright and sharp that whiteness explodes in his vision. He feels the weightlessness of the water before he even registers that he's rolled into the pool, and the velocity makes him sink, sink, sink all the way to the bottom. There's a breath-stealing pain in his face; something is broken.

Come on. Swim!

But his body won't cooperate. He naturally drifts back up, but not fast enough. Water has filled his mouth and nostrils, the taste of chlorine hitting the back of his tongue and burning his eyes. He has no energy to struggle. It's so peaceful down here, so serene. Maybe he should take a nap. He's so very tired. Digging deep, he finds the basal desire to live and kicks his feet. It's like wading through honey. Red tendrils of blood curl like smoke in the water around him. But he can't think about that. He can't think at all.

Just swim.

The surface is within reach. So close. Yet each stroke makes fire burn in his lungs and all he can see are shifting shapes above. His hand breaks the surface of the water, but he can't find a ledge. His eyes close for a moment as he tries for one last burst of energy, but no amount of kicking his leaden, sluggish legs seems to work. Something is blocking him. It's too far away. Too hard. Too much.

Please. I want to live.

His eyes grow heavy. Darkness creeps into his vision like a slow-moving fog. This is it. The end.

As he loses the fight, he registers that there's a pressure on his head. Something is holding him down. He starts to sink again, eyes opening and closing slowly, the world draining away in long, languid blinks. His lungs are on fire. The world is distorted through the water, grotesque and bloated, like he will be soon. This will be the last thing he remembers.

A flash of red. A face.

She's watching him as he drowns, not moving a muscle to help. Waiting. Hoping. There's no air left. He must give in to the pull of the drugs and the comforting nothingness of the water. It's time to sleep. Time to rest.

He has no more fight left.

The past has finally caught up with him.

PART ONE

Chapter One

Earlier

Kylie

I open and close my mouth, but it feels like cotton wool has been stuffed in there. It's sucking the life out of me. My tongue sticks to the roof of my mouth like how the Communion wafers used to when I was a kid and my father dragged me to church on Sunday mornings. Only now, instead of tasting like stale unsweetened wafer, my mouth tastes like the inside of a rubbish bin.

I grind one fist into gritty eyes and find my other arm has gone to sleep. Pins and needles shoot down from my shoulder as I try to open and close my hand, forcing the blood to pump back into where it's been cut off from being stuck under my body. I'm on my back, staring up at a ceiling. I know it's not mine because the white paint doesn't have an ugly crack running through it. It's also missing the cobwebs swaying in the corners and the spot of bubbling from water damage when the apartment above us flooded their bathtub.

Where am I?

With great effort, I roll onto my side, my dead arm still tingling. I'm in a hotel room. The view looks right out over Melbourne's central business district and the city glitters, sunlight bouncing off the office towers and apartment complexes as the Yarra River cuts a snaking line through it all. From up here, the reflection of the sky makes the water look blue when I know, in fact, that it's a muddy, murky brown, like always.

But the view isn't the only beautiful thing here – the inside of the room holds its own. There's a blue velvet couch and a huge telly and—

Holy shit, is that a six-seater dining table?

I push up into a sitting position, my head pounding in protest. This isn't any old hotel room. This is a suite. An expensive one.

What the bloody hell happened last night?

There's a soft knock at the door.

'Housekeeping.'

Shit.

'Just a sec!' I call back.

I'm naked as the day I was born. Swinging my hand down over the edge of the bed, I grope for the dress that lies crumpled on the floor. The black fabric has a chic side panel of wet-look material and it gleams in the bright sunlight. I get off the bed and pull the dress over my head, not even bothering to locate my bra.

Did I even wear a bra last night? I don't remember that. I don't remember *anything*.

My underwear, thankfully, is within easy reach and I pull it up over my thighs and hips, smoothing the dress back down over the top. That's better. I catch a glimpse of myself in a large gilt mirror hanging on the far wall, and I look like something meant to scare small children—tangled mass of red hair, soot-smudged eyes, and a grim expression. I'm paler than usual and there's a smear of red at the corner of my lips. I catch it with my thumb, rubbing to remove it but the action only makes it worse. My head pounds like someone is jamming a fist against the back of my eye, using my skull as a punching bag.

The knocking starts again.

'I said just a sec.' This time my words have an edge to them.

It must be well past the check-out time. So what's new? Dad always used to say my name was Kylie 'Be-there-in-a-sec' Robins. Perpetually late, perpetually disorganised, perpetually on the back foot. Or so people thought. When I was younger, I claimed I didn't care if people underestimated me because then I had the chance to take them by surprise. Nobody suspects the hot mess to pull a rabbit out of a hat.

These days, though, I'm not being underestimated. I am being accurately estimated.

I hear the electronic lock whirr as I grab my handbag from one of the velvet seats by a small round table where a bottle of champagne sits in a silver bucket, the ice long melted. My bag has been tipped over and its contents – a chaotic rainbow of receipts and chocolate bar wrappers and pots of lip balm and bobby pins – are scattered on the couch. I scoop them back in.

On the table, another bottle of champagne lies on

its side, a small dribble of gold liquid shimmering on the glass surface. A third bottle sits on the floor. It has maybe a quarter left in it and I won't lie, if it weren't for the housekeeper standing in the doorway, her judgement boring into me like lasers, I would have taken a swig.

That's another Dad-ism for you: grog is grog – doesn't matter if it comes from a bottle or a bag, drink enough and it'll work just the same.

Maybe that wasn't the best lesson to have taken from him, in hindsight. But for a moment, I seriously contemplate absorbing the housekeeper's disgust and having a sip. My tongue darts out in anticipation. Despite being wildly hungover, I know it will make me feel good. Take the edge off. It always does. Hair of the dog – isn't that what they call it?

'I have to clean the room now,' the woman says. Her dark hair is pulled back into a severe bun and her uniform is perfectly starched. While her voice isn't raised, it's clipped with a slight accent that makes me want to shrink into something small so I can scurry past her without making eye contact.

Why do I give a shit what she thinks of me?

Deeply ingrained need for approval from a mother-type figure? Debilitating people-pleasing tendencies? Remnants of the hopeful stars-in-her-eyes girl I used to be before I married the wrong man and decided booze was better than therapy?

Pick one. Hell, pick all of them.

I sling my bag over my shoulder and stuff my feet into the glossy nude stilettos by the door. They immediately

10

pinch my feet, the patent leather stiff as though they've barely been worn. Confused, I reach down to wiggle them on my foot for a better fit. Then I catch a glimpse of the shiny, untouched red soles.

What the—?

I do *not* have the cash for these kinds of shoes. But they're here, in my room. There's a large shopping bag in front of me, and when I peer inside I see a box that says 'Louboutin' in fancy writing. There are several other items in the bag, things wrapped with fairy-floss tissue paper and others in smaller square boxes with gold embossing.

Inside the shoe box, I find the receipt. Over a thousand bucks for a pair? That's outrageous.

Curious, I dig further. There are several other treasures. A dress from Zimmerman, a bottle of Le Labo perfume, Coco de Mer lingerie in my size. For a moment, I wonder if I'm about to steal something. The shopping bag can't be mine. What if someone else is staying in the room and I've stepped into her shoes and am about to leave with her shopping haul?

But it's clearly past check-out time and no one else is here. On the table with the champagne bottles sit three flutes, one of them bearing a smudge of red lipstick. I try to remember what happened last night, but it's like peering into a thick fog. I see vague shapes moving, but nothing more. No details.

The housekeeper huffs, already ripping the covers off the bed. She probably thinks I'm a hooker. Without weighing the consequences, I grab my handbag and the shopping bag and walk as best I can in the towering

11

shoes. They feel like stilts and my ankles protest at the sharp angle. But as I go past the mirror on the way out of the room, I see that my legs look incredible.

There is always pain in beauty – that's what the director at the ballet company used to say. Nothing that looks good comes easy.

Thankfully, the hallway and lift are both empty and I take a moment to tame my hair back into a ponytail with a spare tie I dig out of my handbag. Using a makeup wipe, I clean up my eyes and the smudged lipstick as best I can. I really need to give up the heavy makeup. It always looks a mess the morning after.

I would know, because the 'morning after' version of me is the only one that feels real anymore; head pounding, stomach churning, regret swelling like a demon I've conjured from the dark depths of my mind. The day I lost Marcus, my entire life fell apart – and not only for the obvious reason. I loved him. I mourned him.

But my mourning was stunted when I found out what he'd done.

I slump back against the lift wall and roll the wrist on my right hand. It's still feeling sluggish from where I've slept on it, but as I gently move the joint around, I hiss in pain. Something doesn't feel right. A shadow of a bruise is forming. I must have fallen. Wouldn't be the first time.

'Won't be the last, either,' I mutter to myself.

Last time I missed the bottom step on a staircase and stumbled, slamming my hand into a wall, I ended up in hospital with a fractured little finger. I had to wear a splint and lie to my boss and all my colleagues that I'd taken a spill after mopping the floor at home. Clumsy Kylie. They knew it was bullshit of course – they'd seen me drink. Even when I thought I was hiding it, they knew.

Nobody was surprised when I got sacked.

A friend has been trying to get me to meet for lunch since our offices are close, but how am I supposed to tell her I'm not working there anymore? I don't think I could stand the pity if I told people the truth . . . that I was shitfaced at a work function and embarrassed my boss in front of a client; that said client then found me puking my guts up in the toilet of a swanky restaurant. That I was crying for my mother while it happened.

The next morning I got called in to the head honcho's office and was handed a box to pack up my desk. I didn't even try to convince them to give me another shot. What's the point? I wasn't going to earn their respect back.

As the lift stops on ground floor, I try to walk out with my head held high. This place is *fancy*. It takes me a minute, but then it clicks where I am: Crown Casino. The hotels rooms here cost a small fortune and the clientele are so *not* my people. I'm pretty sure if I told them I grew up in a crappy one-bedroom rental in Broadmeadows they wouldn't let me in.

I can't deny, however, that the lobby is magnificent. The space is vast and gold-tinted, with a huge floral arrangement surrounded by waiting benches and a behemoth modern chandelier hanging overhead. A woman walks past me, a man trailing behind her with a full set of Louis Vuitton luggage. She's wearing the same shoes as me, but she knows how to walk in them. Now I understand why the champagne bottles had those fancy orange labels on them, rather than the budget kind I usually order for a fun night.

My phone buzzes inside my bag and I fumble for it, wading through the chaos until my fingers brush the vibrating device. I wonder if it might give me a clue as to how I ended up here. But it doesn't. Isabel's name scrolls across the cracked screen and then I cringe when I remember what day it is: our weekly meeting.

The Young Widows Club is an informal support group of women who were widowed in our twenties. We're all approaching thirty now, but we've been meeting for the last three and a bit years.

Every single week.

In those early days, a week was all any of us could manage. Looking further ahead felt impossible because time after death slowed to a thick molasses. We've helped each other through a lot.

'Hey Izzy,' I say, wedging the phone between my ear and my shoulder so I can fish out my sunnies. My eyes are already protesting the light, and I haven't even made it outside yet. 'I'm running a bit behind.'

'No worries,' she says in her quiet, breathy voice. 'I wanted to check that you were still coming today. I only just arrived myself.'

She says that like she's also running late, but it's one minute to the hour so she's right on time. Isabel is one of those rare people who genuinely tries to make others feel better about themselves, even if they're pulling the same old shit they always do. Like I am now.

Good old Kylie 'Be-there-in-a-sec' Robins, at it again.

'I'm definitely coming,' I assure her.

In any other life, I wouldn't be friends with these women. Isabel is too sweet and kind, and Adriana is from another world. But our circumstances have bonded us in a way that none of that superficial stuff ever could. When we're together, those external differences fall away to leave the raw underbelly of who we are.

Broken, battered dolls with an animal side.

Our grief isn't pretty. It isn't romantic. It isn't even always healing. There's no *Eat, Pray, Love* go-and-find-yourself bullshit here.

'Great!' Her voice perks up. 'We've got a new person joining us today. Hannah. I've been telling her all about our group. She can't wait to meet you.'

'I'll be there in twenty minutes,' I say, knowing it will take me at least forty to get to Reservoir. But I don't want them to know where I am and where I've been.

'No rush,' Isabel says sweetly. 'Drive safe.'

As I'm about to put my phone into my bag and get into the taxi line in front of the hotel, my phone buzzes again. This time it's a text.

My darling Kylie, it's Francis. I'm so sorry I had to skip out early this morning. I hope you were comfortable in the room. I'd love to see you again.

I blink.

Who the hell is Francis?

Chapter Two

Adriana

I'm not driving today, which is unusual. I *always* drive. It's a strange relic of my life before, where I needed to prove my worth. I was the chauffeur, the personal assistant, the gofer, the be-everything-to-everyone girl.

The wife.

And I will be a wife again, soon.

I glance at my fiancé, Grant, as he navigates through the vaguely industrial streets of Melbourne's northern suburbs. We've been in the car for almost an hour. Once the small factory loft conversions and tram tracks give way to three-lane roads and high schools and sprawling Kmarts, I know we're getting close. On the nature strip, a couple of cockatoos hop around, fanning their crests and stretching out their pristine white wings, their screeches occasionally cutting in over the gentle hum of light traffic as we idle at a red light. The day is bright and we've rolled the windows down, letting in the balmy breeze and the warble of magpies.

I'm nervous.

I twist my engagement ring around my finger, the three-carat solitaire diamond almost grotesquely large compared to the one I used to wear. The one that's tucked away in a secret drawer in my office with a long-faded photo of my first husband who was a quality-over-quantity kind of man. But Grant insisted I get 'an upgrade' with this one and I'd had to hold back a defensive reply. There's no point arguing with him because it would only make him feel like he has to compete with a dead man. And nobody wins there. So I'd let the reply fizzle on the back of my tongue, filling my throat with sourness.

I know he didn't mean anything by it, other than wanting to treat me. I also know he has a complex about being the second husband and it's my job to make him feel like there's never been anyone else.

Some days, it *does* feel like that. Like the time before meeting him is nothing but a hazy, half-remembered dream. Maybe that's because Grant and I met so soon after my first husband died. In fact, the first time we met was at my husband's funeral. I've never told anyone that. Doesn't it sound awful? I found a second husband while burying the first.

There are times when it disgusts me.

But Grant has the kind of magnetic pull that can only be resisted for so long. He pursued me, charming and insistent, and I said no. And no, again. And no a third time. A fourth time and a fifth time. It felt too soon. Too . . . callous. Yet my situation changed soon after the funeral. My first husband had left me in a precarious financial position – a position I had been in before and to which I never wanted to return – and Grant offered me the perfect solution. So I took it.

And now here I am, about to be a wife again.

It's all happening so fast. Grant proposed out of the blue last week and told me he already had the perfect venue for us – his friend's winery in the Yarra Valley – and they miraculously have a spot open on our anniversary. So romantic. He's got a wedding planner taking care of absolutely everything, leaving me to focus only on finding my perfect dress and picking out an incredible pair of shoes. That's it. That's all I have to do.

Like me, he's a take-charge kind of person.

Even still, his insistence on driving me today is out of the ordinary. Apparently, it's because he's been travelling for work more than usual lately, while he and his business partner set up their new office in Adelaide. I don't mind. He checks in often and we always video call if he's away more than a night. I never feel like he forgets about me, because Grant has a way of making you feel like you're the only woman in the world.

I twist the ring on my finger again, watching the diamond roll to one side, sending tiny fragmented rainbows skittering across the passenger side door. Part of me thinks he's driving me to ensure I don't chicken out and stay home.

Today is my weekly meeting with the Young Widows Club, and I'm the first one to take a chance on another marriage. Grant and I have been together for three years now, but I only got the courage to tell the other widows about him twelve months ago. Their grief made me feel guilty in those early days. Like I was a betrayer for moving on so quickly.

Like it meant I never loved my first husband.

'I'll pick you up at three,' Grant says as he pulls our car up alongside the small set of strip shops in Reservoir where I'm meeting the other women for coffee. Our venue rotates between a small handful of cafés to make it fair since we're scattered across Melbourne. The shops out here are humble, a little bland. Not quite up to the calibre of the places in my neck of the woods.

But you also don't need to pay seven dollars for a flat white out here, either.

'Okay.' I nod.

'You seem nervous.'

I unbuckle my seatbelt. 'I'm not.'

I feel him watching me as I gather my things.

'Adriana.' He places a possessive hand on my thigh.

When I look up, there's nothing but concern in his dark eyes. He's a handsome man, if a little cleaner cut than I'd preferred in my early twenties. Grant has a polish to him—well-cut suits, trim figure, and neatly styled hair that makes him look ready for a corporate photoshoot at any moment. A far cry from the bad boys I once craved, let me tell you. But I've fallen for the details of him. His heavy, serious brows and rich espresso irises rimmed with an almost-black outline. The little scar that prevents his stubble growing in one patch on the right side of his chin. Some people find him intimidating, but I've always found a softness and warmth in his eyes. When he smiles, it crinkles him in a delightful way. And when he laughs, the sound curls inside me like a contented sleeping cat.

'You don't have to wear the ring to your meeting if it makes you uncomfortable,' he says softly, glancing down at my finger.

I twist the diamond around once more. It catches the light, dazzling me for a moment as I'm sure had been his intention when he chose it.

'Of course I want to wear the ring,' I lie. 'It's so beautiful I couldn't bear to leave it at home.'

A proud smile dissolves the seriousness from his face. 'It looks good on you.'

It does. But part of me wonders if it's incredibly insensitive, or at least tacky, to turn up to a widow support group wearing a diamond that cost six figures. Will it seem like I'm rubbing it in their faces? Like I'm flaunting something they can't have? It will, won't it?

Despite the assumptions people often make about me, I'm not that person. I never want my friends to think I believe that I'm better than them. Because I'm not. We're all equals.

'Perhaps it makes me a bit of a caveman, but I want the world to know you're going to be my wife,' Grant says, his voice filled with sincerity. I know, without a doubt, that he loves me. 'I'd shout it from the rooftops if I wouldn't get arrested for public disorder.'

I soften. 'I love that you're never shy about expressing your feelings.'

'Not when it comes to you.' He leans forward to kiss me, catching the edge of my jaw with his hand.

His lips are on mine only for a moment, but in that time I lose myself like I always do. When he touches me it's as if I'm fresh and new again. Reborn. No longer poor

Adriana the young widow. The daughter of a publicly shamed corporate embezzler. Office Ice Queen. A woman made of shattered, jagged, cold pieces.

With him, I am me. Nothing more. Nothing less.

The simplicity of it is addictive. But today I don't linger, because I like being the first to arrive to the club's meetings so I can choose the perfect table and order a few sweet things so when everyone else arrives they feel taken care of. Is it guilt that makes me do this? Or perhaps it's shame for the bad things I've done. The little secrets I keep tucked away, hidden behind layers of lipstick and spritzes of perfume and a cool, confident smile.

Maybe if the widows knew everything about me, they wouldn't want me to be part of the group.

'How did I get so lucky as to find you?' I ask, pecking him on the cheek and pressing my palm to his firm chest.

'I found you, remember?' He laughs. 'And I said to myself, I must know that woman. It's just lucky I'm arrogant enough not to be put off by a rejection or ten.'

'Your persistence certainly paid off.' I push the car door open and set one foot onto the kerb, pausing to look over my shoulder and wink at him.

'Go. Have fun.' His smile is broader – I have done my job. He is reassured. Placated. Secure in his position as the only man in my life, dead or alive. 'I'll be back later to get you.'

'Say hi to Sarah for me.'

His sister is a few suburbs over, in a recently renovated townhouse in Thornbury. Any time we make the trek over to the north side of the city, he likes to go visit her.

'Will do,' he says, waving.

Outside, the weather is mild, a perfect April afternoon. The breeze carries the honeyed scent of wattle blossoms and the minty coolness of eucalyptus right to my nose, and my knee-length skirt wafts around my legs as I walk toward the café's entrance. I step carefully, cautious to ensure my high heels avoid the many gumnuts scattered across the footpath.

Step on one of those and you'll go arse over tit, as Kylie likes to say.

I catch a glimpse of myself in the windowpane of the newsagency as I walk past. Bobbed blond hair (bleached several shades lighter than my natural brown), a high forehead, pearl stud earrings, and a Roman nose with a bump at the bridge that's an unfortunate hint at my mother's Italian ancestry. But I don't believe in messing with my face, so I view my nose as a feature rather than a flaw. The chain strap of my handbag glitters in the late afternoon light. I'm overdressed, as usual. One of the other Young Widows will comment on it, no doubt.

Typical Adriana, always letting her Brighton show.

But I understand what it's like to go without. Not to know how next month's rent will get paid. To walk around Woolworths adding the prices in my head to prevent humiliation at the checkout. To do things that other people would find distasteful for money.

I know it all.

And I will never go back to that place again.

I pause outside the café, nerves fluttering in my

belly. I twist the ring around my finger once more. Twice more. Again. Again. At the last minute, I pull it off my finger and stash it safely away in the side pocket of my handbag.

Today is not the day.

I'm already seated in the back corner of the café with pastel-coloured macarons on a plate in the middle of the table alongside some small bite-sized cakes, when Isabel and another woman walk in. The selection here is good, but the macarons have clearly been shipped in from somewhere else. They taste different when they've been frozen for transportation, rather than baked fresh that morning. The shells should be crisp on the outside, with a soft centre, yet these feel a little stodgy.

'Hey!' Isabel waves as she approaches the table, her arm looped through that of a petite woman with light eyes and plain brown hair pulled back into a limp ponytail. Her fringe falls flatly against her forehead and there's a slight stoop to her shoulders, shrinking her small frame even further. 'This is our new member. Hannah, this is Adriana.'

'Hannah Adamson,' the woman says as we shake hands. 'Nice to meet you.'

At a quick glance, one might mistake Isabel and Hannah for sisters. But on closer inspection, the similarities come more from a vibe rather than any specific features. Both women have soft voices, gentle eye contact and a mousiness to them. But whereas Hannah has fine features, like pinprick freckles and a pointed nose, Isabel is blond with a blunt chin, high cheekbones and a broad mouth that seems at odds with her tendency toward quietness.

Of course, there's also the difference of the scarring. Beneath the thicky-applied foundation, Isabel's facial scars are almost-hidden. In flat lighting, without much to cast a shadow, you might even miss them if you weren't paying attention. But when the light hits the right side of her face, the snaking lines and rough texture are revealed. It's why she always wears her hair down, parted on the side so the bulk of it shields the damaged part of her face.

At the Young Widows Club meetings she pushes her hair back, tucking it behind her ear and allowing herself to be seen as she is, scars and all. Neither Kylie nor I know exactly how she came to be in possession of the scars, and I would never ask. But I wonder sometimes. Car accident, perhaps? Or something else.

'Oh, macarons. Lovely.' Isabel lowers herself into a seat and reaches for a baby-pink confection. 'I always feel like a proper lady when I eat these.'

'How do you and Hannah know each other?' I ask.

For the last three years, it's only been Isabel, Kylie, and me and, to be totally honest, I wasn't so keen on expanding our group. I feel safe with these women. But Isabel is the kind of person who could never leave an injured bird on the side of the road and Hannah, it seems, is the latest defenceless creature she's decided to rescue.

'We met at yoga, actually,' Hannah replies with a nervous smile. She's sitting but hasn't touched the food. 'I moved into a new place a few months back and started taking classes at the community centre. One time the instructor was running late, and we got chatting.'

I'm a little surprised. Isabel isn't really the kind of person to randomly strike up conversation with people – not that I've witnessed, anyway. She's reserved, borderline timid. But I also know that she works as a receptionist, so I guess she must be good at making small talk with strangers.

'And then, uh . . . I guess the topic of why I moved came up and . . .' Hannah's lower lip wobbles.

Oh no. The waterworks are coming.

'Sorry.' Hannah sniffles and accepts a tissue that Isabel has at the ready. 'It's still fresh. He's only been gone four months. Dale . . . that's my husband's name.'

The tears well in her eyes and plop, fat and glistening, onto her cheeks. I've always found it morbidly fascinating to watch someone cry – like you're looking underneath their skin. I cast my eyes down, hearing my mother's voice flash through my mind like a hot knife through fresh cake.

It's not polite to stare, Adriana.

We haven't cried at our meetings in a long time. Truthfully, there never was a lot of tears, even in the early days. We all had our reasons. While I loved my husband, it wasn't an all-consuming kind of love because I'd never gone looking for that. Losing him made me feel adrift. Lost. Abandoned. Confused. The state of our finances after his death made me anxious and desperate. But I didn't experience that aching, pulsing grief of people I saw on TV. In truth, some days I felt nothing but guilt.

Deep, colourless, numbing guilt.

Finding these women, whose grief didn't look like what I saw on TV either, was sweet relief. Kylie had been too filled with rage to cry. She was more likely to hurl coffee cups or knock back a few fingers of Scotch. And Isabel . . . well, sometimes she'd barely said a word. I'd catch her staring into space, lost in her thoughts. Shell-shocked by it all. Trying to find a plan for how to move forward. It made it easier for me to hide how I really felt about my husband's death, to hide the truth of why he was gone.

But Hannah is a crier.

I contemplate which macaron to eat while she composes herself. Lavender jam or pistachio? My gaze flicks back and forth, while I deliberate, eventually settling on the lavender.

'I'm sorry. Maybe this was too soon,' Hannah says, shaking her head and sniffling.

'There's no need to apologise.' Isabel has her arm around Hannah and she squeezes. 'We've all been where you are.'

She looks to me for encouragement and I nod, thanking my past self for deciding to ditch the diamond. That would have been awkward. I glance at the café's entrance. Still no sign of Kylie.

As if reading my mind, Isabel says, 'I called her just before we came in. She's running a little late.'

'So what's new?' I raise my hand to catch the attention of the woman who's coming around the tables taking coffee orders. Out of the corner of my eye, I see Hannah dabbing her eyes and looking relieved that the attention has been drawn away from her. 'No point waiting for

Kylie to order drinks. I'm desperate for some caffeine.'

I order a latte, and Isabel and Hannah both order cappuccinos.

'So, uh . . . Isabel tells me you all met online.' Hannah is sitting straighter now, back in control of her emotions, although I notice that she clutches the wadded tissue in her hand as if certain she may need it again.

'That's right.' I nod. 'I was on my computer a lot after my husband died. Looking for a distraction, I guess. I used to stay up until the wee hours of the morning trawling those advice forums and one day I put up a post about how I felt like my family was judging me. My father had made a few snide comments that I was acting like a spoilt princess who didn't even care that my husband was dead. Of course I was sad, yet . . . I was also empty. Numb. Some days I couldn't feel anything. But it turns out that when you need a friend, the universe provides one. Isabel was there for me. She sent me a DM and told me that she was experiencing the same issues. We bonded right away.'

'And Kylie posted about dealing with the aftermath of finding out that her husband wasn't the man she thought he was . . . and I related to that, too.' Isabel nods, biting down on her lower lip. 'I had complicated feelings about my husband when he passed. It felt like fate, in a way. We weren't only *young* widows, we were misfit widows, too. We needed each other.'

The truth is, we *still* need each other, most days.

I've traipsed all over Melbourne to pick Kylie up when she's too drunk to drive and she came with me to the chemist to buy a pregnancy test when my period

27

was late and I was freaking out. Then there was the time when Isabel completely lost the plot after seeing a mother give her child a whack on the bum while we were out shopping. She'd been inconsolable and I'd held her until she stopped crying even though I didn't know why she was so upset, though I could guess.

These women are my sisters-in-arms and our bond has been forged in fire. In fury. In disbelief. In the ugliest and rawest of human emotions. We have been our worst selves in front of one another and yet we still come to these meetings every week. I don't think I've ever had that kind of unconditional love before.

Which is exactly why I can't tell them truth about how my husband died.

Chapter Three

Isabel

Hannah sits next to me in the car. She shifts and knots her hands together in her lap. The anxious energy is contagious. I feel it invade my body, compelling me to pick at a hangnail while we idle at a red light. My car gives a little shudder and I remind myself, yet again, that I really should take it to the mechanic. The last thing I want is to get stranded.

But even thinking about how much it might cost for them to keep the old gal running is enough to give me hives. Why are cars so bloody expensive to maintain? Too bad my boss recently rejected my request for a pay rise. I work as a receptionist for a freight company and the money is shit, the commute is long and I hate the way the truck drivers leer at me when I walk from my car to the staff entrance.

But none of that matters.

I didn't take the job because of the pay or the location or my colleagues. I took it for a much higher purpose. Unfortunately, choosing a job for those reasons sometimes leaves you short . . . like when your car is wheezing its last breath. And no matter how many times I tweak my budget spreadsheet, I can't find enough for a service.

'Thanks for inviting me today,' Hannah says. 'I promised myself I wasn't going to cry and . . . God, I hope I didn't make an arse out of myself.'

'Don't be silly. Of course you didn't make an arse out of yourself,' I reply with a smile, glancing over at her. 'Tears are part of the grieving process. And having other people around me who've gone through the same thing really helped after Jonathan's accident.'

I tell people that my husband died in a car accident because it's easier than the truth. Less messy than the truth. And because a car accident doesn't encourage questions. It's not like someone is going to come out and say 'Oh, was he on the piss?' to lessen their obligation to feel sorry for me.

Besides, the less I share about my real identity, the better. Not even the Young Widows know the truth of who I am, and they're the people closest to me in the whole world.

'I'm really glad we met,' Hannah says. Sincerity shines out of her like sunlight. 'You have no idea how much I needed a friend the day we started talking.'

She's about six or seven years younger than me, and I hadn't expected to become friends with her when I'd seen her at the community-centre yoga class. The place is ugly and always smells like cleaning fluid, but they charge a fraction of what the proper studios do. I suspect that's why Hannah picked it, too. If her clothes are anything to go on, money seems tight. But she's sweet and we've been going to classes together for a month, grabbing coffee afterwards and getting to know one another.

I wasn't expecting to make room in my life for a new friend, but as soon as I met her I felt like we'd known one another for years. We clicked. It was like we'd been friends in a past life or something corny like that. And I wanted to help her.

'I'm really glad we met, too.' I nod. 'How did you find the others today?'

'Kylie seems nice,' she replies thoughtfully, her head cocked to one side like a puppy. 'There's a certain . . . warmth to her.'

'She's a good person.'

Kylie might be chaotic and chronically late, but she has a big heart. She's the person who will turn up at your house with Chinese takeaway when you've had a long week and who will drag you out for a drink when you're feeling blue. She's always sending funny memes to our group chat to show she's thinking of us, even if she never remembers our birthdays.

After a few beats of silence, Hannah says, 'I don't think Adriana likes me.'

'She takes a while to warm up to people.' I wave my free hand. 'She likes you fine.'

'I just . . . maybe she feels like I'm intruding on your group since you're all such close friends and I've inserted myself.' Hannah sighs and knots her fingers together. 'I don't want to disrupt things.'

I feel her desperation for acceptance like a scent in the air. She's young, vulnerable.

Hannah would probably get carded at a bar or

nightclub even though she's in her twenties. I've never seen her with a lick of makeup – not even mascara – and she always wears plain clothes, like black leggings with white sneakers and a grey zip-up tracksuit top with a hole forming at the elbow. I'd bet the last ten bucks in my bank account Adriana would kill to give her a makeover.

I look at the smooth unblemished skin on Hannah's cheeks and a pang of envy strikes me in the chest. If I wasn't so scarred, I'd let my skin go free like she does.

'I invited you. Therefore, you did *not* insert yourself. There's no rule that says we can't have new people join us.' I lean forwards to check the oncoming traffic before I ease the car around a corner. 'She's reserved, that's all. I think it comes from what happened when she was young.'

'What happened when she was young?' Hannah frowns.

'Her father was some bigwig in the finance industry and he got caught running an embezzlement scheme when she was in high school. It was all over the news when he got thrown in jail. All their assets were seized and she went from being a rich private-school girl to living in commission housing. She told me once that everyone they knew turned their backs on them – all those rich friends and family members and not one would help her and her mother out.'

Hannah's eyes widen. 'That's terrible.'

'The media hounded them a lot, from what I understand. She even had a reporter try to make friends with her when she was in university, only for it to come out that she was researching a story on Adriana's dad.'

I shake my head. 'It's why she's not on social media now. She doesn't even have a Facebook account because she doesn't want strangers being able to contact her.'

I think the widow support forum is the only place she's ever been online – although she didn't use her real name there. From what I can tell, she doesn't have a lot of friends outside the Young Widows, if any at all. Work keeps her busy and she spends most of her free time with either us or Grant. I suspect her guarded nature and trust issues have created a difficult environment in which to make friends. It was only through my persistence in messaging her online that we truly connected.

'No wonder she seems a bit closed off.' Empathy flashes across Hannah's face. 'That's terrible.'

'So don't take her aloofness personally. It's a self-protection mechanism.'

'And we all have those,' Hannah replies.

'You should come to the next meeting.'

I don't know why I'm so adamant about including Hannah in our group. Maybe it's because the first time I met her, the loneliness and anger radiated off her like magnetic waves and I understood those feelings. I connected with those feelings. Some days I *was* those feelings and nothing more.

I never used to be like that. In fact, I was one of those obnoxiously happy, upbeat people who painted the world in rose-coloured hues. If giving people the benefit of the doubt was an Olympic sport, I'd be the Ian Thorpe of it – gold medal optimist and seer of all good things. That stupid trusting nature has ended up being my downfall more than once.

It stopped me looking over my shoulder on a dark city street. Stopped me asking too many questions when Jonathan began acting strangely. Stopped me looking too closely when I found yet another prescription stub in his glovebox.

'Okay, I'll come,' Hannah replies with a nod, though she twists her hands in her lap. 'Thank you.'

'You don't need to thank me.'

My words must be firm enough that she moves on. 'What's her partner like?'

It had come out during the conversation earlier that Adriana was the only one currently in a relationship. She'd seemed very uncomfortable when it was mentioned and had moved the talk on to something else.

'Grant?' I shrug as we roll to a stop at a red light. 'She's never introduced him to the group, but she showed me a photo of them together one time. He's attractive, I guess.'

I don't share the true, ugly feelings that had bubbled up in me when I looked at the photo, because Hannah already seems skittish about joining the group. Personally, I don't think I'd ever be able to move on and especially not so quickly, but if Adriana wants to find love again, that's her business and hers alone. I suspect she has her reasons.

'You've been friends this long but you've never met him in person?' Hannah frowns. It *does* sound a little strange when phrased like that, but the Young Widows Club isn't a typical group of gal pals. We have baggage – enough to open a luggage chain.

'She might come off as aloof, but Adriana is actually very sensitive to people's feelings. I think she worries that it might be upsetting to us if she talks about him too much or tries to force him on the group. I mean, she's not wrong. I'm happy for her, of course, but I don't want to hang out with him.' I shrug. 'The whole "dating again" thing is a touchy subject.'

Frankly, men in general could be considered a touchy subject.

I glance at the side mirror. It reflects back a distorted view of me. My scars look fresh and deep and, for a moment, I swear I can see the blood rolling down my cheeks and the glitter of glass shards embedded in my skin. But then I blink and it's gone. I'm back to being me – scars closed over, trapping the rage inside.

'Death is . . . complicated.' Hannah chews on her bottom lip, teeth tugging at a section of tender skin. I've noticed that sometimes she has sores on her lips from the chewing. 'You think it's clean cut – he's gone and you feel sad. But you feel other things too, some days. Inappropriate things. Things that make you feel like a bad person.'

'It's normal to blame them for leaving,' I say. 'You're not a bad person for having emotions.'

'Are you an angel? Because I swear, after my husband died I thought I was adrift at sea, waiting to drown. *Wanting* to drown. And then I found you and you've been so kind to bring me into your group, and you say all the right things . . .'

'I'm no angel,' I say. 'Trust me.'

With the things I have done and the things I have planned, I may be the very opposite.

* * *

Tonight I'm doing something totally out of the ordinary – I'm drinking at a bar in the city. But fun and frivolity isn't on my schedule. Oh no. It's revenge all the way.

I reach for the bottle of red wine on the table between me and my drinking partner. We're sitting at one of those ridiculous high tables, where you have to balance on a stool, perched like a budgie on a wire. I sway a little, pretending like I've had too much to drink. I've worn a dress I knew would be too hot, so my cheeks will appear flushed and I've been topping up my drinking partner's glass when she's not looking. Then, when she shuffled off to the bathroom, I asked the waiter to bring us another bottle of the same wine.

My drinking buddy didn't notice the switch or that I've been nursing the same glass for the last hour.

'Oh boy, this wine is going to my head. I'm such a lightweight these days.' My colleague, Gabby, fans herself, giggling as I slosh more dark red liquid into her glass.

'Thank you for coming out with me.' I put the bottle down and reach across the table, squeezing her arm and smiling, knowing my teeth are probably tinted red. 'I knew we would get along well outside work.'

Gabby beams and I almost feel bad. Almost . . . but not quite.

What is the most powerful position in a company? CEO, I hear you say. Wrong. Some clever folks might stretch themselves beyond the obvious answer to say something like the CIO – Chief *Information* Officer, for those not down with the acronyms – because technology is the future of every company. Good guess, but also wrong. You might even think it's the person who controls the money. But you'd be wrong again.

The most powerful position in a company is the head executive assistant. They have access to *all* the inside information – the backdoor deals, private emails, political alignments, and dirty little secrets. What they know could topple institutions, and most have no idea how much power they hold or what they could do with the information they have.

But I do.

'Of course,' she gushes. 'I can't even remember the last time I was out for fun. The girls keep me so busy that I've forgotten what it's like to have a social life. That's bloody sad, isn't it?'

'They're such lovely girls and you're a great mum.'

A group of men in their mid-twenties walk past and I see Gabby's eyes follow them hungrily. They don't even glance in our direction. Disappointment flashes across her face but I'm used to being invisible. It's been my lot in life for a long, long time.

Now I use it to my advantage.

Gabby isn't like that, however. She craves attention. It's evident in the sparkly dress she's worn that's slightly too tight so the buttons pull at her breasts and the material stretches across the part of her stomach that's rounded after birthing two babies. It's evident in the way she meticulously curls her hair so it looks like she lives in a shampoo commercial. And in the lash extensions I know she has topped up every other week. I've seen her try to flirt with some of the higher-ups in the office, hoping she might snag herself another husband.

Her first one had an affair with his own cousin, or so I heard.

'It's so nice to get out of the office. I'm in the middle of planning the launch party for the new depot and . . .' She lets out a huff. 'Since when am I a bloody party planner? I'm supposed to manage emails and book meeting rooms, not figure out how to plan a menu that accommodates every dietary allergy under the sun! Seriously, one person said she can't eat anything orange. Is that even a thing?'

I wrinkle my nose in sympathy. 'You'd think that Marketing would be responsible for that.'

'Mr Frenchman doesn't trust them.' Her words are a little slurred and her cheeks are pink like roses. 'I *hate* calling him that. What person in this day and age insists on being called by their title and surname? It's so old-school. He's a pompous arsehole.'

It's a power game. I spotted it a mile away. Our boss wants everyone to know that their station is below him at all times because he gets off on making people feel small. It's like a drug to men like him. An addiction. But I never knew Gabby felt that way. In the office, she's always *yes sir, no sir, three bags full sir*.

'You've worked for him for a long time. You must have some crazy dirt.' I waggle my brows in an exaggerated fashion, leaning in like we're conspirators on the same team. 'All company owners have a skeleton or five hidden away.'

I know for a fact that my big, bad boss *does* have a skeleton hidden away . . .

Me.

But I doubt she knows about that.

'The things I could tell you . . .' She giggles, waving a finger in my face. Then she burps and looks momentarily horrified, but I pretend like I haven't heard it over the thump of the bass-heavy music playing in the background. 'His credit card bills come to the office instead of to his house, you know.'

That's always a red flag. 'What's he hiding? A mistress?'

'Probably a rotating supply of them – you know how men are.' She makes a noise of disgust. 'I saw him looking one of the interns up and down the other day. Pig. He's old enough to be her father.'

Knowledge of an affair or him being a dirty perv isn't the kind of skeleton I'm looking for, because these days nobody gives a hoot about stuff like that. Men cheat all the time. That's boring. I want something juicy. Something incriminating.

'Oh come on, there must be something more interesting than *that*.' I giggle and then I fan myself. It really *is* bloody hot in this dress. Why the hell do fashion companies make dresses in stretch velvet, anyway? It doesn't breathe and I'm sure I look like I'm wearing a cheap Santa outfit. I never wear dresses. Anything that makes men look is a bad idea. 'I know you're on the inside with everything that happens in the company. You've got the most power in that whole place, really.'

She preens. I suspect praise is in short supply in Gabby's life. With an overbearing boss who treats her like a doormat, an ex-husband who never made her feel wanted, and self-absorbed tween brats who couldn't give a shit about anyone but themselves, I know exactly what she needs: to feel seen and important.

She leans in closer. Her eyes have a slightly glazed look that I know well. This is the look Kylie gets when she's called either Adriana or me for a lift. The so-shitfaced-I-forgot-my-own-name look. No more wine for Gabby. I want information, but I don't want her hurting herself. I ease her glass away slightly and she doesn't protest.

I make a mental note to call her an Uber and get her to share the ride information so I know when she's safe and sound at home. This time, guilt does flash through me. I'm not a fan of turning people into collateral damage, and I truly like Gabby. But I have to do this.

'He was running some business on the side a few years back,' she says. 'Nothing to do with the freight company. It's some property investment thing – an apartment building, I think. Out near Moonee Ponds.'

'Right.' I nod.

'He sold off a number of apartments. He even asked me if I wanted to buy one, but they were way out of my price range. Like, almost a million dollars back then.' She snorted. 'He knows what I get paid. How the hell would I afford a million-dollar apartment when it only has two bedrooms? I can't put the girls in together – they'll kill each other.'

'Melbourne is so expensive.' I shake my head in commiseration.

'Yeah, but this was even more expensive than normal. It was supposed to be some "exclusive luxury community" thing.' She snorts. 'Like I would fit into that scene.

Anyway, there was some issue with the zoning. It was supposed to be changed to residential and then they hit delays with the council. There was a protest against the rezoning but work had already started. Then, like, there was some undesirable thing being built on the street right near it. It was a big ol' mess.'

Interesting.

'Did the building ever get finished?'

'Technically, yes. But not to the standard people paid for. And as far as I know, there was an attempt at legal action but nobody ever got their money back. Some nasty clause in the fine print of the contract.' She nods, her eyes losing focus for a second, almost as if she's slipping into a memory. 'One guy turned up at the office screaming that he'd been scammed and that he was going to press criminal charges and blah blah blah.'

'Did he?'

'I don't think so.' Gabby shrugged. 'If he did, I never heard about it. Far as I know, Mr Pompous Arsehole got out of the whole thing without so much as a speck of dust on him. Typical. Men like that never get what's coming to them.'

That sounded *exactly* like the man I knew him to be. A criminal. A predator. A man wrapped in non-stick coating. Nothing could touch him . . . or so he thought.

I'm coming for you. Just you wait and see.

Chapter Four

Hannah

I have a routine when I come to the cemetery. I need it. The sense of order and sameness is the only thing that gets me through each visit.

First I park by the little florist's shop inside the entrance and pick up a bunch of flowers – pink, my favourite colour, because the sight of it helps the world to feel a little less grey. I've been here so often in the last few months that the woman behind the counter greets me by name. I wonder how many other people come as frequently as I do.

Probably not many.

My grief is unwavering. Incurable.

Today I'm tired, however, because my new unit is on the other side of the city and the long drive through thick traffic has worn me down. Thankfully, step two in the routine is to grab a coffee from the little café next to the florist – cappuccino, extra chocolate powder on top. Today, I need it more than usual.

Taking a long, grateful gulp, I head back to my car so

I can drive through the cemetery's gently sweeping roads. I *could* walk, but the grave is all the way over the other side and it's warm today. Unseasonably so. I flick on the air-conditioning, enjoying the feeling of the cool air blowing on my face, and drive, taking a route that's become so familiar it's practically etched into my brain. A gentle curve left, then a right-hand turn, then left around a bend and then right again.

I park my car alongside a large elm tree and walk over to the plaque, identical to the ones either side of it. It's nothing fancy; we didn't have much. But I figure what I might not have in money for an extravagant funeral and gravesite, I can give in time and care.

The next part of my routine involves me clearing out the old flowers, even though I come often enough that they're still looking okay. I always donate the old bunch to a nearby grave, a different one each time because I believe fairness is a lost value. Today it's Elisabeth Dorothea McMasters, born 1925 and deceased in 2011. The plaque bearing her name is dusted with dead leaves and I brush them away, placing the only slightly wilted flowers into the little green plastic pot.

'Enjoy the flowers, Lizzie,' I say, before I head back.

I sit and place the new flowers in an identical green plastic plot, fluffing and tousling them so they look full and healthy. The delicate pink petals bring a brief smile to my face. Then I meticulously sweep the plaque clean with a small brush I bring to each visit, shunting dead leaves and twigs and fallen petals with brown edges onto the grass.

There, that's better.

I trace the letters on the plaque with my finger, breathing in and out as tears come, like they always do.

D-A-L-E A-D-A-M-S-O-N.

'Hi Dale. Did you miss me?'

I clamp my eyes shut and a vision swims in front of me – his hooded eyes, chiselled cheekbones, the short dark hair that never seemed to lie right, and a smile as warm and inviting as the ocean after a hot summer day. God, that smile was infectious. Even in my darkest moments, his smile could light up my world.

I keep a photo of us in my wallet at all times, so it feels like a brief moment of happiness is within easy reach. Some days I wonder if I have been irrevocably broken. The person I loved most in the world and who loved me back with equal ferocity is gone. Forever.

The tears come and I let it happen. He once told me that holding tears in was like shaking up a bottle of soft drink and excepting it not to explode. Eventually, like it or not, that kind of pressure can't be contained. So I cry until I feel wrung out and hollow. There's comfort in the feeling of having nothing left, of being husk-like. Because I can't be obligated to hand anything over. I have nothing to give.

'I went to a meeting yesterday. For widows. It's a support group,' I say, pushing my fringe out of my eyes and tipping my face up to the sky, hoping the sunshine will dry my tears. 'I'm trying to make friends and ask for help like you always encouraged me to.'

Dale was that person who attracted others like a

magnet. Babies loved him, grandmothers loved him, dogs loved him, other blokes loved him. *I* loved him, most of all.

'I've found a new place to live, as well. It's quite different from where we lived before. But I have a nice view of a dog park and the road isn't too busy. The kitchen is great. You would love cooking in it.'

My only reply is the rustle of trees and the slow roll of tyres over bitumen as a car cruises past.

'I wish you were here.' My voice cracks. 'I want to hear your voice.'

The final part of my routine is scratching that itch. I have a recording on my phone. It was a voicemail he left me that I've saved onto my phone for safekeeping.

'Hi, it's me. I'm just leaving work now . . .' I squeeze my eyes shut and my chest heaves, the pain like nothing else I've ever experienced. It's the pain of opportunities lost. Travels never taken. Potential never reached. Birthdays and Christmases never celebrated. *'There's pasta sauce in the fridge. I'll grab some fresh bread on the way home if you want to get dinner started. Love you.'*

It's so mundane. So very ordinary.

He left it having no idea that just ten minutes later a drunk driver would run a red light and plough into his car, killing him instantly. Ripping apart my whole life. Shattering my world.

'I love you, too.' I suck in a breath and look up, watching the trees shudder in the breeze. 'I'll always love you.'

I want nothing more than the recorded voice to

become real, to be whispered right into my ear, with arms wrapped around me. To see his smiling face and the care shining out of his eyes.

Eventually I pull myself together, wipe my tears away and push myself up to a standing position. I'll come back for another hit next week.

But for now, I have a new life to live. A life as a widow.

Chapter Five

Kylie

The apartment feels too bloody small when both of us are home. If I'd thought my run-down childhood rental in the shitty outer western suburbs of Melbourne felt like a prison, then this is a single cell. The walls press in and I find myself shrinking around her. It's not my sister's fault. It's just that Beth notices everything and I'm trying desperately hard not to let her know I've been sacked.

She covered my portion of the rent last month when I told her work had stuffed up my pay and the payroll person was giving me the run-around. But I can't pull that rubbish again. I need to find a new job. Sadly, without a reference, potential employers are looking at me with suspicion. I got to the final stage with a small design agency, only for them to choose the other candidate because they couldn't 'verify my track record'.

Arseholes.

My phone buzzes. It's my group chat with Isabel and Adriana.

ISABEL: *What are you ladies up to on Friday? Dinner at mine? I'm making carbonara.*

ADRIANA: *In!! Your carbonara is *chef's kiss*. Best I've ever had.*

ISABEL: *That's a big compliment coming from an Italian.*

ADRIANA: *Don't tell my nonna. She'll turn in her grave from shame.*

The texts make me smile. Some days Isabel and Adriana feel more like sisters to me than Beth. Maybe it's because they're my equals while my own sister feels like a parental figure. That's not Beth's fault, either. We've never known any different.

KYLIE: *Count me in! Be there with bells on.*

Isabel responds with a string of celebration emojis.

I wander into the main area of the apartment, still wearing my fake work outfit – an old blazer from Myer, which has gone shiny at the elbows, and a slim black dress that covers everything from interviews to dates to funerals. I left the house this morning at a quarter to nine in order to keep up my ruse. But what Beth doesn't know is that I went to Centrelink to meet with someone about finding a job – any job – and then spent the afternoon at the library, killing time. Thankfully, she's working from the office tomorrow instead of from home, so at least I can hang around the house without feeling her watchful eyes on me.

'We're out of coffee again,' Beth says. A fluffy pink bathrobe is wrapped around her broad frame and there's a burn mark on one sleeve – a small blackened circle of scorched fabric that smells like melted plastic even after several washes. I don't remember who caused it. 'And the tea is low. Three bags left and I know you like to make yours strong.'

I watch her reach for a teabag that's sitting on the draining board next to the sink. She pops it into a mug and flicks the kettle on, ready to steep it for the second or third time that day. I thought everyone did that until I went to Adriana's house and watched her wave a peppermint teabag – one of those fancy ones from T2 – in boiling water for barely thirty seconds before tossing it into a bin.

Mum would have been horrified. She could have got at least three cups of tea out of that.

'I'll pick some up tomorrow.' I lean on the counter next to her.

Like me, she's got curly red hair – the kind that tends to be dry and frizzy if you don't take care of it – and freckles. But whereas I've got Mum's slim frame and small bones, Beth is built for farm life, like our dad was. Strong shoulders, thick legs, hands like dinner plates. Her posture is stooped – *that's* what she gets from Mum. She carries the weight of the world on her shoulders, does Beth. Always serious. Always worried. I notice that she's avoiding eye contact as she potters around the kitchen.

Beth isn't exactly warm and fuzzy. Probably because she had to learn responsibility from a young age, when our mum died. She was almost ten when I was born, and I remember her babysitting me instead of going to parties and discos when she was in high school. Then she had to give up her dreams of going to university because she needed to work full time to make sure there was food on the table, since our dad had all but abandoned us by then, even though we didn't have anyone else.

I wonder sometimes if she resents me, the person who's always had to rely on her. The weight around her neck.

'Everything okay?' I ask, tilting my head.

I expect her to respond with a casual 'Yep, all good' but instead her eyes flick guiltily to me. I know what's coming before she even opens her mouth.

'We should start talking about when you're going to get your own place,' she says.

When Marcus died and I couldn't stand to be in our house, she took me in. Even if I'd wanted to stay, I couldn't have afforded the rent on my own, and getting a roommate when I could barely see straight most days didn't seem like a smart idea. Marcus and I had been hoping to buy a small house, but money always ran short. Then he got sick – a brain tumour. Rare. Fast-acting. He was older than me by fifteen years, but still far too young to die. He'd always been conscious of the age gap. In fact, when I first walked up to him at a bar the night we met, he said he was flattered but not interested.

But I could tell he was. Men were always interested in me. For all my shortcomings (and believe me, there are many), I've never failed to get a man's attention.

Marcus was no different.

I saw him again at the same bar the following week. *I'm too old for you*, he said. *It will never work.* I slept with him that night and he told me it was a one-time deal. The third time we slept together he told me I could do better. *I'm a broke mature-age student*, he'd said. *And I've got issues. History. I'm not a knight in shining armour.* But I didn't care that he'd done time for stealing cars. He'd got himself on the straight and narrow, ditched the bad crowd, and gone back to school to get a certificate in business management. Marcus had turned his life around and I thought that was a sign of real strength.

Only it turned out he'd been telling the truth. He *wasn't* a knight in shining armour, that was for sure. After he died, the truth of who he was came out and there was nothing for me to do but drown my sorrows by swimming as fast as I could to the bottom of every wine bottle that crossed my path.

'Kylie?' Beth frowns, the groove in her forehead so deep you could lodge a coin in there. She looks older than her years. She has grey hairs scattered through the red and permanent lines at the corners of her mouth, suggesting she might be in her fifties when she's only in her forties. 'It's time to move on with your life. It's been three years.'

'I know.'

'You say that, but . . .' She sighs. '*Do* you know?'

51

I swallow. At that moment my phone vibrates.

FRANCIS: *I've been thinking about you.*

I hold my breath. We haven't texted since I got his message the morning after the night I can't remember. Part of me has been waiting for someone to call and accuse me of stealing the shopping bag from the hotel room. I shoved it all to the back of my wardrobe like a teenage diary full of pathetic crush confessions and I keep telling myself to take the items back to the stores they came from. I have the receipts and I need the cash. I owe my sister for rent. My mobile phone bill is past due. I'm wearing underwear with holes at the waist and sagging elastic around the bum.

But I'm like Golem hoarding his treasures. I want to be the woman who swans around in expensive heels and wears perfume that leaves a trail and who has a sexy secret under her dress.

FRANCIS: *What are you doing tonight?*

My heart flutters. A night out? It sounds a hell of a lot better than what I've got planned – locking myself in my room and watching YouTube videos and drinking Chardonnay until I pass out.

KYLIE: *Meeting you.*

'Kylie?' Beth tries again, but I'm staring at my phone screen watching the three little dots blink.

'We'll talk later.' I lean in and kiss her cheek. 'Promise.'

I go into my bedroom with my head spinning. Am I really going to meet this man when I have no idea who he is, how we met, or even whether I've stolen things from him? Maybe he wants the items back and I've already worn the thousand-dollar shoes, taking the shine off and rendering them unreturnable? This invite could be a trap.

I hold my breath as a response flashes up on the screen.

FRANCIS: *Wear the dress I bought you.*

Well, that answers one question.

The tram pulls up half a block from the bar where Francis asked me to meet him. Like a lot of the great places in Melbourne, it's down a small, dodgy-looking laneway lined with large green rubbish bins that send a funky scent into the air. It rained earlier and puddles dot the road, reflecting back the lights from overhead.

I step off the tram, careful not to misstep in the precariously high heels. The Zimmerman dress hugs my body as if it's been tailored to my exact measurements, and I feel the soft, high-quality lace of the matching underwear set underneath. It's the most gorgeous powder blue colour and I feel like a million bucks in it.

It's a quick walk to the bar, which has a small entrance with no sign – a sure-fire indicator that it's going to be chockers inside. People from Melbourne love a place like this.

You know the one, around the corner from that old pub with the funny name, down the alley and past the containers. No, mate. Of course there's no sign.

I hover outside the door, nerves fluttering in my belly. I'm not me, tonight. I'm not Kylie-Marie, unemployed dole bludger with a sister who's sick of her hanging around like a bad smell. I'm Kylie, urban goddess who wears expensive clothes and goes to fancy bars and who knows how to have a good time without making a fool of herself.

I push the door open and I'm greeted by a beautiful woman with dark skin and black hair that's shaved on one side and long on the other. A septum piercing catches the light and I see she's dressed in a sleek black dress with a silver zipper down the front. Her lips are coated in dark burgundy lipstick – the kind that looks glamorous on her but which I would get all over my teeth.

'We're full tonight,' she says, firm though not unfriendly.

'I'm meeting someone,' I reply, my fingers automatically reaching for something to fiddle with. They settle on the chain around my neck, which once belonged to my grandmother.

'Name?'

'Francis.' It occurs to me that I don't know his surname. I couldn't even look into the room and point him out. Was he tall? Short? Fat? Thin? Old? Young? I have no bloody clue. My stomach churns and I anticipate the sting of rejection.

Coming here was a bad idea.

'Kylie?'

My name sounds behind me and I turn to find a figure standing in the dark, narrow staircase that leads upstairs. He's wearing black suit pants with a white shirt. No tie. A tan belt highlights his trim waist, with no corporate pudge in sight. It's hard to tell how old he is in the dim lighting, but I'd say older than me by a bit without being *old*-old. The same age as Marcus was, perhaps. There's a smattering of silver at his temples, but the rest of his hair is full and wavy. His smile is devastating and it slices through my nerves like a blade.

He's handsome. Far better looking than I thought he would be, in truth, because I've made some questionable decisions while drunk before. There's a touch of dark stubble dusting his chin and it has the faintest reddish gleam to it.

'That dress is *spectacular* on you.' He holds a hand out and I take it, feeling like Cinderella being helped out of her glass pumpkin carriage. 'Come on, let's have a drink.'

'Enjoy your evening,' the woman with the piercing says, stepping back to allow me entry without smiling. There's something strange about her expression, but the second Francis leads me away, I forget all about it.

The stairs are tricky in my new shoes, but Francis goes slowly as though he's used to escorting women wearing stupidly high heels. When we get to the second floor, I understand why. Here, I don't stand out. All the women are similarly dressed, in expensive shoes, gleaming jewels, and beautiful dresses, with tiny bags suspended from glittering straps.

Can these people tell I'm a fraud? That I'm no more than a redheaded Barbie doll, all dressed up in someone else's clothes?

Francis presses a hand to the small of my back and guides me to the bar. It's gold-edged and sweeping, and people sit perched on velvet stools. The bartenders wear suspenders and bowties, and one of them has a full sleeve of tattoos down one side. We grab two empty seats and are served immediately. I get the impression Francis is known here and the staff are eager to keep him happy.

'What would you like?' he asks me, handing over a cocktail menu that's thicker than those awful books they forced us to read in English class.

'Why don't you pick for me,' I say with a smile.

I can tell this pleases him. Satisfaction flashes across his face like lightning and he withdraws the menu, turning to the bartender and ordering something obscure that I've never heard of. I have a feeling I would have ordered the wrong thing – something tacky and obvious, like a cosmo or an espresso martini – and it's a relief that he's happy to be in charge.

'I managed to find some footage of one of your old performances,' he says as the bartender disappears to make our drinks.

I blink. 'My old performances?'

'Of you doing ballet.'

Oh God, I must have told him that I used to be a dancer. *Jesus.* How much did I drink last time? That part of me is long dead and buried. That's the old me who would painstakingly prepare her pointe shoes for a performance – softening the toe box by pressing down with both hands and then banging it against the ground, sewing on ribbons and elastic, snapping the shank and roughing up the soles so I didn't slip.

There was something therapeutic about that process because a pointe shoe works better when it's been abused. When it's roughed-up and the shine is taken off. I found that comforting back then, that something could be better when it was broken than when it was pretty and new.

'Oh?' I say, wishing I could remember more about our night. 'Which one?'

'It was a modern piece, very artistic. You were incredible.'

I was, for a time.

'It was just a hobby.' I glance toward the bartender, hurrying him up with my eyes. This is not a conversation I want to have sober.

'You never wanted to go professional?' Francis asks. I don't like the way his eyes are looking at me as if searching for a tell or a chink in my armour.

'All young dancers want to go professional.' I smile tightly, trying not to let the grief creep in. I'd overcome a lot to get my scholarship – being too big-chested at a young age (costume makers hated me), not having the money to train at a prestigious school in my younger years, dancing on dead shoes when we couldn't afford new ones, even for important auditions. And when my scholarship ran out and the school chose to give the place to someone else the following year, I'd begged Beth to let me stay on. Begged her to sell whatever we owned so I didn't have to quit.

Too bad we owned nothing of value.

'Only a select few ever make it,' I say dully.

'You were very talented,' he says, which I'm sure is meant as a compliment.

It's simply another area in which I've failed to reach my potential. It's my lot in life. I failed to impress my ballet teachers, failed to keep Marcus interested in me, failed to keep my drinking in check, failed to remain employed.

For a moment, I contemplate sliding down off the velvet stool and walking out. The second Francis understands that whatever he thought he saw in me is an illusion, he'll move on to someone else. But then our drinks appear and I'm tempted by the numbness on offer. Francis reaches for one of the identical glasses and raises it to me, so I can clink with him. I'm too weak to refuse. I bring the drink to my mouth and resist every cell in my body telling me to gulp it down in one greedy go. The flavour is sharp, but there's a hint of warm sweetness underneath it.

'How is it?' he asks, and I know the answer he wants.

'Delicious.' I smile. 'Good choice.'

He beams and his teeth are blindingly white. Like an ad for a dental clinic. Or toothpaste. He holds himself with an air of authority, which is not something I'm usually drawn to. Authority isn't my jam, neither to hold it nor be held down by it. It was one thing I loved about Marcus when we met – he wasn't possessive like some of the younger guys I'd dated. They were insecure and clingy, but he was like a wild horse. Untameable. Free.

Francis looks at me, eyes scanning my face like a laser. My instinct is to squirm. I *hate* being vulnerable – have done ever since I was a kid when my dad used to scream at me that crying was weak. That being a girl made me weak.

'What?' I ask, self-conscious.

'Do you remember our night together?' he asks.

'Why would you ask that?' I smooth my shaking hands down the front of my skirt in an effort to stem my nerves. Can he tell my memory is blank? That I couldn't have picked him out in a crowd? Did I make a complete idiot of myself that night? Probably.

He asked you out tonight, it couldn't have been that bad.

'We drank a *lot*.' He grins and it's roguish and handsome. 'Turns out retail therapy is quite the turn on for me. I usually try not to be quite so poorly behaved on a first date. But you, dear Kylie, know how to party.'

I flush. That's one area where I know I won't fail. Because losing myself is what I do best.

When I found out that Marcus had an aggressive brain tumour, at first I was numb. He was only in his late thirties, with so much time ahead, but everything ground to a halt because of a black mark on a scan. He'd been having headaches. Just a few, here and there. They made him grumpy and some days I woke up to find myself staring at the man I'd fallen in love with, wondering if he was still the same person. Then the blurred vision began. He fell in the middle of the night and hit his head so badly that we rushed to hospital. I was worried he'd broken something, but as soon as we told the doctor how he'd been feeling, I knew something was wrong. It was written all over the older man's face.

Glioblastoma.

A fast-growing and aggressive brain tumour. The diagnosis was delivered with a grim expression and a prognosis that turned my stomach to stone. Survival through to the second year past diagnosis was at a little over 15 per cent.

The end was coming.

I spent the next eighteen months by his side, pouring every ounce of myself into making him comfortable and never wasting an opportunity to tell him that I loved him. I held my tongue when he lashed out, frightened about what was coming, and I never complained about having to work to keep the bills paid, while doing everything around the house and being at his beck and call.

I wanted to do it all. I wanted to give him the best possible last days he could have.

After Marcus died and I found his little black book of lies, I wanted nothing more than to fuck my way into oblivion. He'd been having affairs. Plural. Like, double digits . . . and I don't mean ten or eleven.

I stood at his desk, hands shaking as I flipped page after page after page. My name was in there, from the night we met. Every sexual encounter he'd ever had logged with names and dates and places. One the night before our wedding. One the day after our first anniversary. The times he told me he was going away for work conferences.

Tears had rolled down my cheeks as I tortured myself with it all.

Names I knew. Names of friends. The name of my best friend from high school. The name of a woman who lived down the street. A barista at our favourite café. Name after name after name. They're burned into my brain, every last one of them.

I threw the book at the wall, knocking over a photo of us on his bookshelf. It tumbled and fell, shattering and sending glass over the floorboards. I tore his office apart, looking for every little secret. I wanted to know them all. Wanted to stick them into my heart like needles. Wanted to make sure that the pain was so strong I would never forget it.

He had three kids by three different women, and although I thought we were broke because he was finishing his degree and only working part-time at a pizza place, it turned out he'd been sending money to the women and the kids he'd spawned.

I hadn't seen it coming.

That's why I get drunk and sleep with men whose faces I'll forget in twenty-four hours. I want revenge on a ghost.

'I don't remember much,' I admit, feeling the cocktail starting to work its magic, loosening my limbs and my tongue and dulling my shame until it's nothing but gentle white noise. I take another hearty gulp. 'But I definitely like to party.'

'Then let's have a great time.' With a smile that looks like it might swallow me whole, Marcus lifts his glass in the air. 'To nights we won't remember.'

Despite feeling the barest hint of unease in my gut, I raise my glass before bringing it to my lips and downing the lot.

Chapter Six

Adriana

It's so strange to be here again.

I'm surrounded by gilt mirrors and racks of marshmallow dresses embellished with crystals and lace and translucent beads. The craftsmanship is sublime, the prices enough to make most people's eyes water. Last time I got married, I had a strong vision of what I wanted: a sleek dress to show off my figure, a dramatic veil, and strappy high-heeled sandals from a designer I'd coveted since I was a teenager. Every detail had to be perfect, because I'd been sure in that moment that I'd never do it again.

Once I was married I would *stay* married.

How does the saying go? When man plans, God laughs.

Since I had my perfect day once already, trying to top it seems an impossibility; like setting myself up for failure. In truth, I would have been happy to opt for something simple – perhaps a non-white silk sheath dress custom-made from my favourite seamstress, rather than a bridal store. But when I suggested such a thing to Grant, he looked affronted.

'I don't want you to treat this like a consolation prize, Adriana.' Hurt had splashed across his face like red paint. 'You might have done this before, but I haven't. It's special to me.'

I don't know much about his previous partner, who he was with in his early twenties, except that she accidentally fell pregnant and it ruined their relationship because she wanted to keep the baby and he didn't. She ended up miscarrying and things weren't the same between them after that. It's wild to think he could have become a father when I was still collecting Jonas Brothers posters, because most days I don't feel the difference between us. He's energetic and quick-witted and he has the sex drive of a bull. Truthfully, these days I'm often the one who wants to turn in early or have a quiet weekend instead of going out.

But I know the failed relationship shook him. It's why he's sensitive about my investment in this wedding. It's also why he didn't date anyone seriously for years, preferring to live the unencumbered bachelor lifestyle, free from responsibility. Us falling in love seemed counter to either of our plans – I wasn't sure I wanted to move on so soon and he thought he'd missed his only chance to find a woman who was happy being with someone who didn't want children.

'I have a few options for you here, love.' The kindly older woman who does the bridal fittings wheels a rack over with several options picked out. A tape measure is draped around her neck and she has a pincushion affixed to her wrist with the pearlescent ball heads of the pins poking up.

I remember being jabbed with those pins when my mother's seamstress used to tailor my school uniforms as a child. I'd hated it at the time, the way she used to act like I was a cry-baby if I said *ow* when she stuck me like a pig while pinning the hem of my dress. After my mother pulled me out of that expensive private school because our accounts were frozen and we couldn't pay the fees, I missed everything about it, even the painful fittings.

'There's a few more modern options, with different levels of structure. Some have boning in the bodice to provide shape and lift the breasts. This one, by contrast, is completely fluid.' She pushes the dress across the rack to show it off, and the silk gleams like liquid metal. 'Then this one has a corset-style top but the bottom has a gentle A-line shape, to give you the best of both worlds. I pulled one with sleeves and another with more lace and an open back, so you can get a feel for what you like.'

'That's great. Thank you.' I feel strangely nervous.

'Do you have anyone joining you for the fitting?' she asks. 'Mother of the bride? Maid of Honour? Anything like that?'

'No, it's just me.' I look down for a moment. 'I uh . . . I don't have a family anymore.'

'Well, I'm here to be of whatever help and support you need then.' She smiles warmly and for a second I want to ask her if she would give me a hug. I am desperately lonely in this moment.

'Thank you,' I croak.

She pushes open the heavy velvet curtain to the changing area and selects a dress from the rack. It's the sleek liquid-silk one. 'You should be able to get in and out of this one pretty easily, but call out if you need a hand.'

I head into the changing area and she pulls the curtain shut behind me. For a moment, I can only stare at myself in the mirror, eyes sparkling with tears and cheeks flushed with the effort of holding it all in. Holding it all together.

Why am I being like this?

I shake my head and try to refocus on my goal – to find a dress that makes me feel beautiful and doesn't make Grant question why he wants to marry me. A *first*-wedding dress, not a *second*-wedding dress. I step out of my loafers and strip off my jeans and white linen shirt. I opted to 'work from home' today so I could pop out for the fitting without needing to ask my boss for permission. She's stingy about things like that.

I ditch my bra and slip the dress over my head, letting the silk slither down my body like a lover's touch. My nipples press against the thin fabric. Mm, this one will definitely require some of that 'modesty tape' to make sure I don't poke anyone's eyes out if the weather is chilly.

I tentatively push the velvet curtain back and step out into the bridal shop. The dress is long, since I'm not wearing heels, and I rise up onto my tiptoes so the hem doesn't brush against the floor, and so I can see what it will look like with the extra height. I walk over to a mirror that's set up by the front window, which overlooks High Street in Armadale. Outside, people stroll past with shopping bags hanging off their arms and coffee cups glued to their hands. The number six tram glides past, the bells ringing as it slows to a stop at the traffic lights.

'Oh, don't you look lovely.' A voice catches my attention and I turn, seeing a woman in her fifties looking at me and pressing a hand to her chest. For a moment, I'm frozen by shock. She looks so much like my mother that I have to blink to make sure I'm not hallucinating.

But it's not her, of course. Yes, they both share the same wispy chestnut-brown hair and downturned eyes, as well as fine-boned hands. But this woman is taller and softer, unlike my mother who always had a severe edge to her. Besides, my mother would never say something like 'Don't you look lovely' or any other form of compliment. In an instant I hear her voice in my head.

Pull your shoulders back, Adriana. Those little tits need all the help they can get. Lord knows why he's marrying you anyway! You can't cook for shit and you've got a body like a rail. Not much wife material there.

Also, there's the additional fact that my mother is dead.

Ours was a complicated relationship. I loved her – like you love anyone who becomes a partner in a time of crisis – but I never understood her. And she never understood me. It caused friction. But then she was gone so suddenly and I wasn't sure how I could function without her harsh words and biting remarks, because some days they were the only things that made me feel.

'Uh . . . thank you,' I stammer, smoothing my shaking hands down the front of my dress and trying to shut off the voice in my head. 'They have a wonderful selection here.'

'They really do. My daughter is overwhelmed by the choice.' She gestures to her daughter, a younger carbon copy of herself.

I swallow. Jealousy rockets through me and rage rushes up like a fiery freight train. I clench my hands, forcing myself not to reach out to the vase of flowers sitting by the window. How satisfying it would be to see it shatter into a million little shards against the floor. I don't know how I'm going to get married without any family to witness it.

My sister, whose cancer ensured she didn't live to see her third birthday. My mother, dead. My father . . . I wish he'd gone in her place.

'I'm sure she'll look beautiful no matter what she chooses,' I say, shoving the unhealthy thoughts to one side. My baggage feels heavy today, like it's weighed down with rocks.

The woman smiles. 'Best of luck for your big day. You should go with that dress – it's stunning.'

I stand there, watching her go back to her daughter and my heart aches. When I was a little girl, I used to play with my dolly, pretending it was a real-life baby. My baby. All I'd wanted was a big, happy family. And now, I'm going to stand before a priest and be married, and I won't have a single person who shares my blood there to witness it. And any dreams of being a mother died long before I was old enough to be faced with such choices.

A thump on the window facing the street startles me. Heart thundering in my chest, I turn, expecting to see a naughty child pounding on the glass.

Instead, I see Isabel staring at me with wide eyes.

What the hell is she doing here?

'Hey!' She waves enthusiastically through the window, her mouth agape.

I'm sure I look like a deer in headlights. Sprung. Caught. Guilty as sin. There's no point hiding the diamond now, because the cat is well and truly out of the bag.

'Hi,' I mouth back, waving. Before I can say anything else, she races towards the front door of the bridal shop and comes inside.

I feel sick. I knew that at some point I would have to tell the Young Widows about the wedding, but I've been burying my head in the sand about it. Rubbing a wedding in their faces feels cruel. I came close to telling them about the engagement when Kylie and I went to Isabel's for dinner last Friday, but every time I opened my mouth to utter the words, it was like my throat seized up.

'Fancy seeing you here,' Isabel says as she walks up to me, pressing a hand to her chest and shaking her head.

Her blond hair is loose and it hangs over to the right side of her face, like usual. She's dressed plainly in black pants and a light grey shirt with a pair of chunky, practical shoes. The only piece of adornment is a pair of simple gold hoop earrings. Fashion is not something Isabel cares about, especially for work. She must have come from the office.

But why is she all the way out here?

In her other hand is a small bag from a local jewellery store that I know has *very* expensive pieces. I asked for one of their diamond tennis bracelets for my birthday last year, so I'm familiar with their prices. What the hell is she doing shopping there? I always got the impression she was a little hard up for cash, although she's always been too proud to admit it.

'Hi Izzy.' I muster a smile.

She motions for me to twirl and I do. 'You look incredible.'

I feel almost naked. Totally vulnerable. The dress skims my body, the straps so thin they barely look strong enough to withstand a stiff breeze.

'I . . . uh . . .' I let out a breath.

'Yeah, yeah. You were going to tell us that you're getting hitched.' Her gaze strays to my ring. 'But you were waiting for the right time.'

I let out a laugh. 'Something like that.'

She raises an eyebrow. 'Or maybe not at all?'

'I certainly thought about keeping it a secret forever.' I cringe. Guilt tastes like metal on my tongue. I've bitten my lip. It's blood. Feeling guilty always makes me want to punish myself. I did that a lot after my husband died. 'Am I a terrible person?'

'No.' She shakes her head and reaches in to hug me. I let her and it feels good. 'It means you were worried about our feelings, which says a lot about who you are. You're a good person.'

I pull back and nod, trying to believe it. After years of listening to people say you're a liar and you come from a family of liars, you start to believe it.

'Thanks for being so gracious,' I say. Of course she is, because that's Isabel in a nutshell.

'We already knew you were engaged, anyway.' She laughs at my shock. 'Oh come *on*, Adriana. Really? There was a line on your finger at the meeting the other day because you'd clearly gotten some sun while wearing your new ring. Even Kylie mentioned that she noticed it and that woman is oblivious to everything.'

I feel like an idiot.

'Sorry,' I mumble. 'I wasn't sure how to announce it without sounding like I was rubbing it in. Then Hannah was at the meeting and she was all upset . . .'

Isabel looks at me with an amused twinkle in her eye. In these kinds of moments, with warmth in her expression and her full lips pulled up into a smile, she's quite attractive. 'She thinks you don't like her.'

'I don't know her.' I'm used to people thinking I'm cool and standoffish. They're not wrong. It's a defence mechanism – losing your whole life and all your friends and your house and everything you know in one fell swoop tends to make a person wary of the world. I've done it not once, but twice. 'But I'll try harder next time.'

I make a mental note to include Hannah more, if for no other reason than that I want Isabel to think the best of me. I care about her opinion. A lot.

'She's good people.' Isabel nods, then she takes a step back and gestures towards me with her free hand. 'That dress really *is* spectacular. You look like you belong on a runway.'

This time when I smile it's genuine. At least now if the widows know about the engagement, then I can invite them to the wedding. Maybe I don't have to get married without anyone I love being there to witness it. Surrogate families matter as much as the real kind, in my mind. God knows the Young Widows have done more for me than any of my living blood relations ever have.

They wouldn't be here if they knew what you'd done.

'Grant wanted to treat me,' I say, trying to shake off the intrusive thoughts. 'And we've got a wedding planner taking care of the details. All I have to do is turn up in a pretty dress.'

'Looks like you've come to the right place.' She glances around the bridal store and lets out a soft whistle. I know Isabel's wedding wasn't too grand – she told me that she and her husband were married in a park and she had flowers in her hair that they'd picked that morning and a dress she'd bought at an op-shop.

'Part of me feels like a fraud for doing this all over again and having another extravagant wedding,' I admit. For some reason, this time around I don't feel the same need for all the bells and whistles and attention. Maybe I'm still scarred by all the questions people asked after my husband died – that's the kind of attention nobody would ever want. 'But it's Grant's first time and he wants it to feel special.'

'Of course he does. He's thrilled to be marrying you and why wouldn't he be? You're a catch.'

For some reason, the sweet words make tears well in my eyes. What is *wrong* with me?

'I'm being so strange today.' I shake my head and bring the back of my forefinger gently up to my eyes to catch the moisture there without disturbing my mascara. Isabel fishes a small packet of tissues out of her bag and offers me one. She always has the exact thing you need stashed in her bag at all times – tissues, a Band-Aid, mints, Panadol. 'I feel weirdly emotional about it all.'

'That's understandable.' She nods. 'I'm sure it's bringing up a lot of difficult feelings.'

'I'm supposed to be excited.'

There's desperation in my voice, like a thin thread of unease. I want to ignore it, but I can't. It makes a stone settle weirdly in the pit of my stomach. I miss my mum, even if she doesn't deserve it. I miss my first husband too, which makes me feel like . . . I don't even know what. It might not have been true love, but he was my pillar. And I was his.

But if he were still here, then I wouldn't have met Grant and that doesn't feel right either. It's like there's something in my gut telling me I'm headed for trouble but I don't know why.

'This might be a totally inappropriate question to ask and you can tell me to piss off if you want to,' Isabel says. 'But is everything okay between you and Grant?'

'What do you mean?'

'Is he pushing you into this? Into getting married?'

'No.' My response is automatic.

But . . . is he? I had said to Grant early on that I wasn't in a rush to get married again, because I needed time to process my feelings about losing my first husband. Toby. It hurts even to think his name. What a mess we made of things. It was supposed to be the perfect arrangement, giving us both what we needed, and in the end it . . . was the opposite of that. Even now, I'm not sure how everything went so wrong.

He didn't have to die.

'You want to marry him?' she asks, pushing.

'I do.' I reply stiffly. 'I love Grant very much.'

'Of course you do.' Her eyes drop down. 'Well, I'm thrilled for you. If there's anything I can do to help, you know I'm here for you. You deserve to be happy.'

'Thank you.'

'I, uh, have to get back to work. But we should do a dinner to celebrate and I don't just mean carbonara at my place.' Her face brightens. She always looks happiest when she's got a task to focus on. 'I'll book something nice.'

I bid her goodbye and stand in front of the window, watching as she exits the shop and jogs toward the tram stop. It's spitting now and the sky has turned, a fine mist of rainwater coating the window. I head back toward the changing room to try on another dress, trying to muster some excitement. The rack of options is overwhelming and I flick through the hangers, making them tinkle and chime as they slide along the railing and clink into one another. Eventually after I've examined every dress on the rail, I settle on a dress with a fishtail and a deep V at the back to try on next. The seamstress catches my eye and gestures, letting me know she'll come over in a second to help me.

I step back into the dressing room and yank the velvet curtain closed. My phone chirps with an alert. One new voicemail. There are a few other notifications, too – a missed call from Grant and another from Kylie. I've also got a new email. Expecting it to be a mock-up of the invitation designs, I open my inbox. The subject line sitting at the top makes my throat close up.

YOUR MARRIAGE TO GRANT

I open the email. There's a warning at the top indicating that it's from an email account not in my address book and that it might be spam. But this isn't the kind of spam email pushing grey-market Viagra, catfishers posing as mail-order brides, or bank customer-service people contacting me about a bogus charge. This email is meant for me and me alone.

I don't know the email address. It's one that could be set up easily, without any identification. Nothing but letters and a string of numbers, totally untraceable. Anonymous. And yet the body of the email . . .

It makes my blood run cold.

Grant isn't the man you think he is, Adriana. You're not safe.

Chapter Seven

Isabel

I don't have any business shopping in Armadale. It's far too rich for a receptionist like me, which is probably why Adriana looked so startled to see me. But I was out doing a favour for Gabby. Honestly, I felt like I owed her one after getting her drunk, and the opportunity arose this morning.

The boss needs a gift for his daughter, and Gabby usually runs those kinds of personal errands for him. There's not much to it: take the corporate credit card and go to Tiffany's or Cartier and browse items you could never afford yourself.

Fun times.

Apparently he left a little blue box on Gabby's desk last year because she'd been working as his assistant for ten years. Ten years of putting up with his shit deserves more than a fancy trinket if you ask me. But anyway, today she got called to collect her sick kid from school and he needs the gift tonight.

Not a problem, I said. *Let me take care of it*. Sounds

like he forgot his daughter's birthday was coming up. Bastard. So I ventured out on my lunch break to pick up the three-thousand-dollar Tahitian pearl earrings from a custom jeweller, utterly paranoid that someone was going to rob me. The sense of relief I felt when I got back to my car and locked the doors was immense.

I'm sitting in my car in the staff car park trying to muster the energy to head back inside when my phone vibrates from the little holder affixed to the windscreen with a suction cup.

ADRIANA: *Thanks for not making me feel like an arsehole for not telling you guys about the engagement. I don't deserve you.*

She has no idea that I'm the one who doesn't deserve her. I pull my phone off the holder and type back immediately:

How many times have you come round with ice cream and booze when I needed to vent? You sell yourself short.

Befriending Adriana is like trying to befriend a cat – it can be slow and drawn out, and sometimes you're not sure whether it's working. Even meeting weekly for the Young Widows Club, it took months to get a glimpse of who she really is. And I suspect I haven't seen everything yet. That she's still hiding something important away.

I scrub a hand over my face. She's really getting married again . . .

I was walking back to my car when I happened to stop and look in the window of the bridal store. I'm not even sure *why* I stopped. Usually when I see a place like that, I put my head down and hurry past, a lump clogging the back of my throat. My husband has been dead three and a half years, and it's still raw. Still fresh.

I remember the day I met him. I was sitting in the waiting room of his office like a nervous little mouse. I hadn't wanted to be there. Why were they forcing me? Why? Hadn't I been through enough already? The receptionist had offered me a glass of water and I'd refused, not wanting anything from people who sought to profit from my pain. Not even something that came free from a tap. I'd let my hair hang over my face, my scars so fresh back then that my skin looked like a horror movie.

Minced meat, I heard a boy say one time as I sat across from him on the tram.

The whispers at university were worse. *Schadenfreude* – the German word for the feeling of deriving pleasure from another's misery. I don't want to say that anyone was *happy* about what happened to me, because I don't think that's true. But they certainly didn't mind seizing the opportunities I missed due to not being able to concentrate in class. As I slipped lower on the bell curve, they got higher.

My loss was their gain.

So I dropped out. I gave up my dream of being a lawyer because hiding was easier. I didn't want people to stare. But I wasn't sleeping. Night terrors, you see. I wanted pills and the doctor wouldn't give them to me until I'd made an appointment with a psychologist. Jonathan had poked his head out of his office and called my name and I had expected to find a stuffy old man standing there. But my heart had stopped beating for a second. He was impossibly handsome. Mid-thirties, inky black hair, square jaw, kind eyes. He looked like an older, more refined version of a K-pop star. That day, I'd listened to his soothing voice, trying to steel myself against his care.

But eventually he got past my armour. Past my scars. Past the walls.

'Why did you have to be so weak?' Tears fill my eyes as I sit in my car. The jewellery bag is propped on the passenger seat, looking wholly out of place in the drab, run-down interior of the decade-old vehicle. But I can't get rid of this car.

At one time it was Jonathan's pride and joy, and I'll drive it until the bloody thing falls apart.

Whisking the tears away from eyes, I grab the bag and head back into the office. The front reception desk is being temporarily manned by our current office junior, who's the nephew of the HR manager and always covers my lunch break. I raise my hand in a wave as I walk past, and he looks at me eagerly, hoping to be relieved from his duties soon.

But I still have one more thing to do.

My steps are muted by the ugly patterned carpet that's designed to hide stains from grubby footprints and upended cups of coffee. The truck drivers and mechanics traipse through in their grimy work boots on their way to the staff room, so everything here needs to hide dirt. It's not the worst office I've worked in during my career, but it's easily the blandest. The walls are an unappealing putty beige, and the windows look out at either our fleet of trucks or over the highway. Fluorescent light bathes everything with a sickly, artificial glow, and the scent of sticky, oversweet air freshener and vehicle fumes permeates the air. The desks are separated by low cubical walls that aren't tall enough to afford any actual privacy to the worker bees, yet they still give that dated, closed-in look of an old-school nineties desk farm.

I make my way past the customer service team, which consists of four women in headsets who speak in monotone voices while their acrylic nails tap at their keyboards. The sound is like white noise – a steady *click, click, click* in the background of every workday. Ahead of me, in the far corner, is the boss's office. The walls are glass but there are blinds that he can pull down for sensitive meetings – like the time he had to fire someone who got caught taking pictures of one of the young female admins bending over the copy machine to fix a jam.

Human Resources forced everyone to take sexual harassment training after that incident, and now we have a 'respect for all' policy. How progressive. The HR manager, a man with wire-framed spectacles and greying hair, also made a point of saying that women should wear their skirts long enough so that nothing can possibly show, no matter what position we're in.

Ah, there it is. Respect for all . . . so long as your skirt is long enough.

Not that it affects my wardrobe choices – I rotate between the same three pairs of black pants, washing them each weekend and using the steam setting on my iron to get the creases out without making the fabric shiny because I don't want to waste money on replacing them. I have a personal uniform of sorts: black pants, white or grey shirt, sensible block-heeled shoes, and simple gold hoop earrings.

I dress to blend in.

I walk past Gabby's empty desk, contemplating if I should leave the jewellery bag there and scurry back to my post so the boss can grab it when he leaves. But it doesn't seem wise to leave something so valuable out in the open. The issue is, I don't like going into his office alone. Or at all. And today I feel raw. Untethered. Seeing Adriana dressed in white like a beautiful bride has made me feel sick to my stomach. It's unsettled me.

I don't know why she wants to get married again. I don't know how she can stand it. It reminds me of all I have lost. Of how my husband's death was needless and brutal. Wholly preventable.

I miss him every day. He was my other half. My saviour. In those long, dark days after the incident which took me from a bright, ambitious law student to an aching shell, he was the only person who seemed to understand my pain. Yes, as a psychologist that was his job. Yes, as *my* psychologist it was absolutely inappropriate for him to fall in love with me and for me to want to love him in return.

But he saved me. From myself. From the dark pit of despair that threatened to claim me. From the people who didn't know how to act or what to say, people who used stupid, useless sayings like 'what doesn't kill us makes us stronger' or 'everything happens for a reason'. He was different. Kind. Gentle.

I'd do anything to have him back.

'Isabel?' a voice booms, like a cannon. 'That you?'

Shit. There's no getting out of it now. I've been summoned. I walk towards Mr Frenchman's office door, heart hammering in my chest, a lump clogging the back of my throat. The memories are like hot fingers squeezing my brain, and fear is sticky in my mouth. My palms sweat uselessly as I grip the slippery ribbon handle of the gift bag.

The office door is ajar and I push it, the hinges squeaking in warning. He sits behind a big partner's desk, eyes fixed on the computer in front of him.

'I picked up the earrings for you.' My hands shake as I put the bag on his desk, the ribbon handles flopping daintily to one side.

Gold script writing tells me that *Jewels are a love language* but I wonder how much the man really loves his daughter if he never takes a moment out of his busy day to buy her a present himself. From what I understand, Gabby does the research and selects the present for him no matter who the recipient is.

How is *that* love?

I've never seen his daughter. There's not even a picture on his desk. Maybe their relationship is strained? All I know about her is that she graduated from Melbourne University. Economics degree, I think. Or maybe it was Commerce. Something high powered.

And apparently she likes expensive, shiny baubles.

'Receipt?' he asks, without even looking up. He rarely looks at me. Rarely looks at anyone who isn't part of his inner circle. The rest of us are beneath him.

There have been times when I've been tempted to start tap dancing to see if he'll look at me, but I squash that urge since it serves my purpose to go unnoticed, even when he's sitting right in front of me. I spot some shimmering strands of silver in his hair. It's a harsh reminder of how much time has passed.

Of how long he's got away with what he did.

'It's in the bag, along with Gabby's company credit card.' I'm proud that my voice doesn't shake, even though I feel like a leaf in the wind. 'The jeweller said he hopes your daughter enjoys the earrings.'

'She will.' Why does it sound like a demand, instead of a statement?

For a moment I stand there, frozen to the spot, looking at him. Looking at his three-piece suit and fashionably styled hair and the tiny cut on his chin from where he shaved that morning. There's a minuscule drop of blood crusted there, and it triggers a memory.

The warm stickiness dripping down my face.

The pulsating pain and confusion.

Blue and red lights causing the brick wall beside me to light up like a fairground.

He looks different now, compared to how he looked that night, looming over me as I struggled to push him off; bringing the glass bottle to my face in an effort to subdue me. He's older. Comfortable in the knowledge that he got away with everything. The police certainly never looked in his direction. I didn't know his name, where he was from, or how he managed to catch me unawares.

How he managed to ruin my life in less than ten minutes.

He probably thinks I was a weak little girl who gave up on life. Maybe he thinks I died. He certainly left me for dead. Or maybe he assumed I killed myself, or ended up in a nut house, turned to drugs or drink. Maybe he's never even thought of me at all, after that night.

Maybe he doesn't remember it.

But *I* remember. I think of it often. Of him. Of the pain of being held down. Brutalised. Scarred. Changed.

It was only by luck that I found him one day, years and years later. He was a face staring back at me from a laptop screen and it filled my heart with bright glistening fury. I was already hurting, having lost my Jonathan only weeks earlier. I was raging against the world, and there he was, a gift from the universe. Revenge handed to me on a silver platter.

Go get him, the universe whispered. *He's waiting for you. Make him feel what you felt. Make him lose everything.*

He never expected me to fight back.

More fool him.

Chapter Eight

Adriana

Later that afternoon, I'm still unsettled by the email. Rather than forcing my colleagues to put up with my jittery energy, I reschedule my afternoon meetings and go for a run. By the time I return, my hands are shaking. I tell myself it's because the weather has turned suddenly and the cold has burrowed into my skin, making a home there. That's Melbourne for you – relentlessly unpredictable. The truth is, however, that I've wracked my brains trying to figure out who might have sent me this email but . . . I'm coming up empty. Grant and I don't have a lot of mutual friends. Occasionally we go out for dinner with his sister and her husband, or his business partner, Tom. But that's it.

Beyond that there aren't many people who know us both. And I hardly see anybody from my old life anymore. My old life being the one I had with my first husband – the extrovert, who was always out and about, making friends and influencing people. Since his death, I've pulled into myself, returning to my naturally introverted state. I have minimal contact with my father, and even less with extended family like my aunts and uncles and cousins. Not that there are many I've even seen since I was a teenager – once Dad went to prison, Mum and I were shunned by everyone we knew.

The wedding will be bigger, though, much to my chagrin, because we've expanded the guest list to include people that Grant wants to impress. He's insistent that we invite my father, too. We've argued about it. But he's the man I love, so he and I are all that truly matter. And Isabel and Kylie. Everyone else is simply there to fill out the photos.

You're not safe.

The words echo in my brain. They bother me, like an itch I can't reach, turning my doubt to anger. What coward sends an anonymous message? If there were a real reason that I should be frightened of Grant, then they should bloody well say it to my face. I wonder if it's someone connected to my first husband – maybe his sister. She never liked me. In fact, right before our wedding she told me that she thought I was a no-good gold digger who would only make her brother miserable.

At his funeral, she'd hissed that she'd known I would kill him.

In frustration, I delete the email although I know it won't stop me thinking about it. Then I unlock the front door and step inside. That's when I notice a small suitcase tucked against the wall, a luggage tag still affixed to the side.

'Grant?' I call out.

I hear footsteps above me, and he appears at the top of the stairs still wearing a shirt and dress pants, though he's lost the tie and jacket and cufflinks. The sleeves on his shirt are rolled back, exposing arms that are richly tanned. His mother's side of the family is Greek, and the sun loves him.

'You're home early.' I feel the warmth creep back into me, as it always does when I see him after he's been away. 'How was Adelaide?'

'Boring as batshit, same as always.' He grins and comes down the stairs, reaching for me, even though I'm rain-splattered and sweaty. I'm swept up in his arms, his large body cocooning mine. He smells like citrus cologne and soap, and I notice a slight sheen to his hair that tells me it's freshly washed.

He's been home long enough to shower. Then why is he wearing a shirt and dress pants?

I pull back and look at him. 'You're heading out again?'

'*We're* heading out.' He grins and then he presses his lips to mine, coaxing me into a kiss. I'm still unsettled, but the doubt becomes quiet when he touches me. It's like he takes the volume knob in my brain and turns it down, and the demons settle back into their shadows, placated. 'I booked dinner for us in the city. Great place – you'll love it. Go shower and get changed. We'll head off now and have a drink first.'

'I thought you'd want a night in.' I finger one of the buttons on his shirt, resisting the urge to pop it open and press my palm to his bare chest. For some reason, I feel the need to touch him, to prove that he's real and he's the man I know and love. 'These trips always tire you out.'

'They do. But I missed you.' His lips are on my neck now and he walks me back until I bump against the wall. When he presses me there, I'm like a butterfly specimen – wings stretched out and pinned, beautiful and suspended in time. Preserved forever. 'And while I'd be very happy to help you right out of your clothes and haul you over my shoulder, I know a lady should always be treated to a nice meal before she's ravished.'

'Ravished?' I laugh, letting my head loll back against the wall as his hands skate over my hips. 'Sounds like you've been reading romance novels.'

My mother always loved those books – Nora Roberts, Johanna Lindsey, the little Mills & Boon books with the skinny spines and painted covers. It always struck me as ironic, given how toxic her relationship with my father was. But her nightstand was never free of a small pile of them. I kept some of her spine-cracked favourites when she died.

'What's a better word for it then?' he asks. 'Devoured? Consumed? Ruined?'

Sometimes it does feel like that with him – like I'm turned to dust and spread out on the wind, never to be whole again.

'How about fucked?' I say, drawing the word out, my lips brushing against his ear.

'Be careful, I'll have to wash your mouth out with soap.' His eyes are dark and full of greed. 'Now go upstairs and get ready before I change my mind and tie you to the bed.'

'I wouldn't mind that,' I say, but he leads me by the hand towards the stairs, smacking me affectionately on the bum.

'Go. Now.'

I take the stairs slowly, pausing to watch him over my shoulder. He's staring at me, hands in his pockets, to make sure I do what he says. Part of me wishes he'd give in and follow me. I want to be close to him and there's no moment that we're closer than when his body is pressing mine into our bed. But he remains steadfast, resolved to take me out.

Upstairs, I find a dress hanging from my wardrobe door. It is sage-green silk with big white roses printed on it, a tie at the waist and sleeves that flutter around my shoulders. It's the dress I wore on our first date.

How could this be a man who inspires nasty anonymous emails? He's playful and thoughtful and he always wants to make me feel like the centre of his world. Jealousy. The person who wrote the email is nothing more than someone who's bitter about what we have. What *I* have.

And I won't let it ruin my night.

I shower and get changed and put on some makeup and perfume. Then we call an Uber to take us to dinner. In the back of the car, I can tell Grant missed me because he doesn't stop touching me. Little touches, like tucking a strand of hair behind my ears or brushing the backs of his knuckles against my knee where the slit of my dress falls open. His fingertips trail along my arm. His shoulder and thigh brush mine. He's closer to me than usual.

'You look beautiful, Ri.'

That's his nickname for me, the name he uses when he wants to butter me up. But he doesn't need to put in the extra effort; I'm all his. Tonight, whatever he wants, he can have.

He reaches for my hand, his thumb playing with the diamond on my finger, flicking it back and forth. 'Are you excited about the wedding?'

'Of course.' It's the only appropriate reply, though the question shunts me back to my moment with Isabel in the bridal store and the mixed feelings swirl up once more. 'Why would you ask that?'

'I don't know.' He shakes his head. 'I just had a weird feeling . . . Maybe it's because I've been conditioned to believe that all women go crazy before their weddings and you're acting like things are no different than normal.'

I laugh. 'And that's a bad thing because . . . ?'

'It's not.'

'But you're worried that because I've been married before that this time around it doesn't mean as much.' I squeeze his hand. 'Maybe I'm acting like everything is normal because being with you feels normal. It feels right. I'm excited to be getting married, but ultimately I don't think it will change things between us because we're already in the right place with one another.'

Grant isn't the man you think he is, Adriana. You're not safe.

I want to curse those words out of my mind and I wish I'd never read that email. Grant is a good man.

Yes, sometimes he can be a little domineering and he's a perfectionist who always wants to have his way because it never occurs to him that he might be wrong. I blame his parents for that. But I guess the same could be said of me, in truth. We're both Type A and sometimes it creates sparks because we're flint on flint.

But I *like* those things about him.

'You're wise,' he says, looking at me. I bask in his adoration, letting it warm my skin like sunshine. 'An old soul.'

'My dad used to say that about me.' The words slip out before I can stop them.

I don't talk about my family. Ever.

But I'm saved by the driver pulling to a stop at our destination, and Grant doesn't pry. I open the car door and step out onto the city street, sucking in a big lungful of crisp night air. Loss threatens to overwhelm me. But it's a different kind of loss that I feel when I think of my father, because he's very much alive. Living, breathing, and wreaking havoc on all who dare to get near him.

He's a toxic parasite rather than a human, and he cares about nothing but himself.

It's then that I notice where Grant has brought me – a little Italian restaurant called In Vino Veritas.

In wine there is truth.

It's an old Latin proverb, one I remember my nonno telling me when he was still with us. But it isn't the childhood memory that takes my breath away – it's another memory. One in which I was here with another man: my first husband. I can almost feel the firm grip of his hand on mine, his skin smooth and fingers confident. We came here on our first date, then our one-year anniversary, then the night before our wedding.

It's our place, mine and my first husband's.

'Surprise!' Grant says, wrapping his arm around my waist. 'I know how much you love it here.'

I blink, confused. My mind is distorted, past and present blurring together until I feel like I have a foot in each place at the same time. It's like being torn apart at the seams. 'I never told you I like this restaurant.'

He looks at me strangely. 'Yes, you did.'

But I didn't. I'm *sure* of it.

Because I do everything in my power to keep the 'before times' as far away as possible from the 'now times'. Part of that is because it was easier for me to move on than to deal with how my first husband died, and the note left behind that haunts me to this day.

'I didn't,' I whisper, knowing with absolute certainty that I have never told him about In Vino Veritas.

But Grant simply laughs, tightening his arm around me. 'How else would I know you love this place so much, silly? Come on, let's get inside before the rain starts up again.'

My legs feel like lead, but I take step after step, breath after breath, until we're inside. It hasn't changed. Black-and-white pictures hang on the walls of anyone famous who's ever eaten here, from politicians to footy stars, Olympians to musicians. The tables are covered in white cloths, and candles drip wax as their flames flicker, beckoning people to lean in; to whisper. Low music plays over the speakers and the air is scented with red wine, espresso, sugo rosso, and tiramisu.

'Ah, look who it is.' The owner walks toward us, arms outstretched, and at first, I think he's talking to me. Does he remember me? My hair used to be longer and darker, not the blond bob I have now. And I wore glasses then, before I had laser eye surgery. But the owner breezes past me and envelopes Grant in a big hug, slapping his bear paw of a hand down onto my fiancé's back. 'It's been too long. Come, come. I have the best spot reserved for you.'

My legs wobble as we're led to a booth in the back corner. It's intimate. Sitting here almost feels like you have the place to yourself, even when it's full. I know this because this is the exact table where I used to sit with Toby. He ate here often before we met, and when I agreed to a date, he told me that he wanted to take me to his favourite place in all of Melbourne.

Here. This restaurant. This table.

I slide into the booth seat, tucking the skirt portion of my dress under me so it doesn't wrinkle as I sit on it. It feels like my whole world is tilting on its axis.

'You might remember my beautiful fiancée, Adriana,' Grant says, gesturing to me.

The owner, a man in his fifties with a thick salt-and-pepper moustache that appears to have more hairs than the entirety of his head, looks at me. His dark eyes narrow. 'You look familiar, signorina. How could I have met such a beautiful woman before and not remember her name?'

'I've only eaten here a few times,' I say, looking down.

'Well, it's an absolute pleasure to have you back in

my humble establishment.' He does a little bow, the action causing his belly to pop a little further over the waistband of his pants, straining the buttons of his white shirt and revealing a heavy smattering of dark hair against his olive skin. 'I'll bring you a bottle of wine, on the house.'

'Vito, you don't have to,' Grant says. 'Let me pay.'

'Nonsense.' Vito waves a hand. 'It's my treat.'

He disappears off into the restaurant, barking orders at a good-looking man with a square jaw who stands behind the bar and then he taps a woman on the bum. She turns and grins, pressing up on her tiptoes to kiss him. She's in her fifties, attractive and vibrant. They make a lovely couple.

'Vito is such a character.' Grant chuckles and pours us each a glass of water from the bottle already sitting at the table. 'Although I'm a little insulted he doesn't remember you, given you like this place so much.'

Something is wrong with this picture.

The knowledge of it settles like a stone in my gut. Grant has never pushed me to talk about my life before with my first husband. In fact, the few times it came up he'd almost shied away from the topic, like he couldn't bear the thought that I was with someone before him. It suits me fine because I don't want to rehash the past. I don't want to relive my mistakes. I don't want to add more fuel to the fire of my guilt.

So how does he know this place means something to me?

'It was a long time ago,' I say with a tight smile. 'With Toby.'

I watch for his reaction, waiting to see if there's a flare of jealousy in his eyes or anything else that might clue me in to what the hell is going on right now. But Grant gives me nothing. He nods, already reaching for the menu, which I know he will scan for a few minutes before settling on something basic.

For all his money, he's got a teenager's palate when it comes to food: fish and chips, margherita pizza, chicken parma. No seafood or game meats for my squeamish fiancé. My first husband wasn't like that. He always wanted to try new things and explore his options.

Stop thinking about him.

'Maybe that's how you found out I liked this restaurant,' I say, probing. I'm a naughty little kid, poking a dog with a stick. 'From Toby.'

He looks up, brows wrinkled. 'We never talked about personal stuff. Truthfully, I only met him a few times and it was always in a work setting.'

'You never went out to dinner together? Maybe you came here?'

Grant shakes his head. 'No, never.'

Most people don't know – and will *never* know – that my soon-to-be new husband was a man I met while wearing a black mourning dress and trying to hide the fact that I was a monster responsible for my husband's death. The tears I conjured that day came from my own guilt, more than grief.

I may not have loved my first husband with any romantic passion, but he was a good man. I loved him platonically. I respected him. But I was also angry at him for leaving me with a firestorm of financial problems instead of talking to me about our situation. About the mess he made. About the position he put me in.

I could have helped. I could have done something.

'You know we weren't close, Adriana. I've told you that before. The only reason I was even at his funeral was because Tom said we should go and pay our respects. He was a work acquaintance, that was all.' Grant rakes a hand through his hair. 'It felt like we were imposing, honestly. Then I saw you . . . and I knew why I had ended up there. It wasn't for him; it was for you.'

Love at first sight. It seems grotesque in the context of how we met. Callous. Unforgivable. It's why I don't tell anyone the story of how we came to be a couple, fearful that they will judge me as harshly as I judge myself.

My stomach lurches suddenly. I need a moment.

'Are you okay?' His brow furrows.

'I'm fine.' I know this is the universal woman's way of saying *I am categorically not fine*, but I don't want to ruin things tonight. We're supposed to be having a good time. Celebrating life and our relationship and getting ready for marriage. 'Sorry. I'm being weird tonight. I've been rather emotional lately.'

A knowing look comes over his face and he nods. 'That time of the month?'

'Must be.'

For a moment, I swear my heart stops beating. My period . . . it's late.

Fear crawls up the back of my neck, but I try to reason it away. It's probably nothing. Stress from planning the wedding. Maybe I forgot to switch to the sugar tablets with my contraceptive pill. Easy enough. I've been busy, focused on other things. But a pit forms quietly, heavy and resolute.

I'm pregnant.

'I'm going to head to the ladies' before we order,' I say, sliding back out of the booth, feeling unsteady on my feet.

I rush to the women's toilets and stumble into a stall, dropping to my knees before everything I've eaten that day comes rushing up.

Chapter Nine

The Watcher

Rain dribbles down the back of my neck, slipping into the collar of my tracksuit top. It's only spitting now, so I don't need to stand pressed against the wall anymore. I can be out in the open, getting a better look. Watching.

In one hand I have a coffee cup from the café across the street and in the other is a cigarette. It's been so long since I had one. I really thought I'd kicked the habit this time, but whenever I feel stressed, the desire comes roaring back. I suck in a lungful of it – the comforting, familiar taste. Smoke curls up, obscuring my vision for a moment, but when I blow out, the smoke parts and I see her return to the table.

Adriana.

It's a name befitting a classy woman like her. I can see what the guy likes about her – that slim, fit figure, her cut-glass cheekbones, and that air of sophistication. There's a ring on her finger – a giant, honking rock.

She's wife material for sure. What would she think of me in my baggy jeans and dirty sneakers and my tracksuit top with the bagged-out neckband and the baseball cap? I doubt she'd look twice at me. I'm invisible to a woman like her.

She has no idea I'm watching. That I've been watching for months now.

Wine arrives at the table and two glasses are poured. He reaches for the wine but she doesn't. One of the waitresses – the one with four centimetres of regrowth in her fried, bleached hair – goes to take their orders. After she leaves, he pushes the glass of wine toward her but she shakes her head, pressing a hand to her forehead as though she's not feeling well. I can't see his expression.

Adriana musters a smile. But it's tight. Forced. I know when she smiles for real that her whole face lights up. It's a thing of beauty. This is not a real smile.

She's worried.

And she probably should be.

Chapter Ten

Hannah

I check my reflection in the mirrored doors in my new bedroom. It's hard not to zero in on the things I don't like: the angry red spot on my chin that I couldn't quite cover with concealer, the way my legs feel too short for my body, how my eyes are slightly too close together. I've always been that person, the one who focused on flaws. Dale used to call me out for it.

If you always look for the negative, that's what you'll find.

He was right, of course. But positivity came easy to Dale. Friendship and acceptance came easy to him. For me, it was the opposite. Like the time I decided I had to make the girls at my new school like me. I tried everything, twisting and contorting myself to become someone they would bring into their circle. I even stole money from my grandmother's wallet to buy a pair of fancy jeans I thought would make me fit in.

All it gave me in the end was a verbal lashing from my grandmother and a pair of jeans that made me sad whenever I wore them. The girls still didn't like me.

Maybe that's why I'm so nervous today.

I've pulled out a silky blouse and a fitted black pencil skirt that I keep for job interviews and face-to-face client meetings. I even dusted off a pair of pointed-toe stilettos that I haven't touched since I quit my job in market research when Dale died. I couldn't stand the questions and the sympathetic frowns and the constant *Are you okay?* type questions. I've managed to pick up some freelance work without issue, where I can be a brain for hire and where nobody knows my story.

But today, with a social event on the calendar, I feel a little like my old self – the woman who used to tackle every day with purpose, who had goals and a plan and motivation.

The last few months have felt so dark and endless that there are times when I wonder if I've lost my grip on the old Hannah for good. But slowly she's coming back. Every time I pull out my straightener to do my hair or put on a spritz of perfume or choose to wear a pair of pants with a real waistband instead of leggings, I catch glimpses of her.

So tonight feels special, in a way.

It feels uncomfortably important that these women like me. That I'm accepted. That I'm not alone anymore. It's like being back in school and desperately wishing to be part of the cool group. It's a lot of pressure, I know.

The doorbell chimes and my heart leaps into my throat. I'm going out for dinner with Isabel and Kylie and Adriana to celebrate her engagement. It's nice to be included, and Isabel has offered to give me a lift since we live in adjacent suburbs. When I asked if she wanted to come to mine for a coffee first and she said yes, I was practically giddy with excitement.

If Dale was here, he would chuckle at me for being so excited about such a normal thing.

I fling the door open. 'Hello!'

'Hey!' Isabel smiles. 'This place is cute.'

I'm staying in a two-storey townhouse that's a little skinny and a little dark, but I know it's going to look great when I finish decorating. I've painted the entryway a bright sunshine yellow because that was Dale's favourite colour, and I've bought a lovely print to hang on the wall that shows a field of sunflowers. It feels like sacrilege, in a way, taking delight in a place I bought with his money. Like I'm living off the profits of his death.

Grief is a bitch like that. It tells you nasty things to hold you down.

'Oh, is that your husband?' Her eyes immediately go to the photo resting on the little table in the hallway.

'Yeah.' I pick it up and hand it to her. 'That's my darling Dale.'

I chose the frame specially – it's silver, engraved with flowers and birds, full of so many delicate details I feel like I uncover something new every time I look at it. That was always how I felt about him. He was complicated, rich with texture and feeling. Every time we talked it was like I turned over another small rock in the garden of his life, finding some new treasure or scrap of information. I could have spent the rest of my life learning who he was, peering into every corner of his soul and becoming an expert on him.

Isabel's eyes flick to mine, as if wanting to make sure that I'm okay talking about him. I appreciate the way she's so conscious of everyone's feelings. I smile to reassure her. Hard as it is, I actually like talking about him. It helps to keep the memories fresh because I'm terrified that one day they'll fade.

'He's handsome,' she says, looking closer at the picture. 'And you look like a baby in this photo!'

'I was twenty-one,' I respond. It's a lie.

I was actually eighteen, but I'm aware the age difference between Dale and me might make her uncomfortable. Thankfully, I was wearing makeup in this photo and he had a baby face, especially when he shaved, so I can fudge the numbers. I don't want to deal with any questions around why a guy who was in his early thirties was in a relationship with a teenager. I know it sounds creepy and I don't want them to think badly of him. Or of me.

'And yes, I got married young,' I say.

'So did I and to someone whom people in my life viewed as a bad choice.' Isabel places the photo gently back on the foyer table, making sure it sits perfectly straight. 'So I don't judge.'

I feel my shoulders droop in relief. 'A lot of people do.'

'I know. But people in glass houses shouldn't throw stones, or however that saying goes.' She lifts one small shoulder up into a shrug. I'm a petite person – both in height and frame – and I often feel small around others, but Isabel isn't much bigger than me. The more I get to know her, the more it feels like we could be sisters because we have so much in common. 'Love is far more complicated than the movies would lead us to believe.'

'Disney has a lot to answer for,' I mutter, almost to myself.

Some days I wonder how different my life would have been if women weren't taught from birth to look for a prince. If my mother hadn't loved someone who placed his own needs before hers. If my grandmother hadn't given up a blossoming career to become a homemaker. If I had closed my heart off to Dale when he asked me to come live with him, even though we barely knew each other.

Would I have lived a simpler, easier, less painful life? Probably.

Chapter Eleven

Kylie

Isabel has organised a dinner to celebrate Adriana's upcoming wedding and we're heading to some ritzy place in the city with overpriced cocktails and a dress code. When she sent the email to Hannah and me, asking if we would come, there was no way I could say no.

Adriana has tried to keep the engagement quiet out of respect for our feelings, but she deserves for us to be happy for her, the email had said. I have no idea why Adriana tried to hide the wedding, anyway. Why would we be angry that she's attempting a second chance at a happily ever after? In my mind, Adriana was *always* the one who'd end up married again. She knows what she wants and she goes after it – whether that's sending a coffee back if it wasn't made properly or changing jobs when her boss didn't give her a big enough pay rise.

She's a winner in life. Unlike me.

I'll die before I become 'Mrs' anything ever again. Fuck that. But it doesn't mean I can't celebrate a friend's choices. I wonder if she might stop coming to the meetings once she's married. I hope not. Adriana is a positive influence on the group. She's strong, centred, capable.

I need that energy in my life.

I lift my hand in a wave as I walk towards the table where Hannah and Isabel sit, a smug smile lifting my lips. I'm not the last to arrive! This has *got* to be a first. Lately, I feel like my life is coming together more than ever before. The Louboutins have become my lucky shoes. Since I wasn't able to return them, I've taken to wearing them out any time I need a boost of confidence.

In fact, I wore them to an interview for a receptionist job with a hair salon. They're looking for someone with good admin skills. The interviewer immediately complimented my shoes and told me how she'd always coveted a pair. That bonding moment must have made her overlook the fact that I don't have a reference for my last job and that a reception gig is well below my skillset, because I start tomorrow. Who cares if my uni degree is totally going to waste? I have a job! It's the first step to fixing up the shitshow that is my life.

I've continued to dodge Beth and the conversation about me getting my own place, however. I know I need a solution. But I can only tackle one thing at a time. Now I've secured a job, I can crunch the numbers and see how long it will take me to get on my feet again. And I've promised myself that I will pay Beth back for her kindness once I'm there. I love my sister and I know she's gone over and above for me our entire lives.

I owe her everything.

'Ladies.' I can't help the buoyancy in my step as I approach the table. I lower myself into one of the free seats and sling my bag over the back of the chair. 'Look at me being on time! Who's going to present me with my medal?'

'Gold star for you.' Isabel laughs. 'And don't you look lovely.'

'So do you.'

And she does. Apart from her blond hair hanging over her face like usual, she looks polished. Pretty. A wrap top in a stretchy black and white fabric hugs her small shoulders and chest. She's even rocking a slash of red lipstick.

'Nice to see you, Hannah.' I smile across the table. I'm a little surprised she's here. Adriana is a private person and we don't know Hannah that well yet, but I'm sure Isabel encouraged her to come along, and I certainly don't mind. The more the merrier.

'You too,' she replies, smiling back and holding her hand up in a little wave.

She is also dressed up. Her fine brown hair is out of its usual ponytail and it has a soft wave to it, as though she's used a blow dryer and a round brush. Her ears are adorned with cheap but fun costume earrings, and she wears a light blue silky blouse that suits her complexion. We look the part in this glamorous restaurant – with the velvet-lined booths and white tablecloths and expansive, custom-lit wine shelves that run the entire length of one wall.

I'm already dreading looking at the menu, since my budget probably only extends to a bowl of chips or maybe a salad. But tonight, I'll have to pretend I can afford to be here and hope that my new job pays me quickly. At least I have something lined up. And I'd rather die than admit to the Young Widows that I've been sacked for getting drunk at a work function.

I hate secrets. More than anything.

And yet lately I feel cloaked in them—getting sacked, waking up in a hotel room with no memory of the night before, the shoes, the lingerie, Francis. I'm keeping all those cards close to my chest.

'Where's Adriana?' I ask, reaching for the wine menu.

'I don't know. It's not like her to be late.' Isabel frowns. 'She texted saying she was on her way, but it shouldn't have taken her that long to get here. I hope everything is okay.'

'Maybe we should order a bottle of champagne,' Hannah suggests. 'Have it ready and chilling for when she gets here?'

'Great idea.' I raise my hand to catch the attention of a passing waiter and order the most moderately priced bottle along with four glasses. Even the 'average' stuff here is more than seventy bucks a pop.

Out of the corner of my eye, I see a flustered Adriana rushing over to the table. She looks like a gazelle, long legs flashing from a dress that hits below her knee but is slit in several places to reveal glimpses of toned, tanned thighs as she hustles over. The dress is a stunning silver shade, and she carries a small clutch in one hand – black patent leather – which matches the sandals with pencil-thin heels on her feet.

'Sorry I'm late.' She slides into the last remaining

seat at the table, cheeks pink as if she's been running. Even sweating and frazzled she looks like a goddess, not a hair in her blond bob out of place. 'Grant came home from work and we were chatting and I lost track of time.'

'Lost track of time, eh?' I waggle my brows. 'Is that what they're calling it these days?'

Instead of laughing, Adriana looks green at the mention of sex. Odd. I'd never taken her to be *that* much of a prude.

'Shall we start with some bubbles then?' Isabel suggests, reaching for the champagne.

'I, uh . . . You'll never believe this, but I actually can't drink tonight.' Adriana laughs and the sound is brittle, like an old plastic garden chair. 'I'm on antibiotics and the doctor said no alcohol.'

I smell bullshit. All three of us at the table lower our gazes not-so-covertly to see if Adriana is touching her stomach. She's not, and I notice a flash of irritation in her eyes as I look back up. But she doesn't rush to deny our suspicions or double down on the antibiotics thing. Maybe she's telling the truth. My gut tells me otherwise, however.

Is it such a big deal to be preggers before you get married these days? I wouldn't think so. I would assume at our age, closing in on thirty, a woman who wants to become a mother is already starting to think about the consequences of delaying action.

Not that I fall into that category, mind you. Motherhood is a hard pass for me. Always has been. So maybe I'm off the mark.

'How's the wedding planning going?' Hannah asks, smiling a little too hard as though she's trying to make sure people know she's having fun. Either that or she senses the tension is thick enough to cut with a butter knife and she's one of those people who can't stand an awkward silence. 'I loved planning my wedding.'

'It's fine.' There doesn't seem to be any excitement in her voice.

'Fine?' I ask, exchanging a concerned look with Isabel. 'Shouldn't it be more than fine?'

'Wedding planning can be stressful. There are so many decisions to make,' Hannah interjects with a supportive tone, like she's seen the opportunity to win Adriana's favour and has latched on to it with both hands.

I want to tell her not to try quite so hard, that she doesn't need to win us over. We're not that kind of group. But I worry it might come off like I'm scolding her, so I hold my tongue.

'I was giddy with excitement for months before mine,' I say instead, feeling strangely like I'm telling someone else's story. 'We had the biggest cake I'd ever seen. It was bloody huge. My mother-in-law was a cake decorator and she made every layer look different. Some had sugared roses, another had quilting and diamantes. I felt like a princess.'

I'd had no idea Marcus would break my heart. That I'd turn into someone I couldn't stand to see in the mirror. That my relationship, like everything else I had attempted in life, would fizzle into unsatisfying nothingness.

For a brief moment, I had been joyful and whole, with the future clutched eagerly at my chest, possibility blossoming like roses in a bouquet. But it didn't last. It never lasts.

'It's . . .' Adriana shakes her head.

'What's going on?' Isabel reaches for her hand, always ready to offer comfort.

'I got an email.' Adriana leans forward, her eyes darting to and fro to make sure no one is listening. The restaurant is fairly full and nobody is even looking in our direction. 'About Grant.'

'What do you mean?' I ask, shaking my head. 'What kind of email?'

'An anonymous email saying that he's not the man I think he is.' A line forms between her brows and she presses her lips together. 'And that I'm not safe.'

The table is stunned into silence. I don't know anything about Adriana's fiancé, since she keeps her life very compartmentalised. It took me being friends with her for over a year before I even found out what suburb she lived in, and longer still before she told us about what happened with her father when she was young. I didn't even know her mother had died until almost six months after probate cleared and she needed help to clean out the house. There are some things she's never told us. Like how her husband died.

She's absolutely a closed book and this confession takes me by surprise.

In the lull, our waiter arrives with a bottle of champagne and four flutes. It seems impossibly poor timing, given the conversation, but I don't do anything to dissuade him from popping the cork and pouring our drinks. I'm eager for a taste of the golden liquid and my mouth waters in anticipation.

The glasses are passed around and we say cheers, holding them up to clink against one another, though it feels a little hollow. Adriana places her glass down, untouched.

'Do you have any idea who could have written it?' I ask, pausing to take a sip of my drink. It's cool and effervescent and tastes like heaven. 'Maybe an angry ex? He was married before, right?'

'Not married.' She shakes her head. 'He was engaged in his twenties, but they broke up. I've never met her and it's not like there was some horrible incident where we bumped into her or she tried to get him back or anything like that. I wouldn't even know if we walked past one another in the street.'

'And there was no identifying information in the email?' Isabel asks. Her blond hair hangs partially over her face; the other side – her non-scarred side – is tucked behind her ear, which reveals a small, dainty gold hoop earring. 'No name in the email address itself or anything that might point to who sent it?'

'Nope. It was a Gmail address with a bunch of letters and numbers. There was nothing that hinted *at all* as to who sent it.'

'That's weird.' I shake my head. 'I wonder if it might be a person he pissed off at work. Maybe he sacked someone or refused a pay rise and they're getting revenge by trying to stir up shit in his home life.'

'Hmm . . . I hadn't even thought of that. It's certainly

possible,' she says, her eyes flicking back and forth as though she's considering my suggestion. 'But how would they have got my email address?'

'Your email address is literally your first name dot last name at Gmail dot com,' Isabel points out. 'That's not exactly tough to figure out.'

'True. Although they would still need to know my last name.' She looks confused, but then something clicks. 'Now that I think about it, Grant's sister insisted we do one of those stupid society engagement things for the paper. I didn't want to, but he said I shouldn't start the marriage off fighting with my sister-in-law, so I relented. It mentioned my last name. Anybody could have seen it.'

There's also the fact that with how high-profile Adriana's father's criminal charges were, people might know who she is from the court case. I hadn't known, of course, because I didn't grow up in a family who cared much for staying informed on current events, but plenty of other people would have. I don't want to create any more friction by bringing that up, however, in case she doesn't want to talk about it in front of Hannah.

'Does he have any drama in his family?' Isabel asks. 'Like, one part of the family that doesn't talk to the other?'

'No. And I'm sure that would have come up while we were discussing the guest list,' she says with a sigh. 'If there are issues, then he hasn't mentioned them. But his family seems tightknit.'

I get the impression there's something she's not telling us. An extra bit of information she's wary about disclosing. Perhaps not a full-blown secret, more something tucked away for safekeeping that may or may not come to light later on. I get the feeling Adriana has levels of secrets. Layers of information that she's willing to share and others she'll take to her grave.

'I did wonder if it might be my first husband's sister,' she says eventually.

I squint, trying to remember what I know about her first husband's family. Not much. It seemed like she never got close to them. From memory, there were some issues about his will, a claim that she'd hidden money from his family. Lies, obviously. Adriana wouldn't do something like that.

At least, I don't think she would.

'She was rude at the funeral, right?' Isabel nods, frowning. 'I remember you saying that.'

'She blamed me for his death.' Adriana blows out a breath, and her hand trembles as she reaches for a glass of water. This is the first I've heard of this. She opens her mouth as if to say more, but quickly snaps it shut, trapping her secrets inside.

'Do you think the sister is pissed off that you're moving on with your life, and so she's trying to stuff things up?' Isabel asks.

'Maybe.' Adriana sips her water. 'I wouldn't put it past her.'

'That's ridiculous.' Anger sparks inside me. 'Why shouldn't you move on? It's your life.'

'Agreed,' Hannah chimes in. 'It's your life.'

'You don't have reason to think there's any truth to the email, do you?' I ask. I mean it as rhetorical question, really, because of course she wouldn't believe the anonymous email sender. Why would she marry a guy if she thought he might harm her?

'No.' She shakes her head. 'Of course not.'

I drink my second glass of champagne slowly, determined to keep it together. But every sip feels like a tease. Like an exquisite form of torture. The urge to gulp it all down and pour another, to drown in it, is so strong it's like a physical pull, and my hand twitches in my lap, ready to reach for my glass again.

After Marcus died, the drinking didn't become a problem right away. It was a glass of wine here and there when I felt sad. A treat I dangled in front of myself to get through the workday. A reward when I made it through a weekend without crying. But the slippery slope from a treat to a routine to a habit is swift. It took me by surprise.

Though it shouldn't have. My father drank. My grandfather drank. It's in my blood.

Now I've polished off the rest of the bottle while the others nurse a single glass each, Adriana not drinking at all. I'm dying for another. Drinking is a rollercoaster. The first few glasses are good – they make me feel weightless and the nasty little voice in my head finally shuts up for a moment. But there's a tipping point. It's like being on a seesaw and hovering in that delicious middle, not knowing if you're going to fly up or land back down with a thud.

And I'm starting to fall. Starting to think of all the ways I've stuffed up my life. Too many ways.

I glance over to the bar, watching a guy with bulky arms jostle a cocktail shaker up and down. I can practically hear the ice cubes rattling against metal and the swish of liquid being aerated. My mouth waters. Maybe I can sneak away and have a cheeky shot. There's a second level to this place, and I know there's another bar upstairs. I saw people heading up there when I arrived.

If I tell the girls I need to go to the toilet . . .

'We should get going,' Isabel says all of a sudden, glancing at Hannah who nods in agreement. I check my watch; it's barely nine. She catches me looking and flushes. 'I know it's still early, but I have to be up at six tomorrow for work.'

'Thanks for coming.' Adriana smiles. 'Both of you.'

'Thanks for including me,' Hannah replies, seeming genuinely pleased. 'I can't tell you how nice it is to have a night out and . . . feel normal.'

Isabel reaches for her arm and squeezes as a show of support. Then the women both throw some cash onto the table to cover their portions of the dinner and stand. I get up to give them each a kiss on the cheek and Adriana does the same. I'm half expecting her to make a move to head home as well, but she doesn't reach for her bag.

As we're saying our goodbyes, a group of men walk past us and one mutters something to his mates. I don't catch the words, but whatever they say, Isabel's spine goes ramrod straight. Hannah's mouth pops open and Adriana whirls around.

'What did you say?' she demands.

116

The man stops, shoulders back, chin tilted. He's dressed like those arrogant banker dickheads I see clustered in the cafés on Queen Street – three-piece suit, shiny shoes, gleaming silk tie. He's mid-twenties and looks like he thinks the world should bow at his feet. I know the type. His mates try to pull him away, but he remains steadfast.

'I said your friend's face looks like roadkill.' His eyes – they're bright blue – flick to Isabel and a cruel smirk lifts the corner of his lips. The other men are standing behind him, also dressed in suits. They look uncomfortable.

'Adriana, don't.' Isabel shrinks away, ducking her head, shame lighting a fire in her cheeks. 'It's not worth it.'

'It absolutely *is* worth it,' she says. 'Nobody has the right to talk to you like that.'

I come up beside Isabel and slip an arm around her shoulders, glaring at the man with all the fire I can muster. If it were possible to set him alight with my eyes, he'd be burning like a funeral pyre.

'Listen here, you limp-dicked little boy,' Adriana says coolly, taking a step forward and drawing herself up to her full height. With the heels, she's statuesque. 'I'm going to tell you a secret.'

She leans forward, whispering something into his ear and the man's face goes white as a sheet. He glances at Isabel, mumbles a single-word apology under his breath and then he charges off away from our table, rubbing his nose while his mates trade confused expressions before following him. The tables around look on, curious eyes glancing over our group.

Adriana pulls Isabel into a fierce hug. 'Sorry. I couldn't help myself.'

'It's fine.' Isabel's voice tells me it is absolutely not fine.

'Are you okay?' I ask, but all I get is a tight 'mm hmm' in response.

As they leave, Hannah places a soothing hand on Isabel's back, rubbing in circles, and Adriana says to call tomorrow. Then she drops down into her seat and scrubs a hand over her face as the other two leave, and I take the spot next to her, bringing my drink around to my new seat.

'What did you say to him?' I ask.

'I saw that he had a lanyard for a fintech company tucked into his suit jacket pocket. I know the name of the CEO because I consulted there for six months and I told him the guy was a close personal friend, and I'd get him barred from doing anything more than working in the mailroom if he didn't fuck right off and leave us alone. Oh, and I told him he should dust the coke off his nose if he wants anyone to take him seriously.'

A laugh bubbled up inside me. 'Did he actually have coke under his nose?'

'Not a spec.' She shoots me an evil grin. 'But I read him like a book. They're all the fucking same, those guys.'

I shake my head. 'I never know what to say in situations like that.'

'I can't stand the thought of Isabel feeling badly because some arsehole thinks he's got the right to comment on her appearance.' She's practically bubbling with fury. I'm pretty sure if a nurse were to draw her blood right now, lava would come out instead. 'The gall of it. Like if we're not up to their standards, then it's fine for men to degrade and humiliate us.'

We sit at the table talking for over an hour, just the two of us, eventually moving the conversation on to things like politics, the footy, and her wedding. She clams up when I start asking questions about the latter, however. Especially when I mention Grant.

'You seem more stressed about the email than you're letting on,' I say.

'I'm not stressed,' she replies, tucking a strand of hair behind her ears to reveal a gorgeous pearl drop earring. 'It's . . . I don't even know why I brought it up, to be honest. I wouldn't be marrying Grant if he was a bad guy and it's not like there have been any red flags. I mean, he's probably as close to perfect as a guy can get.'

'Perfect is a lie.' The words slip out before I can think to stop them.

'True.' Adriana isn't offended. A knowing smile raises the corner of her lips. 'Sure, Grant has his issues. He's got a bee in his bonnet about making this wedding a grand affair and he's riding the poor wedding planner like she's a racehorse. But if that's the worst he's got, then I can hardly complain, can I?'

'I hope you didn't dignify the email by writing back.' I frown. 'Anyone who's trying to ruin another person's happiness doesn't deserve a response.'

'I reckon you're right.'

'Look, if there *is* something going on, you know you can talk to us, right?' I don't know why I need to say that out loud, but I do. Frankly, Adriana has her shit together more than I could ever hope to. So I don't exactly know what support or guidance I would offer her . . .

Nobody should be coming to me for advice.

Still, I want her to know she's not alone in the world. Because that's the worst feeling ever. And she deserves better than that. We all do.

'Thank you. And I *do* know that,' she says, nodding. Her fingertip rims the glass of champagne that has sat untouched in front of her all night and the light reflects off the pearly polish on her nails. The bubbles have slowed and only the occasional one now meanders to the surface. 'I hope you know it, too.'

She looks at me pointedly, like there's no doubt in her mind that I've been hiding things. I guess we all do it, because there's something human about wanting to show the best side of ourselves to the world, even if it's a little manufactured. Or *a lot* manufactured.

But just as I have no intention of sharing the ugly truth of my current situation, I'm quite sure she will continue to keep a few skeletons tucked away as well. It's who we are, I guess.

'I do.' I nod.

'I thought of you the other day, actually,' she says, letting the serious tone drop. 'There's a new dance studio near me that does those barre workout classes. I thought we could go together.'

Her smile is hopeful and I feel utterly grateful that these women have put up with my bad behaviour these last few years. No matter how many times I breeze into our catch-ups late or hungover or both, they're still here for me.

'I'd love that,' I reply with a nod.

Adriana looks uncharacteristically misty-eyed for a moment. 'This group is the closest thing I have to a family. I can't even tell you how much it means to me.'

I blink.

'Why do you seem so surprised?' she asks.

'Well . . . I mean, you have your whole secretive thing going on and I don't want to ruin the mystery . . .' I grin, teasing her. 'But I'm glad this means as much to you as it does to me.'

'It does! And I'm *not* secretive,' she protests, laughing. 'And I'm certainly not mysterious.'

'You *so* are. The first time I met you, I was convinced you were some kind of . . .'

'What?'

'Like a spy or something.'

She snorts and it's the most un-Adriana-like sound on the face of the earth. She reaches for her water glass. 'What are you talking about?'

'You literally turned up to our first meeting in a black dress, high heels, red lipstick and a fur coat. I was waiting for you to admit that you'd killed your husband for his money.'

Adriana completely pales. The water glass she'd picked up clatters to the table, landing on the edge of her dessert plate and sending her fork skittering off the edge. Bits of chocolate torte flick across the pristine white tablecloth and we both jump.

121

'Oh my God, I was totally kidding,' I say, shaking my head. Her reaction has unsettled something deep inside me and my mushy brain whirrs like a worn-out gear while I curse myself for the way the bubbles have loosened my tongue. 'That was a *very* off-colour joke. I don't think—'

'It's fine.' She waves a hand.

Good god. How many times has someone said 'it's fine' tonight? It's like we're all swallowing things down, trying to pretend that everything is okay when it's not.

'I'm so sorry,' I try again.

'The fur coat was a bit much, I'll admit. But in my defence, it was faux and I saw it on a fashion blogger who made it look cool. I wasn't going for a black widow vibe on purpose.' She tries to laugh, but the sound is brittle and it cracks, revealing how hard my thoughtless joke struck a nerve.

'That was a really shitty thing to say.' I duck my head.

What is my problem? Why do I always say the wrong thing?

I'm so fucking dumb sometimes.

I look at her, begging her to write my comment off as nothing but the ramblings of a woman who's had too much champagne.

'It's nothing.' She forces a smile. 'I should probably get home, though. It's a work night, after all.'

My cheeks are warm. I'm such a tool. But I hold my tongue from apologising again so I don't seem too pathetic. This is the problem with booze – it loosens me up. On the table next to us, a man raises a glass of amber liquid to his lips and I feel my stomach clench in response. I want something with a little burn to it. All this champagne is making me lightheaded and I need to be brought back down.

'How about I walk you out?' I say. 'I've got to head to the ladies' before I call an Uber.'

And by *ladies*', I mean turn around and head straight back to the bar.

'Sure.' She looks as ready as I am to exit this conversation.

We fix up the bill and I walk her towards the front of the restaurant. Then I wait as she calls an Uber from her phone. We stand awkwardly in the foyer, trying to figure out how to end this derailed conversation, and in a split second, I reach my arms out and hug her. She's stiff, shocked at the sudden display of affection, but then she softens and leans into me. It's a real hug. Not one of those efficient and emotionless squeezes that my sister has given me for most of my life. Not that friendly peck on the cheek to start or end a night. It's not obligatory or reluctant in any way. It's real.

And it feels nice.

Did Adriana have something to do with her husband's death? Surely not.

I banish the question from my mind, cursing myself for even thinking such a question. Being that we're in the city, her driver arrives in a few minutes and I stay until she's out of sight. Just as I'm about to head back towards the bar, my phone buzzes.

FRANCIS: *Where are you tonight? My bed is cold.*
Meet me for a drink?

I type back without hesitation.

KYLIE: *Name the place and I'll be there.*

Chapter Twelve

The Watcher

Adriana looked incredible tonight – like a queen. A goddess. A shining light. While the other women around her were pretty little moths basking in her glow, hoping for a morsel of her attention. When a woman like that smiles at you, it bathes the world in gold.

Her fiancé is *far* from deserving of that smile.

I don't understand why she's made such a bad choice. What does she see in a man like him? What do *all* women see in men like him? Is it the money? The power? The sex? The sports car and holidays to somewhere exclusive and tropical? Are they really so enamoured by material things? They must be. I suspect her friends are no better in that regard.

Why does life always come down to money? It divides us, shuffles us into piles. Rich and poor. Working and unemployed. Thriving and drowning. When really, we're all the same.

If it wasn't for money, my family might still be in one piece.

I'm hidden behind the trunk of a large elm tree, the sweeping headlights of passing cars occasionally lighting me up. This is a nice suburb, if you have a cool two or three million lying around for a house. All the lawns are perfectly manicured. The streetlights all work. Nobody is speeding. Shiny cars with European names clutter the driveways, and there isn't a single piece of rubbish or graffiti in sight.

It's a suburban oasis.

I wait for a moment to see if anyone is coming or going along the footpath, but it's dark now. There's a blanket of inky sky above me and although the street is well-lit, nobody is outside for a walk or chatting to the neighbours over their fence. It's time to go.

I pull my cap down low on my brow to keep my face obscured and walk with intent up the driveway toward the front door. Nobody is home right now, but I don't know how much time I have. It could be minutes. Or it could be hours.

Luckily, I don't need long.

I pull a key out of my pocket. I had it cut a few weeks back when I was following Adriana. She went to a workout class at this bougie place in Brighton. Reformer Pilates. I lifted her keys out of her bag before she went in – a quick little 'bump and excuse me' while she was waiting outside on the street – and then I had a copy cut. The jangling bundle was handed into the Pilates studio receptionist after I 'found them outside on the ground'. I'm sure she was grateful that someone turned her missing item in.

The key slides easily into the lock. I turn it, the

satisfying click telling me I've been granted access. A quick glance over my shoulder confirms that nobody is watching. I let myself inside. A panel on the wall beeps at me, warning that the alarm will sound if I don't punch the code in.

But I've come prepared. I know the number off by heart.

And now I'm in.

Chapter Thirteen

Adriana

I climb into the back of the Uber and pray that the driver doesn't want to chat. He does. He's young, probably a university student, and he seems friendly. Normally I'd be okay making small talk to pass the time but tonight I don't have it in me, so I answer his questions with single-word answers as politely as I can until he gets the hint. Then he turns the music up and I'm able to let my mind wander.

To say there was a strange mood at dinner tonight would be putting it lightly. Kylie seemed to be the only one of us in good spirits and I noticed she was wearing the same Louboutins she wore to our last meeting. Where *did* she get those shoes? Even I would wince dropping that much on a pair of impractical, stilt-like heels. Something weird is going on with her, I can feel it in my bones.

Then there was Isabel with her head in the clouds. Quiet, distracted. In her own world. She's been like that lately. Even when we went around to her place for dinner, there was something off about her mood. It's like she's somewhere else. Like there's a growing distance between us that I don't quite understand.

As for Hannah . . . she's trying so hard. Too hard, my mother would say.

You can't let people know you're desperate to be liked, Adriana, she told me many times. *Only people with nothing to offer are desperate to be liked.*

A psychologist would have a field day with my mother's 'lessons'. The older I get, the more I see how she twisted my view of people and the world. It probably explains how I got into my first marriage and why I've always struggled to open up to new people. To trust.

But aside from all that, I *knew* there would be questions from the women as soon as I refused a drink. Not one of them made any accusations out loud, of course. They didn't need to. God, being a coupled-up woman in your late-twenties is bullshit sometimes. The second you blink, people think you're pregnant.

I wish they were wrong.

I took a pregnancy test the morning after dinner at In Vino Veritas. Positive. I took another again the day after that in the hope it might yield a different result. Positive again. And this morning I stumbled out of bed after Grant had left for work and chucked my guts up for a good fifteen minutes.

This isn't supposed to happen. We're careful – I'm on the pill and we use condoms any time I get sick and need antibiotics. One time the condom broke and we drove right to a twenty-four-hour chemist to get the morning-after pill. I know he doesn't want a kid and the thought of motherhood terrifies me.

I try calling Grant, but he doesn't pick up. About halfway into the journey, I get a call back.

'Hello?'

'Hey.' In the background there's music pulsing and he sounds tired. Irritated. I can tell that only from a single word because he's the kind of guy who wears his emotions on his sleeve. 'How was the dinner?'

'It was nice,' I lie. He doesn't need to know about my turmoil. 'How's Tom?'

I hear my fiancé's business partner in the background shouting. 'No wives allowed!' like he's had *way* too much to drink. I snort. Tom is the kind of guy who likes to pretend he never left his university days behind. I used to worry about him leading Grant into trouble, but he's harmless and his wife has him under her thumb.

Hence the shouting.

'Tom is . . . Tom.' Grant laughs and I find myself chuckling along with him. 'I'll be home later. Are you in an Uber?'

'Yeah.'

'Share the ride with me, okay? I want to know that you get home safe.'

See? Would a terrible guy say things like that? 'I will.'

'I love you.'

'I love you, too,' I say, meaning every word of it.

I tap the button on my phone's screen to end the call and my home page flashes up. It's 10.35 p.m. An early night, all things considered. Wining and dining potential clients is part of Grant's work to grow the business and frankly, tonight I'm happy to be alone for a few more hours. I need time to figure out how I'm going to break the news to him about the baby, but my head is swirling. It feels like I'm drunk even though I haven't touched anything but water.

The Uber whisks me away from the glittering mass of the CBD and out towards Brighton, the waterfront suburb where Grant and I live. Someone is having a party and there are clusters of Mercedes and BMWs and Teslas parked on the street. As the car's headlights sweep around the corner, I spot a couple kissing up against a tree. Her dress is hiked up her thighs and her heels lie prone on the springy grass. The couple shrinks back from the light, laughing and disappearing around the thick trunk, away from prying eyes.

The Uber driver pulls up outside my house and I exit, my ears catching the music pulsing faintly from the next block where the party rages on. The parents are probably away on a posh holiday to the Maldives or Dubai or something. Rich kids throw some wild parties when unsupervised. I remember that from the time before I was forced to leave private school.

Digging my keys out of my handbag, I walk towards the expansive white double doors that mark the entrance to our home. Really, it's Grant's home. He bought the place a decade ago and I've since slotted right in, matching the carefully decorated interior like a thoughtfully purchased side table or bar cart. I haven't changed a thing about the house, even though I've been living here for eighteen months. But I want to broach us buying a place together – something that's truly *ours*.

I want a home that has my mark on it. Still, I have little to complain about. The house is large and comfortable, and it reminds me of the place I grew up in – all the modern conveniences coupled with old-world elegance that I enjoy.

Grant has impeccable taste.

I push my key into the lock, but the door creaks open before I can turn it. I pull my hand away as if I've been burned. Why is the door open? I step back, my eyes frantically scanning the front of the house. Nothing appears disturbed. There are no trampled bushes, no footprints, no signs that anyone has been here.

My keys dangle from the lock and warm golden light spills through the gap. The foyer light is on, like usual. We always leave it on whenever we're out. I nudge the door with my fingertip, widening the gap so I can see the alarm control panel on the wall. It's off.

'Hello?' I call out.

There's no response.

I glance back over my shoulder – the Uber driver is long gone. As I hover on the doorstep, unsure whether it's safe for me to enter, I bite my lip. Maybe Grant forgot to lock the door. But what about the alarm? I shake my head. He's too paranoid about us getting robbed to be so careless. And he confirmed less than fifteen minutes ago that he was out of the house. Only Grant's sister and our cleaner have a key and a code to get inside, but I know our cleaner is currently in Queensland with her family.

'Sarah?' I call out my future sister-in-law's name but only silence greets me.

Shit. What do I do now?

I pull my phone out of my bag and try Grant, but he doesn't pick up. Then I try Sarah's phone and it also goes to voicemail. But there's no ringing coming from inside the house, so I assume that means she's not here. I think about calling Kylie but . . . I'm feeling awkward about the uncomfortable exchange we had at the restaurant. The words struck me so hard in the chest that, for a moment, I lost my breath. She has no idea how close to home she hit.

I didn't kill my husband. I didn't, I didn't, I didn't.

Desperate, I call Isabel, hoping she's still awake.

She answers on the second ring. 'Hey.'

'Oh, you're up.' I let out a relieved sigh.

'Look, don't worry about the thing with that guy. He's a prick and it's certainly not the first time I've had to deal with someone making a nasty comment about my face. Frankly, "roadkill" isn't as bad as some of the things I've heard,' she says, her voice dull with sadness. 'I know you're a real mama bear about stuff like that, but you don't have to fight everyone who looks at me wrong.'

I bite down on my lip. *Did I do the wrong thing by speaking out?* I can't help it. Isabel is the sweetest person I've ever known and seeing her be treated poorly makes something inside me turn to flame.

'Sorry,' I mumble, unsure what else to add.

'I love that you care, truly.' There's a click of something in the background and the sound of metal on porcelain.

'I, uh . . .' I glance into the house. 'Can I ask you a favour?'

'Sure. Is everything okay?'

'I just got home and the front door is unlocked.' I haven't yet spotted any signs of movement or disturbance inside, yet there's a squirming, uncomfortable feeling in my gut. Someone has been here; I can practically smell it in the air – like a barely perceptible trail of perfume or cologne. Almost more of a memory than an actual, tangible scent. 'The alarm is off and Grant's out. I'm a bit unnerved.'

'Do you want me to head over?'

I hear the whistle of a kettle in the background. Isabel lives in Springvale, and it would take her a good thirty minutes to get here.

'No, it's fine. I'm sure I'm being paranoid,' I reply. 'But would you stay on the phone with me while I check it out?'

'Should you be going in alone?' Isabel asks. There's maternal worry in her voice. 'Maybe we should call the police.'

I can only imagine how they would react. One look at me and I'd be pegged as a dumb would-be trophy wife with nothing better to do with her time than let her imagination run wild. *No thank you.*

'I'm sure Grant just forgot to lock up,' I lie.

He would *never* forget something like that.

'Okay,' she relents, but I sense her unease. 'Of course I'll stay on the line. But the second you see anything weird you hang up and call triple 0, okay? Promise.'

'I promise.'

I step into the house and close the door quietly behind me. The foyer has two archways on opposite sides, like sentinels guarding a throne. One leads to the living room and the other leads to a library area, where Grant keeps art, books, and items collected from his travels. Beyond that is the kitchen and his office. There's also a big sweeping staircase up to the next level – wood steps with a cream carpet runner.

I walk hesitantly into the living room. Everything looks as it did when I left, right down to the cup of tea sitting on a coaster with cold dregs in the bottom, the tag hanging listlessly over one side. My heels click as I cross the tiled foyer into the library. Same story there. Everything in its place.

And there would be plenty to steal in this room. There's an antique clock worth a small fortune on one shelf and Grant's favourite Patek Philippe watch on a side table, along with a pair of cufflinks set with small precious stones and his reading glasses. The watch alone is worth close to thirty grand. It would all have been an easy smash-and-grab if someone had broken into the house to rob it.

The fact that it's sitting there makes my heart thump. If someone broke in and didn't steal it, then what were they after? For some reason, that heightens my anxiety.

'Anything?' Isabel asks, her voice tight.

'Not so far.'

I walk towards the kitchen and the seed of paranoia makes my eyes go straight to the knife block but, again, nothing is missing. The last room on the ground floor is Grant's office. At first glance, everything looks normal. There are papers on his desk; haphazard, though I'm sure he would know where everything is.

But when I walk around the desk, all three drawers

hang open. Someone has rifled through the contents. A piece of paper hangs out of one like a tongue poking out, and three more sheets have drifted down onto the carpet. Invoices, it looks like. A cup of paperclips has been overturned in the top drawer, spilling into a leather tray that holds a small collection of fountain pens. There's a rogue bulldog clip and a slide of staples and several Post-it notes featuring Grant's barely legible writing that have collected lint and fluff on the back so they're no longer sticking to anything.

I wouldn't know if anything was taken because I don't come in here often. Grant tends to stay late in the company office, rather than coming home to work, so he's usually only in here on weekends when I prefer to be out and about. Besides, it's quite possible he was looking for something in a rush before he went out for his work do tonight. Perhaps a business card or a note he'd written.

I know the pens alone in the top drawer are worth something – one of them being a vintage Mont Blanc he inherited from his father.

'Ground floor looks okay,' I say to Isabel as I pick up the papers from the floor and toss them onto the desk before closing the desk drawers and heading out of the room. 'Let me check upstairs. I can't hear anything, though. I'm probably being paranoid.'

'Better paranoid than TSTL.'

'What's TSTL?' I start climbing the stairs.

'Too Stupid To Live,' she replies. There's a rustling in the background and a slight metallic sound, like a spoon hitting something. 'You know, like those dumb people in horror movies who go up the stairs instead of out the front door.'

I glance back down to the foyer and front door, my nerves jangling. But I continue on.

The door to my office is open and I can see my desk, neat as a pin, my MacBook sitting on its ergonomic stand and my collection of succulents clustered in one corner. There's a water glass with a smudge of pink at the rim, which is the only sign I've been in the room recently. Everything else is neat and orderly. The other two rooms up here – the main and spare bedrooms – have their doors closed.

I head to my bedroom first, pushing down on the gold handle and easing the door open. The large king bed sits in the middle of the room, perfectly made without a single wrinkle or a pillow out of place. I'm one of those masochists who steams the covers so they look perfectly smooth. But there's something on the bed.

Holding my breath, I approach to see what it is. My heart pounds as I get closer.

What on earth?

It's a small shoe. A baby girl's shoe, to be exact. Inside the single shoe is a piece of paper, folded up and tucked away for safekeeping. With a trembling hand, I reach for it.

'Adriana?' Isabel sounds worried.

But I'm too focused on the note. I put my phone down and unfold the piece of paper. It's lined and ragged at the edge, like it's been torn from a spiral-bound notebook. Black pen is scratched across the page.

Get out while you still can.

I open my mouth, but no words come out. My throat is dry. Parched.

'Adriana?' Isabel's voice is an octave higher now, though it sounds far away since I didn't put the phone on speaker. I pick it up. 'Talk to me. What's going on?'

'There's no one here,' I say into the phone, my eyes laser-locked on the baby shoe and the note now sitting next to it.

'You sure everything's okay?' There's an odd note to her voice but I want to get off this call now. Something niggles at the corner of my mind, but I'm too distracted to pay attention to it.

'Looks like Grant forgot to lock up, that's all.'

'Thank goodness no one robbed the place!' She lets out a long sigh. 'My gosh, how scary! You'll need to have a word with him when he gets home. He can't be doing that. Anyone could get in. I mean, I know you live in a safe suburb and all . . . but still.'

'You're right.' My tongue feels leaden in my mouth and the words have a numb quality to them. I hold my breath and hope Isabel doesn't notice it and push for more information. I feel like I'm about to come apart at the seams. 'Thanks for staying on the line.'

'No worries.' Her reply is relaxed. She has no idea that I'm trembling. My shoulders drop in a brief moment of relief. 'I know you'd do the same for me. Sleep tight, okay?'

'You too.'

I end the call and press my phone to my chest. Someone has been in here. Someone who knows I'm pregnant.

I stare at the note. The handwriting is messy, as though written in a rush. There's nothing particularly distinctive about the paper or the writing itself. I pick up the baby's shoe and turn it over. It's made of pink satin and has a bow, the centre of which is studded with crystals. Now that I look closer, one of the crystals has fallen off, leaving a hard, shining glob of glue behind.

I'm surprised to find that the sole has some dirt smudges on the bottom as if it's been worn. And why is there only one shoe? Then I notice something else. Right near where the side of the bow attaches to the shoe, there's a spot of red. It has seeped into the satin and spread, leaving a softly blurred ring of discolouration. Is that . . . blood?

I don't know what to do.

Should I try calling Grant again? Or wait until morning? Then if I tell him about the shoe, I'll probably also need to tell him about the email.

And the baby.

Something in my gut warns that this is a bad idea. So I take the shoe and the note into my office and pull out the top drawer of my desk. Then I stick my free hand inside and feel for the latch that's hidden on the underside of the desk. When my fingers find the metal, I press and there's a soft *snick*. The false bottom in the top drawer has been released and I can lift it up to expose the small hiding space underneath.

There's not a lot in there. I don't consider myself someone with much to hide from my partner.

My mother, on the other hand . . . The stuff I found in this hidey hole when I was cleaning out her things . . . I kept the desk but tossed the secrets into the rubbish. I didn't want them haunting me.

The items I've chosen to store there have deep personal meaning to me. Meaning beyond my life with Grant, which is why I keep them tucked away. I place the shoe inside and pick up a heavy gold ring – a simple band design – feeling the comforting weight of it in my palm. It's dulled from wear, since my first husband was never precious about his things.

Objects are made to be used, he used to tell me. *There's no point having a wardrobe full of shoes if you're too scared to wear them.*

He hated 'saving' things for special occasions because every day was a special occasion to him. Toby had been diagnosed with testicular cancer when he was twenty-nine and he told me on our first date that he couldn't have children. He also suffered with erectile dysfunction because of the cancer. It was obvious he'd been nervous about telling me, but I had been thrilled. I'd seen what my mother put up with – the lies, the greed, getting wrapped up in my father's crimes and having everything ripped away from her – all for the sake of *love*. A love which, I was sure, was never returned to her. A love that was as toxic as it came, sometimes with an open palm screeching across her face. A love that took the bright woman she once was and twisted her until she was a mean, hollowed-out shell of the mother I knew as a young child.

I was determined never to be so weak as to love a man. As for sex . . . I'd never really understood what the fuss was about. The one boy I'd slept with not long after my eighteenth birthday had been lacklustre at best, more focused on pleasing himself than me. So when Toby said he couldn't give me physical intimacy in that way, it was like being told I couldn't have a vegetable I didn't even like.

Whoop-de-doo.

But the cancer had given him a zest for life that radiated like a warm glow around him. Even though I can't say that I was ever 'in love' with him the romantic way you see in the movies, I deeply appreciated his spirit and his attitude.

He inspired me. We were partners.

I place his ring back into the secret compartment and pull out the envelope that sits beside it. A lump lodges in the back of my throat like it does every I open this drawer. Unlike the note I found tonight, this one is written on thick, high-quality paper with rich black ink from an expensive pen. There are small sections of the paper that have crinkled from droplets of moisture – some from him when he wrote it, and some from me when I read it. I've added more over the years.

> *Adriana,*
>
> *I hoped never to put you in this position. I know ours is an unconventional marriage, and while it might not have been what either of us hoped for as young people with unbroken hearts, I have cherished your companionship.*
>
> *But I can't go on like this.*
>
> *I know the one thing you need from me is financial security. It may sound callous to say that you married*

me for my money, but I know it's the truth. It's a practical truth, even if not a romantic one. I have tried to uphold my end of the bargain and make you happy, as you have made me.

But I have made mistakes. I have so many regrets. I cannot give you what you need and it breaks my heart.

I wish there was another way out, but I feel this is the only exit to this situation. I should never have fallen prey to someone who was only after my money.

Please forgive me.

Your loving husband.

My nostrils flare, my hands shake, and my eyes fill with tears. Guilt washes through me like a wave determined to drag me out to sea. I've carried the burden of knowing I had a hand in his death since the day I found the note. I thought he was so strong when I first met him – to be a man so young and to lose his virility, yet he had the most amazing smile and he showed it often and without reservation. He was warm and kind and generous. He could fill a room with his energy, captivating people all around him.

We slept in separate beds from day one, never able – or even attempting – to consummate our marriage. We both had something else to gain. He gave me the lifestyle I missed from my youth, one of comfort and luxury and status. And I gave him the image he wanted to present to the world: that he was a successful man with a beautiful wife on his arm and a life that others envied.

We worked well. We fit into one another's lives like missing jigsaw puzzle pieces. We supported one another and cheered each other on. We were best friends. But his cancer and the resulting effects were somewhat of a secret. In fact, he confessed that he hadn't planned to tell me about it on our first date but he'd been so awestruck by me that he wanted everything on the table. He proposed on our third date and I said yes without hesitation. The next day he moved me out of my crappy share house in Fitzroy and into his penthouse on Collins Street. He told me I could quit my job, but I wanted to keep working so I could save a nest egg of my own.

Just in case.

I always had a backup plan. An out. I was smarter than my mother and I had learned from her mistakes.

Turns out that I didn't need an out because he pulled the ripcord on me in the end, leaving me to find his body in the home we moved into after our wedding, hanging from the ceiling. Our bank accounts were near on empty and my future was wholly uncertain. I remember sitting on the ground and staring into space, believing I had killed him. Had the pressure to keep me in my ideal lifestyle been too much? What happened to the money? Did it ever really exist? If we were in financial trouble, why didn't he tell me?

A million dollars in cash gone. He'd started taking loans out against the house, too. I sold that beautiful place to cover the debts and pay for his funeral, and was left with little more than I had when I met him. That's when Grant came into my life. He'd appeared at exactly the right moment when I needed someone to help me pick up the pieces.

I refold the letter and place it back into the secret compartment, along with the wedding ring, the baby shoe, and the handwritten note from tonight. It's like a morbid collection of fears and questions.

I will tell Grant . . . soon.

When the time is right.

Chapter Fourteen

Kylie

When I wake up, I know something is wrong.

At first, I can't move. My body is heavy, like I've been wrapped up tight and weighed down with rocks. Like I'm drowning. I blink, pushing past the thick mental fog that tries to lure me back to sleep, but my eyelids droop. Once, twice, three times.

Then a sour stench hits my nose and I recoil, gagging.

With every bit of effort I can muster, I push myself into a seated position and try to get my bearings. I'm in a hotel room – but not the same one I shared with Francis before. This place doesn't look quite as upscale, but it's not exactly a dingy by-the-hour place, either. The walls are beige, as is the carpet, and a brown sofa sits to one side where a mirrored coffee table is cluttered with champagne bottles and flutes. Three, in total.

Three?

I bring my hands to my head, pressing the heels of my hands into my eyes. The pulsing is borderline unbearable and for a moment, I sit, trying to control my breathing enough that I don't cry out from the pain. Or worse, puke.

That's what the smell is. It hits me all of a sudden and I slide off the bed, narrowly missing a sticky yellowish-brown patch on the floor, and stumble into the bathroom. I drop down, gasping as my knees hit the tiled floor, sending shocks up through my body. But the pain is quickly overtaken by the overwhelming feeling of evacuation that comes, swift and brutal. I brace myself against the toilet seat and let it all come up, the familiar burn of acid making my mouth fill with saliva. I heave again.

Sadly, I know this dance well.

My body aches, almost like the feeling of having the flu, where every part of you is so sensitive even the pressure of your own clothing is too much. I flush the toilet and head to the shower, but as I go to strip off my clothes, I discover I'm already naked. Exactly like how I woke up last time.

As the water heats up, I poke my head out of the bathroom. I'm alone. The room is in a state. My clothes – the dress I wore to dinner and the fancy high heels that Francis bought me – are strewn across the floor. My bag is open and the contents have spilled out like they've been ejected with force. Gum wrappers, a lipstick with the lid missing, pens, crumpled receipts, the shiny foil from a Crunchy bar, a packet of Tic Tacs that's opened up, tossing the little white mints across the carpet. The chaos of my life represented by a useless army of ordinary things.

I spot my phone on the floor and try to turn it on, but it's dead. I didn't bring a battery pack with me last night either, because I wasn't expecting to stay out overnight. I glance around the room, hoping there might be a charging cable somewhere, but there's nothing. My wallet has twenty dollars in it and I know the sole credit card in there is maxed out. I used what was left to pay my phone bill and my share of dinner last night.

Shit.

Steam billows out of the bathroom now and I trudge over, feeling like something that's been scraped off the ground. Roadkill. It jolts me back to that awful comment last night and I cringe. My head is home to a set of drums and my mouth feels like sandpaper.

I can't keep doing this.

As I'm about to step into the bathroom, I see an envelope on the side table next to the bed. Frowning, I walk over, bypassing the sticky mess on the floor, and get a closer look at the writing on the front.

Inside is a wad of cash.

I press my fingers to my temple and head into the shower, trying to make sense of it all. Why the bloody hell is there money on the nightstand?

I'd had a bit to drink before I met up with Francis. All that champagne. So yeah, I was already well warmed up by the time we met at the bar. Not the same place as last time, and the details are probably in my phone. I'm pretty sure he texted me the address.

I close my eyes and let the water pound against my head, running through my hair and down my body. Only flashes come to me. Francis, pulling me close, squeezing my arse. More drinks. There was another guy with us – but his face is blurry in my head. Tall, messy dark hair . . . maybe. He was wearing a suit. I remember shrinking away when he brought my hand to his lips.

Why can't I remember his face?

There was a woman, too. She seemed familiar, but her image swims in my mind. Dark hair, pretty . . . I think.

The shower has dispensers mounted to the wall for shampoo, conditioner, and body wash. I squirt some of the latter into my palm and begin to smooth it over my body, wincing. I wonder if I'm starting to get sick, with how tired and achy I feel, but when I run my palm to the inside of my thigh, I hiss through my front teeth.

'Ow!' Looking down, I find bruising on the inside of my leg – one mark about the size of a thumbprint and two smaller marks. The skin is mottled purple and red.

All I can do is stare. My mind is like a sheet of white paper and nothing in my memory bank matches an injury like this. Yes, I'm prone to being clumsy and falling when I drink, and I probably wouldn't have thought twice about a sore wrist or ankle or a banged-up knee.

But this . . .

I immediately need to vomit again. It rushes out of me and splashes against the floor of the shower, more bile than anything else. The water swirls it around the drain and I kneel, hunched over with one palm pressed against the tiles, wet hair hanging over my shoulders, my mind whirling like the water.

This isn't a clumsy injury. This is an *intimate* injury.

But is it, though? I wonder if maybe Francis and I got rough last night. Drinking can make me a little

148

sexually aggressive, or so I've been told. Usually I don't remember. Perhaps I wanted it rough.

Then why are tears filling my eyes? Why are there three champagne flutes on the coffee table? Why is there money on the nightstand?

And why do I feel like something terrible happened?

A tear rolls down my cheek and I let it get washed away. Something needs to change; I can't keep drinking like this. I can't keep waking up and not remembering what happened. It's one thing to get wasted sitting on my bed and not remembering what I watched on Netflix, but it's entirely another thing not to remember sleeping with a man . . . twice. I have to know how I got the bruise on my thigh.

Maybe it's nothing.

I close my eyes and wonder if I can let myself believe it. My heart wants to believe it. But there's a little voice in the back of my head saying that something is wrong and I've heard that voice before. I've *ignored* that voice before.

When it told me there was a reason Marcus guarded his phone, I ignored it.

When it told me I should move money into an account only I could access, I ignored it.

When it told me the drinking was becoming a problem, I ignored it.

'Something happened,' I say, my voice lost to the steady drum of water and the thick screen of steam. 'I know something happened.'

* * *

149

One thousand dollars.

That's how much money is in the envelope. I count it three times, sure it will suddenly vanish from my hands in a thick puff of smoke. But it's still sitting there. Twenty perfect fifty-dollar notes. They're bright gold, unwrinkled, fresh from the mint.

I put the money back on the nightstand and stare at it. The alarm clock shows that it's only eight-thirty in the morning, so I'm not being rushed to check out today. My gaze swings to the discolouration on the carpet from where I've tried to clean up after myself. At least, I *assume* it's my mess.

From what I've seen, Francis hardly seems the type to chuck up in a hotel room.

I've hidden the glasses away, out of my line of sight, because the third glass makes something twist and churn in my stomach. What should I do? I reach down between my legs and press my fingers against the bruise, biting down on my lower lip to stifle a cry of pain. Despite my mental pleading, it doesn't bring anything else to mind. No new memories. Not even a flicker.

I wish my phone was on so I could see a message from Francis saying that there was some big mistake. That he hasn't left money for me like I'm a sex worker. That there was no third person in the room with us. That the bruise was an accident, a little rough foreplay that went too far in the heat of the moment. That everything is fine.

I pull my dress on, grateful I wore something to dinner that wouldn't look out of place in an office. Walking out of a hotel room in something shiny and

150

sparkly would feel like more than I could endure in this moment. I'm vulnerable enough – I don't need people judging me for my poor decisions any more than I'm already judging myself.

I slip my feet into my high heels, shove my personal effects back into my handbag and stare, again, at the wad of cash. My mouth is dry and my pulse beats unsteadily. That money would do me a world of good. And what else can I do? Leave it here so that some lucky cleaner stuffs it into their pocket? I swipe the envelope and stash it away in my bag, hating myself even more than I did a moment ago.

I glance guiltily at the patch on the floor before I check myself in the mirror – thankfully, I feel worse than I look. My red hair is slightly frizzy from being air dried and I washed my makeup off in the shower, so I seem fresh-faced, if a little tired. Without foundation, my freckles are more pronounced. Like a mist of cinnamon-coloured paint. There are bags under my hazel eyes, but anyone looking might simply mistake me for an overworked management consultant.

If only.

Sighing, I walk out of the hotel room and let the door shut quietly behind me. Room 406. I assume Francis has taken care of the bill.

As I head down the hallway to the lift bay, there's an older woman standing outside one room with a trolley filled with bath towels and sheets and other room refreshments. She looks at me, her gaze immediately narrowing. There's a large mole on her chin and her black hair shows a good centimetre of pure silver at the roots. As I get closer, she opens her mouth as if she's going to say something. But then she snaps it shut again. I look down at myself, worried I'm somehow flashing my underwear or committing another public faux pas. But everything appears in order.

'Hello.' I nod politely as I get close and she nods in return, her eyes not meeting mine.

A strange intuition settles into my gut. I feel like I've seen this woman before, but I can't place it. I stop in the middle of the corridor and look back, but she's let herself into one of the rooms. The cart sits outside, unattended.

I shake my head and keep going. The hotel appears to be some kind of corporate conference gathering point, because I find myself waiting behind a group of men and women in suits with lime-green lanyards around their necks. A quick glance tells me it's some kind of technology conference. This probably also explains why the decor of the hotel is simple and unfussy – indicating it's a place of business rather than pleasure.

But for some reason, that makes me feel even more uneasy about last night. Francis doesn't strike me as the kind of man to sleep in a moderate three-star conference hotel. The one at Crown Casino seemed to fit him better.

Why don't I remember coming here with him?

The lift dings and I step in behind the group, shrinking to the side of the carriage as I spot one of the men eyeing me up and down. I drop my gaze to the floor, hoping he won't engage. When we arrive at ground level, I see the foyer of this hotel is much less opulent than the Crown Casino hotel. It has a few tub chairs arranged to one side, an abstract painting in fifty shades of beige hanging on the wall and a check-in desk with a bored-looking attendant standing behind it. She glances at her nails, eyes a little glazed.

Right as I'm about to walk through the automatic doors that lead out to the street, I stop. I don't know why, but something compels me to turn around. In four short steps, I close the distance to the counter and the woman looks up, a half-hearted smile on her face. 'Hi. Can I help you?'

'Yes, uh . . .' I'm not sure where the words are coming from, exactly. It's like I'm following some hunch that's buried so deep I barely know what it is. 'Did my boyfriend take care of the bill for our room? We were in 406 last night.'

The woman looks down at her screen, long French-tipped nails tapping over the keyboards. The *click* sound gets under my skin and I press my fingertips to my temple. I need coffee and every painkiller I can get my hands on.

'Room 406 has been taken care of.' The woman nods.

'Can you confirm the name it was booked under?' I ask.

'Francis John.'

It sounds like a false name. Or John as in . . .

I think of the cash in my bag and my stomach lurches again. I need to get my phone turned on and find out what the hell happened last night.

Chapter Fifteen

Isabel

I hate visiting the cemetery.

In truth, I haven't come here all that often since the funeral. I visited once right after, and I'd felt so hollowed out that I hadn't even found it in myself to cry. Then I came once on his birthday and then once more when I was so angry I didn't know what else to do.

Yet I know the path to the headstone without having to stop and think or navigate any wrong turns. I ease my car along the gentle sweeping curves of the Springvale Botanical Cemetery until I spot the cluster of standard rose bushes where he lies.

Jonathan loved roses.

He was a bit of an old soul like that. Loved his record player and vintage silver teapot and leatherbound books and holding out my chair when we went to restaurants. I found those parts of him charming. Nostalgic, even. There was a steadiness to him, like the big exposed beams in our house that made me feel secure and protected.

Until that night.

I get out of the car and slam the door shut behind me. The grass is springy and lush, revived from its crispy, crunchy summertime state with the rain we've had recently. There are still a few little brown patches here and there, but with more rain due in the coming months, it will turn into something out of a fairy tale. Well, except for the graves.

I find Jonathan's spot and stop, dropping down to my knees and not caring at all that I'm going to get grass patches on my leggings. I press my hand to the plaque on the ground.

JONATHAN PARK
BELOVED HUSBAND AND KIND HEART TO ALL

For a moment I can still see his face in front of me: the jet-black hair and strong jaw; the dark, expressive eyes he inherited from his Korean father and the warm golden olive skin and comforting smile that he inherited from his Spanish mother. I can see the glint in his eye that he used to get whenever he teased me and the smile that would turn to smoke when he pulled me towards our bed. He was a superb lover, always finding the perfect balance between hard and soft, never pushing me too far but not letting me become complacent, either.

Tears well in my eyes and spill onto my cheeks. Some days I miss him so much it's like I've shot a hole in my chest and my insides have turned to ash, blowing out of me any time I try to feel. Some days the loss is so bright and so sharp that I can't taste food or smell the eucalyptus in the air.

'When is it going to stop?' I ask him. Because I'd always asked him those questions.

When will I stop being angry?
When will I believe it wasn't my fault?
When will I be able to move on?

After the first time we kissed, he told me that he could no longer be my psychologist. What he'd done was unethical, a massive breach of his duties. One kiss – the barest brush of lips – had changed things. He wrote me a few recommendations for people he knew in the industry who specialised with victims of sexual assault and told me that I would be in good hands.

I didn't see him for almost three years. It was only by chance that we bumped into one another at a bar. I was still in therapy and making steady gains and he was recently single. I asked to buy him a drink as a thank-you for setting me on the right path and we married the following year. It was blissful. He was a fantastic cook, well-read, hyper competitive at board games, while I was chaos most of the time and he enjoyed my unpredictability.

One night he went out to a gala dinner for some industry award thing. He didn't drink much, generally, and chose to drive. It was not long after dusk and he was heading there straight from work. His clinic was in a leafy suburb, prone to native wildlife, especially kangaroos. I hate the damn things, with their long powerful tails and large feet, and their affinity for coming towards headlights. There was one on the side of the road and he moved into the other lane to avoid it, but his wheel hit something else – a dead kangaroo that he'd missed while focusing on the live one. The car swerved and the back end clipped a large gum tree, causing him to spin and hit another tree. The impact pitched Jonathan forwards and the seatbelt yanked him back.

It saved his life, that seatbelt. But the accident was severe. His back was ruined. The pain was immense.

For the next year, I watched the man I loved dissolve in front of me. I watched him turn from being an open, honest, and forthright person to a man who would hide pills in his desk drawer and hop from one doctor to another looking for opioid prescriptions. A temper flared where there had not been one before and he withdrew, curling into himself like an echidna protecting its soft insides with a spiny outer layer.

I press my hand to the cool surface of his plaque.

The morning he died, I found him on our bedroom floor, vomit down his shirt and pooling on the carpet. He wasn't moving. I shook him, crying his name and using all the strength I could muster in my body to wrack his shoulders back and forth. Then I called triple 0. I remember screaming at the ambulance from the street, waving my arms hysterically.

After that, it was all a blur. They couldn't revive him.

I will never know if it was an accident or not. There was no letter, no suicide note. Nothing to indicate he'd done it on purpose. All I knew was that he was miserable and that the pain stopped him from sleeping or standing or sitting too long. But I figured that he was a psychologist, so if things were really that bad . . .

Surely he would have got help.

Surely.

Surely.

'I miss you,' I whisper, closing my eyes as more tears spill onto my cheeks. 'I'm sorry I didn't try harder.'

I could have read the signs better, kept track of his pill popping, forced him to speak to someone, asserted myself. But in that moment, I was trying to do for him what he had done for me – kindness, patience, understanding. I tried to be soft and gentle for him as he had been for me.

And I think I buried my head in the sand. I tried to tell myself that pain made people act strangely, and that it was okay that he sulked and yelled if that's how he needed to deal with things. I tried to be everything he needed.

But maybe I was the opposite. Maybe I let him die by not being strong enough. By not speaking up.

I don't think Jonathan would be proud of what I'm planning, but I don't know any other way to be. I'm adrift. Untethered. I'm a husk with nothing to keep me alive except a thirst for revenge. My shoulders shake as I let it all out, both hands now pressed into the plaque as I brace myself against it. Just when I think I'm empty, there's more. More hurt. More loathing. More questions. My tears splatter his name like rain drops.

Without him, there's nothing to stop me hurtling towards my darkest desires.

When I get back home, my face is swollen and puffy from crying. I keep my sunglasses on so I don't frighten my neighbour's small children who are playing in their front yard as I park the car and walk up the driveway of my modest house. It's not the same one I lived in with Jonathan. After he died, I couldn't stand to be in the house where we were once so happy. So I sold up and moved somewhere small and indistinct, losing myself in the nothingness of builders' beige walls, hardy renters' carpet, and bland bathrooms.

Inside, the air feels musty. I used to love burning candles of all scents – vanilla, lemon, sage, berry – and I had an entire cupboard dedicated to them. At least once a week Jonathan would come home with a new one for me that he'd seen in a gift store or specialty shop. He'd always present it to me with sparkling eyes, eager for my excited smile and the way my eyes would flutter shut when I stuck my nose into the box to breathe in the scent.

These days my house smells like the stale remnants of whatever I cooked or reheated the previous night for dinner.

The pocket on my denim jacket vibrates and I pull my phone out. It's Adriana.

ADRIANA: *Thanks again for being there for me last night. It was nothing to worry about in the end, a simple mistake.*

I raise an eyebrow. Leaving the door open to a house like that is more than a simple mistake. It's inviting trouble. Something about the whole thing has left me with a strange feeling and lately the secrets are piling up. First the engagement, now the pregnancy she's doing a terrible job of hiding. I still can't believe she told us about that email – it's highly out of character for her. And I don't think for a second that this is the end of her list of secrets. Kylie seems to have a number of her own, too – like why she hasn't emailed us from her work email address in weeks and where the designer shoes she can't afford have come from.

But I can't judge, I'm keeping plenty of secrets from the Young Widows, too. Secrets like who I really am and what I have planned.

ISABEL: *If Grant needs a lecture about safety, you can send him my way.*

She responds with a laughing emoji.

I'd like to give the guy a lecture about more than safety, truth be told. But I know Adriana won't appreciate me butting into her business.

I dump my handbag and keys on the kitchen table and spy an envelope, untouched and pristine white, lying on the breakfast bar. It's been there for a week while I gather the strength to open it. So many times I thought about throwing it away, crumpling it in my fist or jamming it through the shredder. I feel this way every time the envelope comes, with the same neat handwriting with curling lines spelling out my full name.

Susanna Isabel Park.

It makes me cringe. I haven't gone by Susanna in years, and this is the only place where I have to endure the name. In the outside world, I have 'Isabel' listed as

160

my preferred name everywhere and have even thought about having it legally changed, if the administration weren't such a headache. After my attack, I found out that my grandmother – Dad's mum – was actually the one who chose my name, and ever since I've hated it.

Susanna, a wife in the Book of Daniel, was a biblical figure who was accosted by two men. They tried to convince her to have sex with them, and when she refused, they attempted to punish her with false cries of adultery. She was saved from execution by Daniel and a mistake involving the description of a tree, and the two men were ultimately put to death. My grandmother found this so inspiring – *Upholding virtue and truth is so important, Susanna* and *You are named after the very triumph of morality, Susanna* – that she convinced my parents to name me after this woman.

All I see is how my life echoes this story. I am a woman who was punished for refusing a man, a man who tried to put me to death with his own hands, and now I am on a path of justice. I am both Susanna and Daniel – both a victim and my own saviour.

I tear open the envelope. Inside is a photo of a little girl, blond-haired and blue eyed. She's seven now, with a gap between her teeth and light brown hair past her shoulders. The colour seems to shift every time I receive a photo, always on her birthday. As a baby, she was blond. By the time she made it to kindergarten, her hair was a pale caramel. Now it's a deeper toffee, with sections that have been lightened by the sun and others that hint at her father's darker colouring.

The letter enclosed tells me that 'Poppy' is doing well

at school and that she's shown an aptitude for sports, so they've put her into a softball team. It's not the name I chose for her, secretly and in my heart. I never said it out loud as I carried this baby, because I never had any intention of keeping her. I wanted her to go to a good home, one where she wouldn't be looked at as the product of great pain and suffering.

I didn't want her to bear that mark. That stain.

Her new parents are good people and they have means. They have given her a life far better than I could have, with money for any whim she has and the best education our state has to offer. They plan to tell her she's adopted when she's a little older and will keep in touch with me in case she ever has questions. They know how I came to be pregnant. In fact, the wife's sister was one of the receptionists at the clinic where I met Jonathan, and she was the one who helped me set up the adoption.

I take the photo and the letter and carefully tuck them away in a locked box where I keep everything related to the child I never held. There's a small collection of photos graduating from a chubby-cheeked baby to a now seven-year-old little princess. I have the hospital bracelet I wore the day I gave birth in there, too, and a single onesie that I bought in a store one day with a plan to give it to my child, though I never mustered up the courage.

I close the lid on the box and slide it back into place, wedged at the top of my refrigerator and out of sight.

'I'm doing this for both of us, baby girl,' I say. 'Your father is going down.'

Chapter Sixteen

Adriana

I've tried four different brands of tests, from three different chemists. Twice each over the course of a week and a half since I figured out my period was late. I *keep* taking them in the hopes that one of them will return a different result and I can say 'Phew, dodged a bullet there!' But no matter how much water and coffee I drink and how many times I wee on the little plastic sticks, they've all come back with the same result.

I'm pregnant. It's as true now as it was several nights ago when I went to dinner with the girls.

I've never been comfortable with idea of motherhood. It's like a dress that doesn't quite fit; it pinches in spots and restricts my movement. It stifles me, makes me sweat. It's claustrophobic.

The pressure. The judgement. The expectation.

I'm frightened of it.

Maybe that's because I don't have a good example to go on. My own mother never perfectly fit that role, either. She tried – I know she did. But it chafed her.

The memories are faded now and as much as I try to bring them back to life, it's like I'm colouring over the top of them, trying to create an oil painting from crayons and dried-out watercolour pens.

I sit on the toilet and stare at the edge of one wrapper, bright blue and white, poking out from under the wad of tissues I've crumpled up and pressed down over the top of the discarded packaging to hide it inside the small rubbish bin. I don't know what I'm going to say to Grant.

He doesn't want children.

The close call he had twenty-something years ago was enough to show him that he doesn't want to become a father. We've even talked about him getting the snip so we don't have to worry about it anymore.

How could this have happened? I know the pill is only 99 per cent effective but still . . . how could I be *that* unlucky?

I drop my head into my hands, pressing the heels of my palms into my eye sockets in the hope it might stop the pounding there. The pressure hurts and yet it feels like I need it, because feeling nothing is far scarier than feeling pain.

'Adriana?' Grant's voice floats in through the gap under the bathroom door.

Shit. I thought he was going out again tonight. I spring off the toilet and pull my undies up, before grabbing the rubbish bin and sweeping the latest test – and all the wrappers, instruction papers and so on – into it. Then I stuff more tissues on top to cover it up. I need to think about how I'm going to break the news to him.

'One sec,' I reply, flushing the toilet and washing my hands, taking longer than I need to try to gather myself.

I grab my blue silk bathrobe from the hook on the back of the door and slip it over my shoulders. Taking one last look in the mirror, I blow out a long breath and force myself to relax. My blond hair is limp and there are bags under my eyes. My nose looks even more pronounced against my pale, slightly sallow skin. I'm a mess.

I have to figure out how to break the news to Grant, but that doesn't mean I have to do it right now. If I can get through tonight without losing it, then I can sit down and make a plan.

I *will* figure this out.

I open the en-suite door and step into the bedroom. Everything is perfectly in its place. Our king bed made with luxurious cream and grey bedding, every one of the half-dozen pillows in its correct place. The white carpet is plush and fluffy, there's no excess clutter on the custom hardwood nightstands. All the art on the walls is precisely level. It could be a picture of a home in a magazine.

Grant stands in the doorway, still wearing his suit from a long day in the office. His hair is rumpled, a sure sign it's been a frustrating day, because he tends to drive his fingers through the strands whenever he's upset. The knot of his tie is loosened too, and the top button of his shirt sits open. There's a tension to his expression.

'I thought you were heading out tonight?' I say, hoping my voice sounds light and breezy.

'I cancelled.'

'Is everything okay?' My stomach knots immediately because I know, without a doubt, that everything is not okay with my fiancé. I can feel it crackling in the air, like a storm that's about to burst through the clouds.

Oh God. What if he's seen one of the pregnancy tests I've thrown out? Or what if he went snooping in my inbox and trawled through my deleted emails and saw the one telling me I'm not safe with him?

I'm being ridiculous. That would *never* happen. The stress about my unwanted pregnancy and the break-in and the creepy baby shoe and keeping all these secrets are getting to me.

Everything will be fine. You triple-check the alarm and the locks now, and nobody has contacted you since. Just chill.

'It was a rough day in the office,' he replies. But he's remote. Cool. 'I . . . never mind.'

'Tell me.' I walk over to him and press a hand to his chest. 'If you need to talk, I'm here for you.'

A warmth suffuses his expression and he places his hand over mine. For the first time in my life, I crave physical intimacy from a man. When I was younger I thought sex was something to be put up with, and then after marrying Toby, I never knew any different because it was never on the table. Aside from the physical complications of his cancer, neither of us wanted to try. It wasn't that kind of relationship. But Grant has taught me to understand my desires. To understand pleasure. To understand the delicious feeling of giving yourself over to another person. It's addictive.

166

I never wanted to fall in love. I never wanted to be like my mother, so besotted with a man that I would sacrifice everything for him. And really, I'm not there yet. But Grant tempts me closer to that place, even though I know better. Sometimes it scares me how easily he seems to slip past my defences, raking aside my walls and my excuses like a man cutting his way through the jungle with a machete.

'You've got such a big heart, Adriana.' He cups my face.

'It's all yours, I promise.' I press up onto my toes and brush my lips against his. 'Now stop beating around the bush.'

'Lately I've felt like something has been off between us.'

My stomach churns. Does he know about the break-in? Was something missing from his office? Has he found the secret compartment in my desk?

I find it hard to swallow. 'Oh?'

'Ever since we went to dinner.'

'At In Vino Veritas?' I frown. 'How so?'

'I swear you told me about that place, but when we went there you got all confused and distant. I thought maybe I'd made a mistake. But then I remembered . . .' He swallows and looks down at me. 'You used to go there with Toby, right?'

I blink. How could he know that?

'I bumped into him one time and he was there with you for your anniversary. I noticed you sitting with him and . . .' He lets out a laugh. 'I was so fucking jealous that he had a woman as exquisite as you at his table.

I must have confused you telling me you liked that place with actually seeing you there before.'

I search my mind, trying to remember a time when we spoke to any business acquaintances of Toby's while out at dinner, but there were so many instances like that they all blur into one. And why would I remember such a banal thing? Maybe he didn't even speak with us that night, and only noticed we were there for a distance.

'I don't remember . . .' I shake my head.

'I didn't interrupt your special night.' He rakes a hand through his hair. 'I said hello to Toby when he walked past my table on the way to the men's room and he said you were on a special night out, but I didn't speak directly to you.'

It fits my memory, as I met Grant for the first time at Toby's funeral. He never mentioned that he'd seen me before, but I guess that probably wouldn't have been an appropriate thing to say to a grieving widow. But for some reason, there's an aspect of his story that sits oddly. Like he's telling me a half-truth or maybe even an 80 per cent truth.

He's leaving something out. Something important.

'I don't know why I needed to clarify that.' He rakes his hand through his hair again. No wonder it's such a mess today. 'But things were feeling weird between us and I wanted to clear the air. You seemed upset the other night.'

'I wasn't, and nothing is weird between us,' I assure him, knowing it's a lie.

We're keeping things from each other and we're not even married yet. It's not a good sign. But I can't deal with this right now. I have too much in my head. Too many questions. Too much uncertainty.

'Good.' He seems relieved. Bending down, he presses his lips to mine and kisses me hard. I let him. 'I don't want there to be any skeletons hanging around when we get married. No secrets or lies, okay? I've done that once before and I don't want to go down that road again.'

'Me neither.'

But I fear, even as I say those words, that we've already taken a detour off the highway of truth and we're speeding towards a tangled web that's waiting to wreck us both.

I wake in the middle of the night, fists clutching the bedsheets and sweat dampening my body. My heart batters against my ribcage and my breath comes in gulps, like I've made a mad dash in the rain. The dream swims in front of my eyes – Toby's body hanging from the beam in our kitchen, swaying back and forth, eyes bulging, skin tinted purple. I tried to reach for him, but my feet were glued to the floor. Tears streaked down my face, stinging my eyes, and a scream burned the back of the throat.

But then Toby's head snapped towards me and his eyes bulged as he roared my name. His face twisted and distorted, morphing until his features resembled Grant's. That's when I woke up, gasping.

I reach for Grant out of instinct, something I've never done before. I'm prone to bad dreams, you see. But normally I get out of bed and compose myself with a glass of water and the feeling of a cool compress on the back of my neck or my forehead. Independently. Quietly.

I try not to rely on others. Especially not men.

But in this moment I need him. I reach for my fiancé, but my hand meets only cool, empty sheets. Rolling, I blink into the darkness and grope around. But there's nothing. I push up to a sitting position and give my eyes a moment to adjust, and the room slowly comes into focus, dark, fuzzy blobs slowly taking shape until I can see the chest of drawers, the mirror, the chair.

Swinging my legs over the edge of the bed and standing, my soles are cushioned by thick carpet. No light comes from under the en-suite door. 'Grant?'

There's no response.

I go to the bedroom door and push it open, slowly so it doesn't creak, and I spot a glimmer of gold coming from downstairs. Stepping out onto the landing, I peer over the railing. The light in Grant's office is on – not the overhead one, I don't think. Just a lamp. The glow is dim. Soft.

He's talking to someone, his voice low.

I wish I'd taken note of the time on the clock by my bed, but it has to be the middle of the night. Outside, the inky black sky feels like it's closing in, darkness making even the sound of my own breath feel like clashing cymbals. I creep to the edge of the stairs, straining to listen. His voice is muffled. Something in my gut compels me to go listen.

I take one step down the stairs, then another, keeping one hand gripping the railing and one palm pressed to my chest as if it might slow my thundering heart. But it doesn't. I take another step, then another. One, two, three more. I reach ground level and raise my heels up, tiptoeing with great care so I don't draw his attention. I'm outside his office now, my ears almost ringing from trying so hard to listen.

'Was it *you*?' The voice doesn't even sound like it belongs to him. It's vicious. Disembodied. 'Did you break into my fucking house?'

He knows.

I hold my breath.

'Oh, don't give me that bullshit.' He lets out a snort. 'I know someone was in here and they were looking for something. The only person I know who'd want anything in my office is you.'

I have no idea who is on the other end of the line. One of the bookcases rattles slightly as he paces.

'Don't bring Adriana into this. Don't even say her name.'

I freeze. I can't blink, can't breathe. Does he know about the note? About the baby shoe?

'Keep out of my business. I won't play these games. Not now. Not ever.'

The silence is like a knife. It slices through the air, splitting it open and letting tension pour into the house. I can feel it ringing in my ears. There's a squeak and a dull thud as Grant drops down into his desk chair, and a clattering sound follows that's probably him tossing his mobile phone across the desk.

I need to get back to bed before he catches me.

Quiet as a spider, I creep back to the stairs and up

to the bedroom. He knows about the break-in and yet he hasn't said a word to me.

See, I knew we were keeping secrets.

Chapter Seventeen

Isabel

Today is the day. I'm lightheaded with anticipation.

Only this event could make me excited to stay at work late while the management team has their big quarterly planning meeting. Normally I can't get out of here quickly enough. But not today.

Usually Gabby takes the minutes for the planning meetings and the junior executive assistant, Amanda, who looks after the rest of the c-suite executives, stays around to order food, make coffees, and do other menial work, while also being responsible for any calls that come through the company's main phone line.

Today, however, Amanda's kid has a school play and I, the diligent employee that I am, have volunteered to be office gofer for an evening. This means that while everyone is holed up in the boardroom for hours on end, I'll have the place to myself.

Why is this important?

Because I'm going to break into the boss's office and go fishing.

Ever since Gabby told me about that apartment building project that went belly up, I've been thinking about it. Obsessing over it. I have a quirk, you see, where a thought becomes a burr. It gets stuck, hooked into the twisting, turning tendrils of my brain, and I can't shake it.

So I think and I think and I think.

My husband used to call it 'intrusive thoughts' and I had many of them back then. Back when he was a professional brain fixer and I was a broken doll. I'd become obsessed with finding the man who attacked me in the city alley that night. The man who ruined my life. My dreams. My face. I would spend hours bleary-eyed in front of the computer looking for him. Of course I didn't have much to go on – only the image of his face that was clear as a bell in my memory bank. The hard downturned eyes, the nose with a Roman bump, the mole on his left cheek, teeth that were mostly straight except for a slight slant of the upper right incisor where it had been chipped. His face was burned into my brain.

While he lives in there, you will never be free of that night, Jonathan used to say to me. *If you want to move on with your life, you need to let him out.*

And I had. Or, at least, I thought I had. Sitting on Jonathan's couch week after week while his soothing voice slowly pulled me from the wreckage of my mind, I thought I'd found the handle of that mental cage and told my attacker to get the fuck out. For two whole years I stopped seeing his face in my dreams.

Then Jonathan betrayed me by dying. All those lessons he taught me – how to take back control of my

174

own life, how to make small steps towards progress, how to reward incremental improvement – went out the window after his car accident. The chronic pain turned him into a different person. A raging beast. The pills became his escape. And then he started to love the pills more than he loved me, and suddenly my demons started showing up again. My attacker wandered back into the cage in my mind.

And when I found Jonathan on the floor, with no pulse, lying in a pool of his own vomit, I knew nothing but revenge would stop me from following him into the light.

Which is why I have to follow this lead and see where it goes. I won't get my revenge with fists because I know not to engage in a fight I can't win. Instead, I need to find the thing that will pull my boss's perfect image apart at the seams. I want to ruin everything he loves.

And the time is now.

'Hey Gabby.' I smile and approach her desk, a stack of letters in my hand. It's three-fifteen and I can sense the anticipatory hum in the office. The worker bees are ready to be done for the day. 'The mail delivery guy came.'

'Thanks, Isabel.' She looks up, her eyes slightly glazed behind a pair of thick rimmed glasses.

'Everything okay?' I ask. 'You look . . .'

She sighs. 'Exhausted?'

'I was going to say stressed.' I pull a sympathetic face. 'You've been working long hours lately.'

I know because I've been coming in to work to find emails in my inbox from her that were sent after 10 p.m.

'It's only while the expansion is going on.' She waves a hand. 'I'll be fine. I've got a holiday planned next month and that's the light at the end of the tunnel for me.'

'Oh nice. Where are you going?' I lean against her desk, getting a little further into her personal space. It's taken her a while to fully trust me, but one thing I'm good at is gaining people's trust.

I know not to push too hard, too soon. Relationships are built bit by bit, incrementally over time. Patience, here, really is a virtue and I am nothing if not patient. I know how to lie in wait like nobody else. Biding my time. Planning my next move. Ever since we went out for a drink, she's been more open with me.

'To the Gold Coast.' Gabby gets a faraway look in her eyes, like she's already there, sand between her toes and the ocean lapping at her feet. 'The girls are going to come with me and my sister will meet us there. It's going to be glorious. Well, except for the lines at Dreamworld, but that'll only be one day out of the trip, thankfully.'

My eyes stray to the drawer in her desk. I've tried to hang around a few times and see if she'll open it in front of me, but so far she hasn't. I need her to do it now, however.

'Hey, I don't suppose you have any chewing gum or mints on you?' I cover my mouth as if embarrassed. 'I think they put too much garlic aioli on my panini at lunch.'

'Did you get it from the Italian deli?' She shakes her head. 'That happened to me one time. I swear, no one would come near me for the rest of the day.'

Her hand drifts down to the set of drawers at the side of her desk, where a key sits in the lock, a small glittery key chain dangling from it. We have a security policy that mandates we clear our desks of any personal effects and lock our drawers at the end of each workday. This is the exact reason I haven't been able to get into her drawers to snoop around myself. I tried picking the lock one time, but it was *not* as easy as the guy made it look on YouTube.

'I've got Tic Tacs or some Extra chewing gum,' Gabby says.

I can only see the Tic Tacs sitting on top, so she might have to rifle for the gum. The drawer is kind of a mess, which surprises me. Gabby is someone who always seems to have her ducks in a row. At least, that's how it looks from the outside. Though I know better than anyone that one's external appearance might purposefully say nothing about them.

'Gum would be amazing, thank you. You're a lifesaver.'

She slides her hand under some papers and my eyes dart across the contents of the drawer, catching the faintest glint of light on metal. Another key! There's a tag attached to it, and while I don't catch what's written on the tag, I'm positive it's the spare key for the boss's office. Now I know for sure that she keeps it in her desk drawer.

She finds the pack of Extra and holds it open towards me so I can slide out a piece of the wrapped gum.

'Thank you.' I shoot her a grateful smile and she returns it readily.

'No, thank *you* for agreeing to stay back tonight.' She sighs. 'And Amanda said to pass on her thanks, too. She said she owes you one.'

'It's nothing.' I wave my hand good-naturedly. 'I'm happy to help.'

As I walk back to my desk, nobody paying me any mind, a plan begins to form.

As the end of the day rolls around, I watch everyone stream out of the office. By 5.30 p.m. the place is almost empty.

I set the company's main phone number to ring on all the desk phones in the office, so I can answer any calls no matter where I am, and head into the boardroom to make sure everything is set up for the meeting. There are jugs of water and clean glasses, the whiteboard is clear, tissue boxes full, and the rubbish bin empty. Overhead, a fluorescent light flickers gently. I top up the bowls of mints, one at each end of the long oval table, and in an hour I will place an order for food using the company credit card and bring it into the room, with plates and cutlery from the staff room.

With everything in place, I exit the boardroom in time for the management team to enter. The team consists of ten people – all men, none younger than fifty – and they pile into the room with laptops and coffee cups, shirts creased from hours of sitting at their desks. Most of them look like that's all they do, with bellies pushing against their waistbands, skin pale and dry. The guy who runs the finance department must be closing in on seventy, and the backs of his hands are covered in sun-spotted skin.

Not one of them makes eye contact with me.

'Thanks again for doing this,' Gabby says as she unplugs her laptop from her desk and tucks it under one arm.

'It's no problem at all.' I smile, keeping my eyes on Gabby. I wait by her desk as she gathers her things, leaving her drawer unlocked.

'Taking minutes is *so* boring,' she says, her voice low. 'Make sure you nudge me if you come in later and I've fallen asleep.'

I laugh and then quickly cover my mouth with my hand. She winks at me and disappears into the boardroom, which is on the same side of the floor as the boss's office and Gabby's desk. This means that if anyone comes out, they could easily spot me rifling through her drawers. I have to be quick. Stealthy. I also have to be patient and bide my time while everyone settles in for the meeting, to make sure nobody pops out to grab a forgotten pen or a charging cable. But I also can't leave it too long, lest anyone duck out for a toilet break.

I'm practically holding my breath as the stragglers file into the room.

I busy myself with pottering around the office and in the first fifteen minutes, I'm called into the boardroom twice – once to replace a glass that the CFO decided was dirty (it was not) and a second time to help someone adjust a chair. Gabby shoots me an apologetic look the second time, because she knows as well as I do how ridiculous it is for a fully grown man who earns well over six figures not to be able to adjust his own chair. But she's busy tapping away at her keyboard, recording the droning presentation from the Head of Business Development.

Mr Frenchman sits at the head of the table, looking crisp despite the fact that it's been a warm day and the air-conditioning is struggling to keep up. His shirt is unwrinkled, his tie still perfectly knotted at his neck, and his salt-flecked hair is full and neat. He exudes confidence. Sometimes I wonder where it comes from, the ability to command the attention of those around you. I have never been that person. Likely, I never will be.

I duck my head and leave them to their business as soon as the chair situation is sorted. The company phone rings and it creates an echo as the sound comes from multiple desk phones. It seems strange that in this day and age we even have desk phones anymore, but this company isn't exactly at the technological forefront. Jogging over to Gabby's desk, I take the call there. That way if anyone comes out of the boardroom, I have a legitimate reason to be standing there. But nobody leaves the room. I take the message from one of our bigger international clients and write it on a Post-it note, leaving it stuck to Gabby's computer.

My gaze flicks to the boardroom door. It's closed and the muffled back and forth tells me the meeting is fully underway now. They're all settled in, focused on work.

I reach down to Gabby's drawer and pull it open to stare at the mess. A packet of cigarettes is wedged to one side, partially hidden. Interesting. I've never seen her smoke at work and haven't ever smelled that tell-tale stale stench lingering on her. I wonder if this is a new habit – stress-induced, perhaps. Trying not to make any noise, I rifle around for the key as quietly as possible which isn't an easy task with all the crap in there. For a moment my heart sinks, and I think she must have taken it with her without me noticing, but then I see a glimmer.

The key.

Scooping it up, I close the drawer and look back over to the boardroom. The muffled talking continues. There's a frosted panel either side of the door, and the blurry shapes remain mostly still. My heart is thudding so loudly it creates a drumbeat in my ears that momentarily drowns out the sounds of talking. I toy with the key, palms sweating.

I have to go now.

I hustle to the front desk and grab the USB hard drive that's sitting tucked into the side pocket of my work bag. Dropping it into the deep pockets of the flowy black pants I'm wearing – literally the only item in my wardrobe with pockets big enough to conceal the drive – I walk over to the closed door bearing my boss's name and slide the key into the lock. The company doesn't have security cameras inside the office – something I know from getting friendly with the tech guy one time. All the cameras are focused on the more valuable areas of the business: the yard where all the trucks are kept and the maintenance wing, which houses expensive tools and truck parts. There's one camera trained on the entrance to the property from the main road and another focused on the reception area, to keep track of who's coming and going from the building.

But that's it. There's nothing inside this office worth stealing . . . unless you're me.

I take one more look over my shoulder and decide to go for it. The key turns easily in the lock and there's a soft click as the mechanism releases. I push the door open and slip inside, closing it behind me. If anyone comes looking, I'll make out like I was in the bathroom. Given the sexist hiring practices of this company, the only one likely to go looking for me there is Gabby.

The office is meticulously clean and the air smells faintly of cologne. It's the same one he wore years ago and it turns my stomach, bringing a rush of memories to the forefront of my mind. But I can't afford to get sidetracked now. I have a goal to achieve.

The desk is practically bare, save for a large monitor and a laptop stand, which sits empty. There's a leather pen holder and matching in-tray with a few papers inside it, some colourful flags poking out of the small stack. In the corner of the room is a coat stand, which holds a trench coat, the distinctive checked pattern of the lining telling me it cost a small fortune. Under the desk, tucked neatly against the wall, is a black leather satchel.

I crouch down beside it and ease the latch open so I can peek inside. There sits a laptop – much slimmer and fancier than the ones we use in the office.

'Bingo,' I whisper.

I pause for a few heartbeats, listening to the point that I'm almost straining. But there's nothing. No footsteps, no voices getting louder. Letting out a breath, I look back down at the satchel. It's now or never.

I pull the laptop out and set it down on the floor, easing the top up. Keeping crouched behind the desk, I press the power button. To my surprise, the computer is asleep rather than fully turned off and it immediately shows the log-in screen. I suck in a breath.

This is where my plans could all fall apart. I have to hope that my boss doesn't take his personal security too seriously, because, otherwise, I'm fucked.

Please work. Please work. Please work.

A few months back, we ran a company-wide password audit. Turns out, 63 per cent of people in the company used a person's name as their password and a further 82 per cent hadn't changed their password in more than twelve months, even when prompted. They've since rolled out a program that forces workers to change their passwords every sixty days, but when I asked the IT team how I could help to encourage a more security-conscious work culture – something I didn't actually give two shits about, but I want to ingratiate myself with useful people – the poor IT boffin had sighed.

Sometimes I wonder what the point is, he'd said in frustration. *Our own CEO does exactly the same thing we're trying to tell staff not to do. I had to change the password requirements to force him to use more than letters. You'd think he'd care more!*

This filled me with hope that his personal laptop would have a similarly weak password.

I type in the name of his partner. A little red message flashes up on the screen. Wrong password. *Shit*. I was *sure* that would be it. I try his own name, but no dice there, either. I have to be careful not to get locked out, because then he'll know someone tried to break in.

It's probably something stupid like a childhood pet's name or maybe the nickname he had in high school. Or . . . Maybe he uses his daughter's name. Gabby told me her name the day I went to buy the earrings, so I type it in and hit enter, squinting my eyes shut and praying I got the spelling right. If this doesn't work, I'll be at a dead end.

I crack one eye open and have to stifle a yelp of joy. I'm in.

I take the USB drive out and plug it in. It's time to go fishing.

I look through the computer for anything useful. Every so often I stop and listen, but the office is quiet. The laptop screen tells me I've probably got another half an hour before I need to go in and take everyone's orders for dinner. Japanese food tonight.

The folders on the computer are arranged with a logical system that allows me to navigate through everything with methodical precision. Helpful as my boss's anal-retentiveness is, it won't mean a thing if I don't find any dirt. There *has* to be something. I've waited too bloody long to fail now. All this time I've been working for him, building trust with Gabby and getting the information from her, has been solely in order to get the justice the police were never able to give me; so I can get revenge on the man who ruined my life.

My rapist. The father of the child I gave up for adoption. The attacker who brutalised my face.

I *have* to see him fall.

Just as I feel the sinking disappointment that maybe there's nothing here – maybe he's been too careful? – I stumble across a folder marked 'insurance'. I expect to find policy documents inside, but quickly it's clear that this kind of insurance *isn't* about dental and optical coverage.

It's pay dirt.

Chapter Eighteen

Adriana

I want to know who Grant was talking to, but he keeps his phone under close guard, always tucking it away in a pocket inside his jacket or in his pants. I've tried calling the phone company, only to find out that my name isn't listed on the account and so they won't tell me a thing. Even his iPad is locked with a passcode I don't know.

I've never taken much notice of that before. Is that normal for two people about to get married to not share their passwords? Do people usually do that when they're in long-term relationships or am I looking for red flags where there are none? Well, other than the anonymous email and late-night phone call and the fact that my husband seems to know more about my relationship with my first husband than I previously thought.

Those *definitely* feel like red flags.

It's Wednesday morning and Grant is off at a golf tournament with some clients and other industry people. Thankfully he was out of the house early because there was no way I would have been able to hide the morning sickness today. It battered me about, leaving me shaking and weak on the bathroom floor. I've called in sick. Again.

Grant isn't the only one I need to tell about this pregnancy. My boss is starting to get suspicious.

Now I find myself standing at the bottom of the staircase, staring into his office. The house feels vast and quiet, and outside I hear the caw of cockatoos and the warble of magpies and the buzz of someone cutting their grass. The hum of real life.

I was supposed to be heading to a makeup trial for the wedding this evening, but I've called the makeup artist and feigned a stomach bug so she would let me reschedule. The best lies have a little truth in them, or so Mum used to say.

I can't even stand to think about the wedding right now. I need to know what Grant is hiding from me and I need to know *before* I marry him. My father kept secrets from my mother and me for years – things that came out into the light like insects scattering when the rock is lifted, things we learned when he was handcuffed and escorted out of our house, while my mother watched on, crying. Useless. The neighbours watched too, snickering behind their hands, curtains parted and mobile phones pressed to ears as they spread the word beyond our street. They took pleasure in witnessing my family fall apart, gobbling up our misery like cake.

I always knew there was something off about him,

they said, even after they'd come to our parties and eaten our food.

You can't trust new money, they said, even after they'd taken his advice for their stock portfolios and property investments.

I would have known what was going on if it were me, they'd said, as they scorned my mother and ejected her from their social groups.

I can't let myself be put in that position. Not now. Not ever.

My mobile phone trills from the kitchen bench and I pick it up. It's Kylie.

'Hey,' I say, tucking the phone between my ear and my shoulder. 'How are you?'

'I'm okay.' She sounds a little distant, as though she's got the phone on speaker and she's standing elsewhere in the room. 'I wanted to check in.'

We haven't spoken since the awkward end to my celebratory dinner.

'I, uh . . .' She's closer now and the call becomes clearer, as if she's brought the phone up to her ear. 'I feel really shit about the other night. I had a bit too much champers and it was supposed to be a joke, but it came out all wrong.'

'Kylie, it's okay. I know you didn't mean it.'

'No, it's not okay.' I hear the guilt in her voice. It coats the words in sticky emotion, making it sound like she's on the verge of tears. 'I can't keep doing shit like this and expecting you to still be my friend.'

I've never known what to say when it comes to Kylie's drinking. I'm sure she hides the worst of it, only letting

188

us see her being fun, tipsy Kylie. Or, at worst, hungover-party-girl Kylie. But addiction is often like an iceberg. The tip that pokes through to visibility is only a fraction of what's really going on behind the scenes.

It scares me. What she must be dealing with that I can't see . . .

'I just want you to be well, babe.' I mean it, every single word. 'Forget about what you said. I'm not mad. But I think—'

'I know I need to stop.' I can hear the tears in her voice.

'Maybe you could try one of those meetings so you don't feel like you're going it alone,' I suggest gently. The last thing I want is for her to feel alienated by her friends, when what she truly needs is our support. 'I don't know if they let friends come along for moral support, but if they do I'd be happy to come with you. I can sit and hold your hand if it would help.'

'Thank you.' She sniffles. 'I feel so stupid.'

'Don't say that. We all do things in life that aren't . . . optimal. But that's what friends are for, right? To help you up when you've had a stumble. I know you'd do the same for me.'

The words echo what Isabel said to me the night of the break-in. That's what our group is – women who would do anything for one another.

For some reason, the thought makes me look down at my belly. Why didn't I tell them I was pregnant? Why am I hiding the stuff about Grant? And the break-in, the baby shoe? I'm a hypocrite. Why do secrets feel easier than the truth?

'I would do the same for you,' she says and I believe

189

her with all my heart. 'Thanks for putting up with me.'

'I don't put up with you. You're not a chore, Kylie. I *want* your friendship, okay? I'd be sad if we ever stopped being friends.'

'So you're not going to leave the group when you get married?' she asks in a small voice.

'Are you kidding me? Not on your life.' I shake my head vehemently, even though she can't see it. 'We're not friends because we're widows. Not now, anyway. That might be how it started, but we're real friends now. I'm not going to get married and suddenly think I'm too good for you. That will never happen.'

There's a sigh on the other end of the line and I can tell I've appeased her fears. At least for the moment. But the silence hangs, like there's something she wants to say. I can feel the crackle of tension. What is she not telling me?

'I don't know what I'd do without this group,' she says eventually.

'Whatever you need, Isabel and I are here for you. Remember that.'

'I will, thanks.'

We chat for a few more minutes and find a time that works for both of us to go to a barre class together before ending the call. After I've punched the activity into my Google calendar, I continue to toy with my phone, turning it over and over in my hands. The action reflects the whirring in my mind. I can't let go of the late-night phone call.

I wander into Grant's home office and look around, not sure exactly what I'm hoping to find. Everything looks much the same – desk in the centre of the room, heavy wood bookshelves on either side, and a window behind that overlooks the sprawling greenery of the back yard. His desk chair sits slightly away from the desk, facing one of the bookshelves as though he were sitting there contemplating something. There's a floor lamp in one corner, with a gold stand and green shade, and the colour is repeated in a large piece of art that hangs on the opposite wall to the window. The canvas is modern and stark, yet oddly calming with its splashes of tonal greens and blues.

One thing that does catch my attention, however, is that Grant's desk looks oddly neat. One might even call it sparse. Usually there are at least a couple of papers scattered on top and handwritten Post-it notes stuck to the base of the desk lamp and a moderate stack of invoices and other business documents in the leather in-tray, along with some mail that needs to be opened. Today, however, the in-tray only holds a single sheet of paper and the surface of the desk is completely clear.

I pad across the plush carpet and peer into the in-tray. The solo item is a bill for the cleaning company we use to detail our cars. Grant is old-school and always asks for printed invoices. Even with the ones that come via email, he prints them out and files them away in a large filing cabinet, where they will sit for the lifespan that they're relevant to our taxes before being archived in boxes that line the shelves in our garage.

It's one habit he has that feels like a strange relic of another time.

I reach down and try one of the desk's drawers and

I'm surprised to find it won't open. Crouching down, I spy a small lock on the top drawer that I have never noticed before. The drawers don't lock individually, so that one lock secures all three of them. No amount of jiggling – nor my poor attempts at using one of the bobby pins from my hair – causes the lock to give in. Sitting back on my heels, I stare at the drawers, dumbfounded.

Since when did he start locking things away?

Maybe he's concerned that whoever broke into our house is coming back. The thought fills me with an icy uneasiness and I glance over my shoulder, as if expecting to see that someone has snuck in behind me. But there's nobody there.

I look over at the filing cabinet, which I've never opened before. Grant manages all the household bills because everything was set up before I arrived and he's never let me contribute a cent. The only paperwork I have is my own tax paperwork, which is upstairs in my office. Everything else . . . well, I've never had anything to do with it. I try one of the drawers and it slides open easily, even though the cabinet clearly has a lock on it. There are five drawers, each deep enough to hold the hanging folders which are neatly labelled inside. I walk my fingertips across the metal edgings, pushing each file back one by one as I look over the labels in Grant's chicken-scratch handwriting: household bills, mobile phone bills, mortgage statements, house insurance, contents insurance, car insurance, travel insurance, health insurance.

Normal things.

There's a folder for all the documentation for his

extensive luxury watch collection, including all the warranty agreements, instruction booklets and authenticity certificates. Another folder contains the warranties and instruction manuals for all the white goods in the house, and a further two folders are dedicated to the cars we own and contain the service history, registration information, and even a couple of paid speeding tickets.

One whole drawer is nothing but folders of personal tax documents in chronological order for the last seven years. I consider walking away without even looking in the last two drawers, because there doesn't seem to be anything of interest here. The locked drawers are more likely to hold something important, but I'm the kind of person who's inclined to finish a task once I start it, so I pull open the second-to-last drawer of the filing cabinet and look inside.

This one contains the same stuff – mostly superannuation reports and a fat folder containing probate information from his father's estate. But once I push the folders around, they hit something in the back of the drawer. I pull all the files forwards, cringing at the screech of metal on metal, and reach my hand into the back of the drawer. My fingertips touch something cold and hard.

I grope at a small tin box and pull it out. It's also locked, but this time with a combination code.

What is going on?

My thumb brushes over the wheels of the combination lock, which needs six digits to get inside. The numbers appear to be set on a random code – 9-2-3-9-1-0 – but knowing my attention-to-detail husband, this isn't any random number. It's probably set to a specific combination so he knows if anyone moves the dials. And given someone *has* been in our house, looking through his things, I'm sure he's even more conscious of it than ever.

I take the pen from the crystal holder on his desk and quickly scrawl the numbers on the inside of my palm so I can return the dials back to this specific combination when I put the box back into the filing cabinet. Then I drop into his chair and start trying to work out the combination. I try my birthday, then his, then the date of our upcoming wedding, our anniversary, our first date, and even the day we met, aka my first husband's funeral. The lock doesn't budge.

In a last-ditch effort, I try 1-2-3-4-5-6 but of course that doesn't work, either.

The box feels heavy in my hands, as though it contains the weight of my worries, and I'm so frustrated that tears prick the backs of my eyes. Maybe I should have responded to the email and asked for more information about why my fiancé is supposedly dangerous. If the anonymous sender was serious, then—

I hear vibrations. They're coming from one of the locked drawers.

I put the box down and head over to the desk, crouching down to get a better listen. There's a device buzzing in the top drawer and I'm sure it's a mobile phone. The buzzing continues and I press my palm to the wood, feeling it rattle.

Did Grant leave his cell phone at home?

194

The vibrating stops and a few seconds later there's the short *buzz-buzz* of a message, likely someone leaving a voicemail. With a hardening sensation in my gut, I pull my own phone out of my pocket and dial Grant's number. It rings, but there's no buzzing coming from the drawer. The call goes to Grant's voicemail and I leave a scattered message, asking him to text and let me know if he's planning to be home for dinner even though we talked about it before he left.

I stare at the drawer. He has a second phone.

For a moment I contemplate throwing the metal box through the window as a way to release the pent-up emotion inside me, but I rein it in. I tamp it down. I count to twenty and breathe slowly in and out, swallowing my emotions like I've done my entire life, until nothing exists on the outside except the perfect, shiny exterior of the woman I want people to think I am.

But inside I am fire. I am fury.

The man I love is morphing right before my eyes into a stranger and it feels like I've stepped into my mother's shoes.

Maybe it's something innocent – some old childhood photos and mementos in the box and a work phone in the drawer. *Maybe you're making a mountain out of a molehill.*

There's only one way to find out.

I start trying to get the code through a methodical process – 0-0-0-0-0-1, 0-0-0-0-0-2, 0-0-0-0-0-3 – and give up by 0-0-0-5-6-5. My palms are sweaty, there's a churning in my gut, and I'm almost ready to return the code to its original state and give up. But then something

195

catches in my memory, like a tissue snagging on a bush filled with thistles.

The alarm code for the house.

Or rather, *one* of the alarm codes for the house, because there are multiple. One for him, one for me, one that his sister has in case of emergencies, and one for our cleaner. My code is my mother's birthday, which I chose at his request when I first moved in. *Why do we need more than one code?* I'd asked. I'd thought it odd. The house I'd grown up in had an alarm panel and we'd all used the same code. I still remember it, even now.

Call me paranoid, he'd said, *but it's a security thing. If something ever happened to you, I'd know exactly when you came and went from the house rather than getting the information mixed up by a cleaner or my sister coming and going.*

I remember laughing, at first. How paranoid. How fantastical. If something happened to me . . . like what? I'd stopped laughing when it became apparent that he wasn't joking.

My mother was kidnapped once, he'd said. *Right from our living room. The cops had their timeline all wrong because my grandpa came to the house and let himself in. But that's when we first found out about his dementia, because he swore black and blue he hadn't been there. The cops weren't working with the right information. We were lucky we got her back.*

His mother had been found forty-eight hours later, thank God, shaken but unhurt. Physically, anyway. It was a ransom attempt gone wrong. Grant's father had been a wealthy businessman with ties that were less than squeaky clean, and that day it had come back to bite him. Apparently after that incident everyone in the family was assigned their own code so each person could be tracked coming and going from the house. It was a habit Grant planned to keep.

As far as I knew, he was under the impression that I didn't know his code, since I had my own. There'd never been any need for me to know his. But I'd seen him punch it in a few times and wondered whether it had any meaning, like mine did.

2-5-1-1-8-0.

It's a number that doesn't make any sense to me, but maybe it's more than a random number. Maybe it's a date – 25 November 1980. Maybe it means something important to Grant.

I try the combination. The lock releases.

My hands tremble as I ease the lid open, almost squinting with worry about what I might find inside. But it's nothing unusual. A collection of photographs in varying shapes and sizes lines the bottom of the box. There are some faded and yellowed ones that look like they're from a time period before I was born, and a man in a powder blue suit, matching vest, and a super-wide tie holds a baby with a mop of dark hair. There's another, taken from the same night, with that same man and a woman whose hair is luscious and dark, falling around her shoulders in voluminous waves.

There's a photo of Grant on his graduation day, his proud smile echoed in his father's face. Both men are tall and broad-shouldered, with square jaws and proud noses. Beside him, his mother is slight. A wisp of a woman with pitch black hair, soulful dark eyes, and light olive skin. Sun flares dance across the picture, the lush green grounds of the university stretched out behind them.

There are a few Polaroids – Grant drinking with his friends, Grant standing beside his first car, Grant dressed up as a groomsman for his sister's wedding, Grant holding a baby.

I wonder if that's his niece, Kira. She's seventeen now. It's hard to tell how long ago the photo was taken, so I flip it over to see if anything is written on the back. There's a date in the corner: 21 June. No year.

The little girl in the photo has a little tuft of golden hair, and she's dressed in a frothy pink tutu-type skirt and a T-shirt with glittery writing on it. She has little white socks with a frill and appears to be missing a shoe. Besides Grant, there is a woman standing slightly out of frame and as well as a cluster of balloons in pink and silver. I can't see much of the woman's face, save for some curly hair and part of her jaw. The baby stares up at Grant adoringly. It's a sweet photo. I'm about to drop it back down into the box when something catches my attention.

The woman off to the side . . . she's holding a baby's shoe. The missing shoe the little girl kicked off, presumably. Whereas the angle of the child only shows the sole of the shoe, in the woman's hand I can see all the details. The pink satin, the bow, the crystals.

It's identical to the one hiding in my drawer upstairs.

Chapter Nineteen

Kylie

Almost a week after waking up in the conference hotel, I still have no idea what happened. My bruise has transitioned from an angry purple to a sickly green brown and I poke at it constantly, wishing it was a button that could reactivate my memory. When I turned my phone on, there were no answers. The only thing I could find was a single photograph of Francis and me about to kiss. Someone must have used my phone to take it, or else they sent it to me, but I can't find any corresponding messages. Maybe they AirDropped it to my phone? I'm not sure.

In it, we're sitting at a bar; his martini glass is full and mine is near empty. His hand is on my knee, the other cupping my face. At first glance, I look happy. But when I peer closer, something feels off. The bar is not the same one where I met him, and I have no recollection of it at all. Even the hand on my knee looks like it's digging in a little too hard, his fingers pressing into my flesh.

It makes me think of the bruise.

He's texted me a few times, all flirty and friendly, like nothing weird happened at all. I find myself writing back, strangely compelled to keep in contact with him, although I dodged his invitation last night to go out for a drink, claiming I had something on with my new colleagues. It was a lie, but he didn't know that. And he'd seemed annoyed, getting curt with me and then ending the call soon after.

But I'm going to put it out of my mind today.

I need a moment to feel . . . normal. To do normal things, like hang out with a friend and chat about mundane things like the weather and the traffic and the latest episode of *MasterChef Australia* or *The Block*. Low-stakes stuff.

I sit on the tram, watching Melbourne roll past. It's still light out and the golden glow bounces off the windscreens of cars driving in the opposite direction, flaring like camera flashes. Tall buildings give way to green trees swaying on the side of the footpath and people walk around, little dogs on leashes, and kids in prams, and girls in checked school-uniform dresses skipping and holding hands. It's a normal evening.

Except for the bruise.

I tear my mind away from what I don't know and try to focus on something positive. I've completed three shifts at the hair salon so far, and I like it there. The people are friendly and the clientele is nice – mostly older, well-to-do women. The boss even gave me a little goodie bag on my first day, containing samples from the hair product brand they stock. The shifts crawl by and it seems a horrific waste of my business degree and of the years I spent getting a foothold on the corporate ladder, but at least I'm employed. At least I'm doing *something*.

I *will* dig myself out of this hole.

And I'm not going to ignore the worry that churns in my gut. Not like last time. Not like I did with Marcus. Despite the low hum of anxiety in the back of my mind about what happened, I actually feel more in control than I have in a long time. I want to be a functioning adult again. I want to be independent and have a life I'm proud of again. Since Marcus first got his diagnosis almost five years ago, even those most basic ambitions have lain so dormant I thought they were dead.

Part of me died when he did – not just because I lost him, but because I sacrificed everything for him in those last eighteen months. I worked myself to the bone trying to keep it all afloat; trying to keep the bills paid, and to stay optimistic for his sake and to forgo anything I wanted so that we could put his needs first.

Appointments, medication, whims, outbursts.

The night he died, I sat with him and held his hand. He told me that I was the most incredible woman on the face of the earth and that he was grateful I was stronger than him. I was so very tried. His death seemed almost a relief in a way, because seeing the tumour rapidly eroding him broke my heart.

I knew the wound would take a long time to heal. But I never expected it to fester. I never expected to find out that before Marcus's diagnosis he'd bedded anyone with legs to open and written it all down on some sordid little scorecard.

I loved him with everything I had and he betrayed it all.

The electronic voice on the tram announces the next stop, and I reach for a green pole to push the stop request button. Several people stand, crowding the exits as we slow, and I follow them onto the street. God, if there was ever a place I don't belong it's at a posh shopping strip in Toorak, going to an exercise class that costs more than my public-transport budget for the week.

But thankfully they were having one of those 'free trial month' offers, so I signed up and put a reminder into my calendar to cancel before I get charged. I have to admit, the studio is gorgeous. It's all white walls and pearlescent details and it has a reception area with leafy green monstera plants in baby-pink pots. Three pink velvet couches line the waiting area and there's a station to fill your water bottle and another with complimentary mints, individually wrapped biscuits, and fancy hand sanitiser – the kind that somehow doesn't smell like rubbing alcohol. Black-and-white photos of ballerinas in sleek black leotards striking modern poses adorn the back wall. It appears the studio runs both proper dance class *and* dance-inspired exercise classes, catering to clients young and old. A sign on the wall announces that they have an adult ballet class starting, aimed at people who've trained in dance as youngsters and who are looking to get back into it.

It tugs at something deep in me. I would love to do that!

202

There's a sole pair of pointe shoes sitting in my wardrobe, still in the wrapper with the satin shiny, the shank intact, and the ribbons pristine. The receipt in the bag tells me I bought them almost ten years ago. I put them on every so often, sliding them out of the plastic and slipping my feet inside, admiring my handiwork in the sewing of the ribbons and elastic. I point and flex, my feet straining against the hard structure of the shoe as I rise up onto my toes, but only on carpet so I can protect their perfect condition. They're a piece of my past that I've had trouble letting go of. Part of *myself* that I've had trouble letting go of.

I spot Adriana sitting on one of the chairs, dressed head-to-toe in Lululemon and looking like she stepped out of a 'fitspo' Instagram photoshoot. Her blond bob is half-clipped back, since the bottom ends aren't long enough to be pulled into a ponytail, and her makeup-free face is glowing with health. She has a pair of small diamond studs in her ears and her engagement ring glimmers in the light.

But she's staring off into space in the strangest way, brows knitted and bottom lip rolling between her teeth. I glance down at her stomach, but it's washboard flat, as usual. There are dark circles under her eyes and I notice her fingers are drumming against her thigh.

'Hey,' I say, dropping down next to her.

She jumps as if I've crept up on her in a dark alley. 'You startled me!'

'Jumpy much.' I laugh as I bend down and slip off my battered old Converse sneakers, which are more grey than white now, to change into the sticky-bottomed socks the website recommended we wear. Adriana already has hers on.

I open my bag and rifle through the chaos inside to find the socks – I'd tossed a banana in for a snack later and it mixes around with a little pack of Skittles, some chewing-gum packets and wrappers, a paperback with a cracked spine and dog-eared pages I borrowed from my sister, two bits of mail I'm scared to open, a packet of tissues that exploded everywhere, a couple of lip glosses, perfume samples that have been in there for God only knows how long . . .

'Your handbag is the stuff of nightmares,' Adriana says, wrinkling her nose. 'Literally.'

'What's wrong with it?' I ask as I finally retrieve the socks. My messiness is something I've made peace with over the years. Even when I lived with Marcus, every drawer in our house was like this.

I always neglect to throw things out and the second I take my bag off my shoulder, I forget all about it, even if I've promised myself I'm going to clean it out. Of all my flaws, it's low down on the priority list to change.

'It's so disorganised.'

I roll my eyes at her. 'Sorry I don't have a spreadsheet to track my bowel movements like you do.'

She snorts. 'That's disgusting.'

'I wouldn't put it past you,' I mutter.

Now it's her turn to roll her eyes. 'Are you excited to get back to the barre after such a long time? You *must* be excited – you actually turned up on time.'

'Hey!' I nudge her with my elbow. 'Rude.'

'It's true, though.' She lifts one shoulder into a shrug and smiles. I can't argue; she's not wrong.

'It's been *so* long.' I glance at the glass door to the main studio where the class ahead of us is finishing up. 'I'm sure I won't remember anything.'

It's a lie.

I remember everything.

The way my body used to feel when I would glide across the stage in a grand jeté. The rush of a perfect set of fouetté turns. The power and strength of executing a grand adage. I remember the pain of blisters, the satisfying ache in my muscles, the giddy nerves as I waited in the wings for my cue. I remember the camaraderie between the dancers in the changing rooms as we helped each other with our makeup and costumes, the way thundering applause felt like tribal drums in my chest, and how frustrating it was to get a rip in your tights right before an audition.

'I bet you'll show everyone up.' Adriana rises as the students begin to pour out of the studio. 'Come on, let's get a spot by the window.'

She hurries on ahead, getting into the room before the other students, and I scramble to catch up, almost tripping over my own two feet. Whoever told you that dancers were graceful outside the ballet studio was lying. The teacher waves to us as we all pile in. She's wearing a black long-sleeved leotard with a pair of tracksuit pants over the top, the legs rolled up to the knees, and soft ballet shoes. Her feet are slightly turned out in that way all ballet dancers tend to unconsciously do.

'Welcome everyone,' she says, smiling. 'My name is Irena and I'll be leading your class today. Grab a spot anywhere that's free. We have little marks on the floor to show you how far apart to stand so you don't accidentally hit anyone during the exercises.'

'Let's go here.' Adriana urges me to follow her and we stand right in front of the big window that overlooks the street. Rich early-evening sunshine pours in through the glass and it warms my face.

'Aren't you worried about people watching us through the window?' I say as we place our water bottles and bags on the floor, out of the way of our feet. I run my hand along the smooth wood of the barre and memories fire and spark in my brain.

My first time in pointe shoes. My first solo performance. Spotting Beth in the audience, a proud smile on her face. My father sitting next to her, looking bored. The school principal's pitying eyes when he told me my scholarship wouldn't continue.

'Why would I be worried about that? I'm going to copy you the whole time.' She winks at me.

'You shouldn't use me as an example of anything,' I mutter.

But as I stand at the barre and settle into first position, my arms rounding, hands growing soft and feet and legs turning out, I feel myself evolve into the old me – a young girl with dreams and hopes and ambitions. Someone with milestones to live for and plans for the future. I desperately want to be this person again.

'I can spot a trained dancer from the way they hold

their hands.' The teacher approaches, smiling at me. 'And what a lovely turn out you have.'

I flush. 'Thank you. It's been a long time.'

'Where did you train?'

'The Melbourne Institute of Dance.' I don't reveal where I went on to study later with my scholarship, since that's too painful to even mention.

She nods. 'I'm delighted to have you in my class. If you ever want to get back into the practice, we do have adult classes here.'

'Thank you.'

The teacher wishes us both a good class, before moving on to greet the next group of students. I run my hands down my body. I've worn one of my old Bloch leotards – a maroon one with three-quarter sleeves and a little gathering at the V-shaped neck. Over the top, I've pulled on some black leggings with a slight pattern to them. Despite feeling like Toorak is the last suburb I belong in, I feel welcome here in the studio. I feel . . . like the old me.

'See,' Adriana says, shooting me a smug look. 'I knew you'd be good at this. I'm going to look like a gangly baby giraffe next to you.'

'Hardly.'

Adriana is one of those annoying people who's good at everything the first time she tries it. The Young Widows Club once went to a 'paint and sip' evening, and the paintings Isabel and I produced looked like a kindergarten finger-painting lesson gone wrong. But Adriana's could have been hung in an art gallery without looking out of place.

'Just watch I don't take your head off,' she says with a slight cringe. 'Grant once told me I have two left feet.'

There's something dark in her voice that seems at odds with what should be a light-hearted joke. I'm about to ask her if everything is okay at home when the instructor starts up the music. A soft modern classical piece plays through unseen speakers in the studio's walls. An excited tingle runs down my spine.

'Let's begin with some warm-up exercises,' Irena says, her voice commanding the attention of the room. Everyone quietens. 'We're going to take our arms up, two, three, four, and down, two, three, four.'

I stand facing the front of the studio, following along with the simple movements. The studio is at street-level, and out of the corner of my eye I see people walking to and fro. Some linger and have a sticky beak, and I catch a little girl watching in awe as we turn to face the other side, her slender arm outstretched as she points and smiles.

Ten minutes into the class, I am wholly relaxed and at ease. It's like I shed my issues at the door and as soon as the music started, I fell into a familiar, beautiful escape. In the past it was an escape from my father's temper and his drinking and the aching loss of my mother. Escape from the school classroom where I always felt behind and the playground where I struggled to make friends. Now it's escape from the ever-present itch for a drink. From the anxiety I feel when I've said something stupid while inebriated. From the constant feeling that I'm a failure.

Here, I can just *be*.

We face the barre for the next exercise and my shoulders are low, away from my ears, and my hands drift softly to the wood. It's like coming home. Like shrugging off a too-tight pair of shoes. The relief. The freedom.

As I lean to one side, a man walks across the window and stops dead in his tracks. He's tall, with a wild mop of dark hair, a hard jaw, and a small scar that cuts across his eyebrow in a way that makes him seem menacing. He stares and I stare back. There's something oddly familiar about him, yet I can't put my finger on how I might know him. Maybe he's a customer at the salon? Or maybe he was a client from my old job?

The classical music plays on but I'm frozen, suspended in a memory just out of reach. Neither of those options feels right. I didn't meet him at work – my gut tells me that much. He shakes his head as if in disbelief and then he hurries away from the window, head down and shoulders hunched defensively forward. My mind whirrs, like a tyre stuck in mud.

Then something jolts in my brain.

Everything is spinning, spinning, spinning. I'm on a carnival ride, but there are no lights and I can't smell fairy floss or the salty ocean air of Rye Beach. It's dark and warm. Soft. I feel like I'm wading through quicksand.

Where am I?

'Kylie.' Someone gives me a shake.

My eyes blink open. The darkness is of my own making. My eyes droop again and blackness blots everything out. I try to blink. Once, twice, three times. The world is fuzzy. Murky.

'Kylie, wake up.' It's Francis. He's leaning over me, one hand on my shoulder, shaking me.

I'm so sleepy. It's warm in this bed and I want to let slumber lure me away from the real world. Sleep is better. Safer. But then someone is yanking me by my arms, holding my wrist tight. I feel cool air on my thighs and I know something is wrong. I want to get back into that warmth.

'What . . . ?' My mouth is dry and it tastes funny. 'No.'

I'm being moved around, shoved and pulled into position. There's a hard pressure on my leg. It hurts.

I force my eyes open and this time there are two faces. Francis and another man . . . He has wild hair and a scar across his eyebrow.

He's the third champagne glass.

I gasp and lean forward to get a better look out of the window, ballet exercises forgotten, as the man disappears into the crowded street.

Chapter Twenty

Isabel

Since accessing my boss's computer, I've been able to form a picture of what happened with his building project on the wall of my spare room. After shoving the furniture to one side, I took a trip to Kmart and bought the biggest corkboard I could find. Then I printed out every single document I downloaded onto my portable drive. It takes hours and the printer runs out of ink halfway through, so I take a quick trip to Officeworks for a new cartridge and then get back to it.

The sound of the printer and the smell of freshly printed ink and warm paper fills the room. I empty a box of colourful pins into a soup bowl so they're easier to grab, and I have a pack of rainbow highlighters at the ready. As I read, I make notes and pin the important pieces on the board. There are emails, contracts, screen captures of text messages, Facebook DMs, and property listings. There's research into prospective buyers, reports from banks, transcripts from a legal hearing, letters of complaint, death threats, land evaluations, blueprints, and checklists.

I am a tin-foil hat short of being a full conspiracy theorist.

But a story unfolds: a luxury apartment complex in Melbourne's western suburbs, close to the airport so highflyers can get from first class to their own sofa in less than twenty minutes, right near the leafy Brimbank Park and Maribyrnong River. Big ideas, flashy brochures, lucrative incentives to financial planners and mortgage brokers if they brought in clients with money to burn. These 'investment seminars' were hosted in luxury venues, with custom catering and glamorous models hired to pose as employees of the property company in order to woo male investors.

Fucking gag.

The project is a grand vision with a grand name to match: D'Or Prime Residences. From the rudimentary French I took in high school, I figure the translation is something along the lines of 'premium gold' residences . . . or maybe golden premium. Perhaps there isn't a direct translation because they've simply slapped some fancy-sounding words together knowing people are buying into the vision, rather than the reality.

Oh, the irony.

The studio apartments start at a million dollars, with the penthouse floor being upwards of three and a half. The complex houses a yoga studio, an infinity pool, a 'Zen garden' (whatever the hell that means), a fully decked-out movie theatre, a private airport shuttle service, lock boxes with twenty-four-hour security, and even a wine vault. The renderings look like a piece of art, and it's easy to see how someone might be suckered into the idea of living such a fantasy life.

The end state. The residence that says you've made it to the top.

But the photos of the actual building in its near-completed form are nothing like the renderings. The garden is sad, with swaths of concrete that look closer to a shopping-centre car park than anything Zen. The insides of the apartments aren't much better, with strange corners, columns in random places and fine cracks in the walls. The 'high-end' fittings appear poorly installed and several complaint letters show that the apartments aren't even the correct size, with some of the private terraces being merely a third of the metreage promised.

Then a homeless shelter was built down the street.

The builders knew it was coming and there are emails confirming they did everything in their power to try to stop it, and when they failed, they turned their attention to delaying the shelter so their buyers would be in the building before news broke. One email referenced a stat (though it was unverified) that homeless shelters can cause as much as a 10 per cent drop in value for nearby homes. I imagine that's more likely due to people's prejudice than any actual impacts on crime rates, but ultimately financial value is decided by people with biases, and the builders knew it.

By the time they approached the building's lock-up stage, the apartments were worth *far* less than what people had paid. Then the pandemic hit in 2020. The share market took a nosedive. Recession loomed. For a while apartment prices stagnated. People who'd planned to flip the apartments were saddled with the difficult choice of losing money to offload a subpar property or trying to rent it out to stay afloat. Owner-occupiers were faced with a similar choice: lose money or move into a place that wasn't what they'd paid for. Some emails indicated that the D'Or Prime buyers were not necessarily real-estate-savvy rich folks, rather people who'd bought into the dream of having the life they desperately wanted and could only afford if they leveraged themselves to the hilt.

Experienced investors probably saw this for what it was: a gilded lily.

I sit cross-legged on the floor, looking at the chaos around me. My board is coming together with the main pieces of information and I have a series of folders organising the rest into categories. The builders got away with their deceptions thanks to being hidden behind a shell company that protected the identity of the major players and then conveniently became bankrupt when the shit hit the fan.

But my dear, meticulous boss has everything needed to spill the tea.

I'm not exactly sure how I'm going to use this information yet. From what I can tell, they went into building this property with at least semi-good intentions. Nothing I've seen leads me to believe it was set to be a scam from the beginning, which I had initially suspected. But at some point they must have seen their dreams of a luxury compound start to crumble. And in fact, both my boss and one of the other business partners sold off the apartment they'd intended to keep for themselves when this happened, a sure red flag that things were not going according to plan.

None of that is the kind of revenge I need, however. It's not enough. There's *always* a rotation of stories on *A Current Affair* about builders screwing over buyers or contractors absconding with cash, but it never goes anywhere. The contracts are predatory and most people sign their lives away without fully understanding what they're giving up, and if things go bad, the shell company gets dissolved.

Big whoop.

But my gut tells me there's something more here. I have to keep digging.

I'm only torn away from my research because I have to get to yoga class. Aside from the Young Widows Club meetings, it's the highlight of my week. An hour for me where I don't allow anything else to creep into my head – not the past, not my blood lust for revenge, not Jonathan. Nobody.

It's *my* time.

I lie on my back, following the slow in and out of my breath, as gentle music plays over the speakers in the community-centre fitness room. Beneath me, the thin mat cushions my bones and I sink, sink, sink into nothingness. My eyes are closed and everything fades. I'm floating. Dissolving. Disappearing.

It's blissful.

'Izzy?' There's a hand at my shoulder and a gentle shake.

My eyes pop open and I see Hannah staring down at me. 'Uhh . . .'

'You drifted off there for a minute.'

Around us, everyone is already standing, rolling up their mats and gathering their things. The lights are on and I squint into the brightness, my head foggy from the interrupted, though unintentional, nap.

'Oops.' I let out a self-conscious laugh. 'I must be tired.'

'We don't have to go for coffee, if you're not feeling up to it,' Hannah says, her brow crinkled with concern.

It's become our ritual – yoga class, then coffee and something sweet. There's a cute café across the road from the community centre and, while it's nothing fancy, they make a really good cappuccino with extra chocolate sprinkled on top. Just the way I like it.

'Let's still go,' I say, getting to my feet. 'I like the coffee time as much as the yoga class.'

She beams. 'Me too.'

I pull a jumper over my workout top and get all my stuff together. On the way out, I thank the yoga instructor and she waves, telling us she's looking forward to seeing us next week. I really like this place. It's humble, unpretentious – there's not an overpriced Lululemon item in sight – and most of the people in the class are older ladies and men, fifties and up. It's not competitive and nobody worries about how many stomach rolls they have when they're contorting themselves into the various positions.

It suits me to a tee.

Hannah and I settle in at the café across the street.

'Is everything okay? You seemed a bit out of sorts before yoga.'

'Oh that.' She shakes her head. Her brown hair is pulled back into a plait, which hangs over one shoulder. It makes her look young. 'Just family drama.'

'Oh?' I raise an eyebrow.

I don't know much about Hannah's family. I've asked about them a few times, but I got the impression it was a sore point. But today it feels like she needs to get something off her chest.

'Growing up, I lived with my grandparents in Cranbourne. My mum died when I was a baby and she and my dad weren't together. But then Pa passed away when I was twelve. Nan didn't cope so well after he was gone, so we moved away.' She bobs her head. 'I wanted to reach out to my dad then to see if I could go and live with him, but he never made any effort to build a relationship with me. I guess I always thought that having a biological connection with someone would mean that there was love there, even if you were separated. I was wrong about that, though.'

'I'm so sorry. That's a lot of loss for one person.' I shake my head. It makes me wonder if my daughter will one day have these questions. Will she seek me out? Want to know me? Will she harbour anger and resentment that I gave her away and didn't have contact with her? 'I was raised by my grandmother, too. But we . . . well, we don't see eye to eye.'

Understatement of the century. I wonder what might have happened if she hadn't had so much influence over me. Unlike Hannah, I *did* have my parents but they were never home because they both worked multiple jobs to make ends meet and to pay for me to go to a good school. All they ever wanted was for me to be educated and have a better life than they did. They sacrificed everything for it . . . only for me to drop out of university after the attack.

They've never judged me. But sometimes I wonder . . . do they think it was all a waste?

'It's tough, isn't it?' She sighs. 'Whenever I speak to him, it's like I'm still a child. He doesn't respect me or my opinion.'

'Trust me, I get it.' I reach out and squeeze her hand. 'My grandmother is the same.'

It's why I haven't been to see her in over a year. Mum always tries to convince me to go with her, but I can't bring myself to do it. The old woman always has something horrible to say about Jonathan and how he was a no-good drug addict, and how I should get surgery to fix my face so I can find another husband.

There's too much water under the bridge. Too much resentment.

'I've always believed family is the most important thing in life. If you don't care about your own family then what's the point of anything? Why else are we on this earth, if not to be part of a group?'

'I don't think blood determines everybody's group, though. A found family can be as meaningful as a real one, if not more. Kylie and Adriana are that for me.'

'Really?' She looks at me, long and deep, as if she knows something I'd thought nobody could know.

It makes something slide down my spine – a tiny drop of unease. Like condensation formed from my actions, accumulating quietly, building up without my noticing. But there's no way she could possibly know my secrets – the secrets that not even Kylie and Adriana know. The secrets that would tear my own found family apart if they came to light.

The secrets that are worse than how I got my scars.

'You're so right. There are bonds far greater than blood – like marriage.' Her gaze drifts as she sinks into thought and my unease melts away.

I'm being paranoid.

When you eat revenge for breakfast, lunch, and dinner, you start to think that everyone around you has an ulterior motive, that everyone is lying in wait. But Hannah is simply a person with a complicated family and understandable grief at losing her husband, and I'm projecting my own issues onto her.

At least, that's what I think is happening.

Chapter Twenty-One

Kylie

I don't know how I convinced Adriana that I was okay to go home by myself.

After I saw that man and something deep in my brain cracked open and revealed a memory, I raced out of the studio into the street. But he was gone. Was he even there in the first place or had I imagined it? Was the memory real? It certainly *felt* real.

Adriana came running out after me, like a worried mother hen, and I claimed I thought I saw an animal about to be hit by a car. Unsurprisingly, she didn't seem to buy that explanation. I was, after all, shaking like I was suffering from hypothermia. Instead of forcing me back into the class, though, she collected our things and insisted we go to a café so I could have a drink of water and something to eat.

Now, an hour later, after much reassurance that I would be okay, I start the long journey home on the tram by myself. She makes me promise to text when I get home, and I do as soon as I step out onto the street.

The tram bells ding behind me as the metallic beast glides off into the intersection, leaving me standing alone. My sister's apartment building is a squat brown cube on a corner, with laundry flapping like fairground garlands on the tiny balconies facing the street. I head to the main entrance, key in hand, and skip the lift because climbing two flights of stairs is better than risking getting stuck in the rickety tin can masquerading as a form of transportation.

Fool me once, and all that.

I can tell Beth is home the second I walk in the door, even though she's nowhere to be seen. There's a cup of tea in the process of brewing, steam still rising up in delicate tendrils from a blue mug with a chip on the handle and the little Bushells tag dangling over one side. She's started dinner preparations. A head of broccoli sits on the kitchen counter, a wooden cutting block and knife close by. There's a packet of meat – probably chicken, since it's cheapest.

'Beth?' I call out. The apartment is so small that there's only a few possibilities of where she could be.

Her room is closest to the front door and I poke my head inside. Empty. I can see into the bathroom from here, and she's not there, either. Something hard and heavy settles into the pit of my stomach, and I take a step towards my room – formerly her office – which I have taken over since Marcus died.

She comes out of the door before I make it over, cheeks red and a line carved between her brows. In her hand sits the wad of cash in the envelope. I feel my vision blur at the edges as heat rushes up into my face. This is bad.

221

'What the fuck, Kylie?'

She never swears.

I spot the fancy shopping bag sitting on my bed, the contents spilling out onto the floral polyester doona on the pull-out bed, like some gross display of my shortcomings.

'Why were you going through my things?' I can't even muster an indignant tone because shame has taken prime place in my chest.

'I was looking for that top you borrowed. The red one.' The money looks as though it weighs as much as a house brick in her hand. For a second, I think she might hurl it at me. 'I've got an important meeting tomorrow and I wanted to wear it.'

'It's at the dry-cleaner's.'

'I know. I found the stub.'

I swallow. The top is at the dry-cleaner's because I wore it out and chucked up all over myself in the taxi on the ride home. I'd been hoping to get it back and into her wardrobe before she knew it was missing. But that isn't important right now. Part of me is furious that she was combing through my things, invading my privacy, but the other part of me knows I deserve as much. If not more.

I'm living in her home, eating her food, preying on her good will, and not paying my portion of the rent. Shame roars inside me, the burn of humiliation as hot as an inferno.

'How many lies have you been telling me?' Her voice quakes. She looks like our mother – angry, sad, desperate. It's a combination I know well. 'Do you know what I

222

did before I went through your things, huh? I went to see you at work so we could grab a coffee.'

Oh shit.

'And they told me that you were sacked weeks ago.' Her voice rises with each word, the crescendo reaching a brain-piercing pitch. It's like being jabbed in the skull with a steak knife. '*Weeks* ago, Kylie. And yet every morning you leave the house all dressed up in your blazer and heels, never saying a word to me. In fact, just the other day you were telling me that you couldn't stop and get the groceries on the way home because you had to stay late for a meeting.'

She's practically vibrating with anger. It distorts the air around her and I want nothing more than to shrink into the floor and disappear forever.

'Beth—'

'And now I find bags of shopping in the back of your wardrobe and all this money. I don't know what I'm angrier about! That you *can* pay your part of the rent or the fact that the money is clearly coming from something illegal. At the very least, something you're ashamed of enough that you don't want to tell me about it. Oh, and that you've been spending up a storm at Crown Casino. Designer clothing? Seriously? While I struggle to keep the bills paid and let you mooch off me like you're a lazy bloody teenager?'

The resentment pours out of her, fast and hot, tears glittering like diamonds in her eyes. The anger I can take. Anger is comfortable and familiar to me. I know it burns fiercely and then it dies down for a while. But disappointment lingers, never fading. Never shrinking.

223

In fact, it grows when you ignore it and I know that Beth has been watering hers like it's a beloved houseplant.

'Is it drugs?' she asks, shaking her head. 'Sex work? I don't want to know, actually. Thinking of you doing either of those things . . .'

How can I possibly answer her questions? My eyes drop to the floor. If there was a hole, I'd crawl into it like the failure I am. I can feel her gaze like a torch shining on the top of my head, her emotions a swirling summer storm. They're pulling at me, tearing at me, picking apart the stitches on my barely held-together confidence.

'It was a gift,' I mutter, not knowing whether it's a lie or the truth.

'The money?'

'And the things.' I look up and she's gaping at me in disbelief.

'Gifts? From who?'

'A guy I've been seeing.' A guy who potentially bruised me. A guy who seems to vanish in the middle of the night while I'm passed out. A guy who gets mad when I don't want to see him. 'His name is Francis.'

'You're serious?'

'I was going to give the money to you, Beth. I . . . I swear.'

'I honestly don't know whether I can believe a word coming out of your mouth right now.' She thrusts the envelope towards me but I don't reach for it. 'You've been wilfully lying to me about your job. Your boss seemed worried about you, Kylie. He says you were drinking heavily at a work function. He says you need help.'

'You really think a guy who sacked me gives a fuck about what I need? It's not like he did anything to help me.' My lips curl into a sneer.

I'll bet that arsehole took great pleasure in outing me to my sister and then pretending like he was worried about my wellbeing. He didn't seem too worried when he pulled me into his office and told me that 'people like me' were a blight on society and that he would never stand for having someone with such a disgusting problem on his team. I probably could have taken action against him for discrimination, but the truth is, I don't have any fight left in me.

'He isn't really the problem here. The problem is that I took you in because you needed support and yet in that time you've done nothing to help yourself or improve your situation. I know you drink a bit – we all do in this family. But clearly the situation is bad. Or maybe our family has a warped sense of what's normal.' She shakes her head, her frizzy hair – the red heavily faded and threaded with silver – shudders with the action. 'Whatever the case, me coddling you doesn't seem to be doing you any good.'

'It *has* done me good,' I protest. Along with the Young Widows, Beth has kept me from falling even deeper into despair. I don't know what might have happened if she hadn't let me come live with her.

I love my sister more than anything.

'I disagree. You have a drinking problem, you lost your job and you're "dating" a man who pays you. That is very bloody far from my definition of good.' Her lips press into a line. 'I don't know how this all started to spiral out of control, but I can't enable you any further.'

'I'm serious about the money,' I say, gesturing to the envelope. Desperation clings to the air around me and I know she can smell it. That only seems to make her retreat more. 'It's yours. Take it all.'

Her gaze flicks over me and the frown deepens. Her disappointment hurts like I've physically cut myself. It hurts like the bruise on my leg. It hurts like the ache in my soul. Beth has only ever tried to look after me, tried to set me on the straight and narrow. She sacrificed a lot to take care of me after Mum died, and now I've proven myself to be a liar who's abusing her kindness.

Like Marcus did to you.

The comparison makes me feel sick to my stomach.

'Start looking for somewhere else to live,' she says, throwing the wad of cash onto my bed. Then she pushes past me and heads to the door. 'Put the money towards the first month's rent. I want you out of here as soon as possible.'

A second later, the front door slams and I sink down to the floor, clutching the money to my chest as my eyes fill with tears.

Beth doesn't come home that night. I suspect she's gone to stay with her best friend who lives a few streets over. The apartment feels like a tomb without her. So many nights I holed up in my makeshift bedroom, sneaking in wine from the bottle shop and drinking to the sound of mind-numbing reality shows playing on the other side of the wall. How many times have

I wished for silence? How many times have I cranked up my music to drown out the sounds of *The Bachelor* or *Love Island*?

I'd kill to hear it now – Beth's soft chuckle, the sound of popcorn popping in the microwave, the squawk of those stupid women debasing themselves for television.

I can hardly judge. I'm no better.

I wrap my fingers around the neck of bottle of Pinot Noir and bring it to my lips. I'm hazy. My taste is distorted. My face is starting to numb and the sinking sensation of falling into oblivion is finally coming to me. Finally, finally. It takes longer these days, more drinks to get to this point. I'm dressed in my underwear, wearing the Louboutins with the gifts from Francis scattered on the floor around me.

I stare at the bruise.

It started out looking like a thumbprint, though now it's grown blurry.

At that moment, my phone buzzes and I snatch it up, wondering if it's Beth responding to the pathetic *Please come home* message I sent after having multiple calls go unanswered. But it's not Beth. It's Francis.

FRANCIS: *What are you doing tonight?*

I take another swig of the wine bottle and stare at my phone, the screen wavering in front of my tear-filled eyes. I squint, trying to make it sit still. Then, probably because I'm drunk and hurting and looking for trouble, I call him instead of texting back.

He picks up on the third ring.

'Kylie, darling.' His voice is smooth like a fine whisky, warm and inviting. It offers more oblivion.

In the background I hear muffled noises, laughter, music. It sounds like he might be at a restaurant, but a low-key place. Or maybe one of those fine-dining spots that are quieter and more intimate.

'Where are you?' I ask.

'I'm out for dinner with friends.' The sounds fade, as if he's walking away from the action. 'But I'm bored. I want to see you again.'

I feel cruel. Claw-tipped. 'Your friends must be boring, then.'

He laughs. 'I mean, I wouldn't say it to their faces but . . .'

I bring the wine to my lips again, my stomach already protesting from all the alcohol given I haven't eaten anything aside from a pizza roll I scoffed down during my ten-minute break at work hours ago. I feel slightly sick. Is it the wine or the sound of his voice? For some reason, my gut is screaming at me not to meet up with him.

'Why did you leave money on my nightstand?' I ask, the words spilling out of me because my filter has been washed away in a sea of red.

My question is met with silence. I pull the phone away from my ear to see if the call has dropped, but it hasn't.

'Francis?'

'The money . . .' I can tell he's scrambling, which seems odd. If he left me the money, then why doesn't he have a ready answer? 'It was a gift, darling.'

'Like the shoes and the dress?' My voice is uncertain, wobbly. I want to believe him.

'Yes, yes. Exactly.' His confidence is restored and it tweaks something in my brain. There's an issue with this situation. Something I can't see. 'I know you lost your job and I wanted to help.'

Did I really tell him that? I cringe.

'This isn't, like, a . . .' I don't even want to say the words. 'You're not looking for a sugar-daddy thing, right?'

'I'm hardly old or sad enough to have to pay for a date.' He sounds a little insulted. 'And you're not even young enough to be a sugar baby.'

'I'm young at heart,' I say, my worlds a little slurred.

His laugh has an edge to it, like he's growing frustrated with my questions. I feel a darkness under the whisky smoothness, like there's a monster lurking within. I fight the urge to hang up.

'Yes,' he says. 'You certainly are.'

It's not a compliment.

'That's probably why I can't remember what happened last time we went out,' I say.

'We had a few drinks at the bar and then I took you to a hotel and we had an amazing time.' He says it so matter-of-factly, like he truly believes what he's saying.

But as I look down at the bruise again, I'm not sure I can believe him. My mind skips back to the room – to the money, the pool of vomit on the floor, the third champagne glass.

'What about your friend that joined us?' I ask.

The image of the man with the wild hair and the scar swims in front of me.

'What friend?' His tone is sharp now. An undercurrent of tension crackles in the air, like he's worried about something.

'There were three glasses in the room . . .'

'Oh that,' he scoffs. 'One of the glasses was dirty so we asked them to bring a fresh one. There was no one else there.'

But then why wouldn't they have taken the dirty glass away? Francis is lying to me.

'Why would I want to share you with anyone else?' The smooth sound is back again. But it's a sticky smoothness. It clings to me and threatens to suck me down like quicksand.

I can't trust it. I can't trust him.

'Don't leave me hanging,' he says. 'We'll have a good time, I promise. And if the money freaked you out, I'm sorry. I was just trying to help.'

For a moment I almost believe it, because a too-generous boyfriend is so much better than any other possibility. Maybe it was simply rough sex and too much wine and nothing more. Maybe the man with the scar met us for a drink at the bar. Or perhaps he was the Uber driver who took us to the hotel.

What if it's all in my head?

'What should I wear?' I ask, my will-power fading as I give in to the need for someone to hold me. For someone not to think I'm a failure. 'Something sexy?'

'Yes.' The word is like a snake's hiss. 'Wear that sexy red underwear again. I want to see you spread out on my bed looking like dessert.'

I glance at the pile of dirty clothing on the floor

from that night, clothing I haven't been able to bring myself to wash. My bra and matching underwear sit on top, in a pile. They're both black.

I don't own any red underwear.

Chapter Twenty-Two

Hannah

For this week's Young Widows Club meeting, we've decided to do something a little different. The weather has warmed up again and so, instead of meeting at a café, we're having a picnic in the Royal Botanic Gardens. It's one of my favourite spots in the city, with its lush green grounds, big leafy trees, vibrant flowers, and endless hidden corners to explore. In fact, I'd always hoped to get married here one day, but that dream was shelved after I moved out to the country to live with Dale.

He hated the city, but I never lost my love for this place.

To rub salt in the wound, there's a wedding going on as I walk along St Kilda Road towards our meeting spot. A woman in a billowing white dress stands near the famous floral clock, flanked by four bridesmaids, two on each side, who wear floor-length dresses in pale lilac. Each one is slightly different – one with flutter sleeves, one with an asymmetrical neckline, one with bows at her shoulders, and another with a plunging V-neck. Presumably the designs have been chosen to reflect the bridesmaids' individual personalities in some way.

Asymmetrical Girl is probably the 'unique' or 'creative' one. Flutter Sleeves is likely a bit more conservative – maybe she's the mum of the group – and Bow Ties is the pretty girl who advises everyone on what shade of lipstick looks best. My bet is that Plunge Girl is probably the only single one of the group and she's hoping to get lucky with one of the groomsmen.

I drag my gaze away and keep walking, almost straight into a familiar figure. Adriana. She's carrying a fairy-floss pink cardboard box with the name of a popular bakery scrolling down the side and has a canvas shopping tote slung over one arm, the neck of a bottle of soft drink sticking out of it.

I'm almost startled by how striking she is – not artificially pretty, with plumped-up lips and eyelash extensions like a lot of the women I see walking around in the city, but more memorable than that. Her eyes are slightly wide-set and her blond hair always has the most incredible, healthy shine to it, never with a hint of regrowth, even though the colour of her eyebrows tells me she's naturally a brunette. When Isabel mentioned she was only twenty-eight, I was surprised. Not that she looks older, really, but there's a confidence to her. A centred maturity. The way she stood up to those horrible men in the restaurant was . . . well, I've always wanted to be like that. Sure of myself, confident. Able to stand my ground with the people who try to hurt me and those I love.

Practice makes perfect, I guess. I'm trying my best.

'Are you okay?' she asks, her eyes flicking back and forth between me and the bridal party like she's expecting me to burst into tears.

I think of Dale and my lip trembles. Him handing me a bunch of flowers on my birthday. Holding me tight when we had to put our elderly dog down. Curling up on the couch with me for our weekly movie night. The sparkle in his eyes when he put dinner on the table, proud that he'd made something I would enjoy. I wonder how long it's going to be before those memories don't trigger sadness anymore. Maybe that won't ever go away. He would be devastated to know that's what his name does to me now.

He always wanted me to be happy.

'Yeah, I, uh . . .' I shake my head, trying to get the words back in the right order. 'I'm fine.'

'I should have thought about what this place would be like on a Saturday before I suggested it. There's always a bloody wedding here.' She shakes her head.

'I take it you're not getting married here, then?' I ask as we walk. My gut clenches and part of me hopes she says no. The thought of having to come here for their wedding while it takes place in *my* dream spot . . .

You haven't even been invited yet. Jeez. Calm down.

'Out in public like this with anyone who walks past stopping to watch? Uh, no.' She shakes her head. 'I know some brides love that aspect of it, the strangers coming up to say congratulations and whatnot. Feeling like a celebrity. But not me. I couldn't think of anything worse.'

'Not one for the spotlight, then?' I ask. We stroll along the path, keeping out of the way of the joggers and mums with prams coming in the other direction.

'Not at all.' She shoots me a wry look. 'What about you?'

I shake my head. 'No, I'm not one for the spotlight either. My husband always said I was the human personification of a hermit crab.'

She laughs. 'That's cute.'

'He was always saying funny things like that.' I look down the path ahead of us and shrug the green canvas shopping bag higher up on my shoulder. I might have gone a little overboard with all the baked goods and lollies I've brought and the bag is starting to feel quite heavy.

You don't have to buy your way in, Dale always used to say. *Just let people see who you are and they'll want you in their life, like I did.*

Of course he had to say that, but it was still nice to hear it. I've always felt like I was the odd girl out – at school, at university, in the workplace, in the small tightknit Kinglake community I moved to with Dale. I never fit in. Ever. I was always too shy, lacking the natural warmth to make others gravitate towards me the way they did to him. I'm not charismatic or charming or any of those things.

Starting over in Melbourne has felt really tough, because it's poking at all my sore points when I'm already feeling raw and vulnerable. I guess that's why I really want the other young widows to accept me. Because then all the discomfort will feel worth it.

235

Getting an invite to Adriana's wedding would really cement my acceptance in the group. But I would never press the issue, never ask. That would be tacky. Or gauche, as Nan used to say. She loved that word.

'Have you bought a dress yet?' I ask, my mind refusing to leave the whole wedding thing behind.

'Yeah, I have. It's strange doing it a second time around . . .' She bites down on her lip, her eyes pulling away from me and drifting off somewhere in the distance. 'I guess I got everything I wanted the first time, so it's been an exercise in reassessment. What do I want *now*, in this second phase of my life?'

'How did you and your husband meet?' I ask.

I'm *very* curious about her answer.

From what Isabel has told me, she, Adriana, and Kylie have all been widowed between three and four years. Isabel and Kylie seem to have made no moves to start a new relationship – at least, not that they've disclosed. Yet Adriana has found someone and is ready to walk down the aisle again. It seems quick. I wonder whether she was the driver of the new relationship, or if that came from him.

'One of those happenstance things,' she says, her gaze pulling back to me. I sense a wall going up, a shift in her eyes that locks me out, and a slight dullness to her tone that doesn't invite further questions. 'Fate, really.'

That's a vague answer. Perhaps she's worried I'm going to judge her – I'm not. I know how persuasive men can be. I would never have left the city if not for Dale's insistence that our lives would be better in Kinglake.

'Speaking of which,' she says, turning to dig something

out of her bag. It's a white envelope with a delicate pearly sheen to it. I suck in a breath as she hands it over. 'I wasn't sure if this was appropriate, but I talked to Isabel and . . . well, it's an invite to my wedding. If that's too soon for you I *totally* understand. No obligation at all. I wouldn't have wanted to go to a wedding after my husband passed, either.'

I'm so elated I almost miss how uncomfortable she looks. Later, I will ponder why this is. But in the moment I am too awestruck and grateful to be accepted into her circle that it doesn't quite register.

'Thank you so much.' I beam up at her as if she's handed me a piece of gold. Or, at the very least, something truly valuable. And really, she has. 'I will absolutely be there.'

Chapter Twenty-Three

Adriana

I sit in my doctor's office, my back braced against the padded chair in the waiting room, eyes fixed on a poster chart on the wall that shows the development of a foetus over the lifespan of a pregnancy. It all looks quite alien to me. The clinic has a largely female clientele, from the people I've seen coming in and out of this waiting room over the years. Aside from two GPs, there's also a fertility specialist here one day a week.

I usually avoid coming on Thursdays for that exact reason.

But Dr Phuong is booked solid at the moment and this is the only slot I could get for the next two weeks. So I'm here, still in my black shift dress and sharp-shouldered blazer that tells people at work to take me seriously, and a pair of inky-black pointed-toe stilettos. I look like the Grim Reaper compared to the other women here, with their bulbous bellies and swollen feet and tender faces.

I have never felt more unsure of myself. Or more out of place.

One of the women sitting across from me takes a call and speaks in low tones, stress immediately lining her face as she argues with the person on the other end of the line. I figure it's her husband from the way she says 'sweetie' with a cutting tone. I remember my mother being like that with my father when she was mad. He used to love riling her up, because it made him feel powerful to see her fury and then to douse it with his manipulation. He was an emotional arsonist, starting fires left and right because he loved to watch the flames.

Am I about to end up with a husband like that? Is history getting ready to repeat itself?

I think of the photograph. The one of him holding the baby with the shoe so similar to the one deposited on our bed. Life isn't making sense right now. But the wedding is so close I'm still going through the motions – like sending the invitations out because he's been hounding me to do it before it's too late.

Last night I dug out the old photos that Grant keeps in an album in his office, several of which are of his sister and his niece when she was born. I couldn't find a single one of the baby wearing those shoes, nor any of Grant holding that little girl. If it was his niece, why would he single out that one photo to lock away, rather than keeping it in an album where his other family photos reside?

'Adriana Gallo.' Dr Phuong calls my name from the end of the hallway, her face warm and welcoming. I still go by my maiden name. Toby and I agreed I'd keep it because it was a name I'd chosen.

239

You see, Gallo is actually my mother's surname. I stormed up to Births, Deaths and Marriages the day after my eighteenth birthday and had my name legally changed, because the thought of spending another year bearing my father's name made me feel sick to my stomach. I wanted to erase him from my life, but I couldn't do that if every time I needed to show my driver's licence, his legacy was staring right back at me.

I became Adriana Gallo by choice.

Dr Phuong leads the way to a small examination room with a desk and two chairs on one side and a bed protected with disposable covers on the other. She takes a seat at the desk and gestures for me to take one of the empty spots near her. 'We have your test results back and I can confirm that you are indeed pregnant.'

I nod, grateful that she doesn't immediately say 'congratulations' like many people do, because I'm not sure I'd be able to hide how I feel. I'm sure some might interpret the omission as cold or unfeeling, but it's how she allows the patient to remain in control of their narrative. It's a small thing, but it shows what a keen understanding she has of the complications of being a woman.

Despite what society thinks, not all of us have dreamed of motherhood since we were little girls.

'I'm going to book you in for some general bloodwork to ensure all your levels are looking good. We'll check your blood count and infection markers. I'll also refer you to a radiology clinic to have a dating ultrasound so we know how far along you are.'

I nod, biting down on my lower lip so hard I taste the metallic tang of blood.

'Let me print you out some of our guidelines on the types of vitamins we recommend, as well. It might seem like a lot of information, but you can have a read over it in your own time and then let me know if you have any questions, okay? I'm here to help.'

Dr. Phuong's tone is professional but warm. Everything about her from her neat black ponytail to her steady hands and the firm but comforting eye contact exudes capability and care. It seems as natural as breathing for her, and, for a moment, I feel like I could be swept along by her calm, methodical approach. Maybe everything *will* be okay.

'There are several options for antenatal care and check-ups. If you have an obstetrician that you'd like to see, then that's great. If not, we can partner with the hospital and take a shared approach.'

'I, uh, yeah, okay.'

Her eyes flick up to mine and I can see the cogs turning in her brain. She might be able to tell from my general demeanour that I'm not exactly thrilled by this life update.

Panic swirls in my stomach.

'Is everything okay, Adriana?' she asks, a small crinkle forming at her forehead.

'My husband doesn't want this baby,' I blurt out. The second the words are out I want to snatch them back. It's like I've exposed something that I don't want anyone else to see, especially not someone as respectable as Dr Phuong.

'Pregnancy can come as a shock if it's not something that has been planned,' she says gently. 'How do *you* feel about it?'

'I don't know.' It's the only honest answer I can give. I've never seen myself as a mother. Never felt that yearning for children like other women do. I'm not maternal or a natural caregiver. I'm just like my own mother . . . and that terrifies me. 'It definitely wasn't planned.'

She nods. 'Well, the good news is that I can refer you to someone who might be able to help you sort through your feelings. It's completely normal to have to process what's going on, and a lot of my patients find that talking to a professional helps. Nobody is here to judge you.'

I feel my shoulders release a little. 'Thank you.'

'As your doctor, I will support you no matter which route you take.' Something flickers in her eyes, a little flash of concern, like lightning way out in the distance. 'Your husband knows about the pregnancy?'

'Not yet,' I whisper.

'Do you have concerns about telling him?'

Yes. But not like she thinks. Grant would never hurt me. It makes me momentarily sad that she even has to ask.

'I'm concerned to tell him because I know he doesn't want children and it's going to be an uncomfortable conversation for our relationship, but I'm not concerned for my safety,' I say. 'I appreciate you asking, however.'

She nods. 'That's my job.'

I suspect it is, but Dr Phuong gives the impression that she genuinely cares about the answer and not just

242

out of medical duty. Maybe that's not how it is, but I allow myself in that moment to feel that she really does care about the outcome of all this.

'Let's book you in for that bloodwork. I'm also going to write you out a referral to the radiology clinic for the ultrasound and another for a psychologist who specialises in antenatal counselling. Try to book your appointments as soon as you can.'

I nod.

She checks the test and then reaches for the tray on her printer to collect the information about pregnancy vitamins. Then she starts running through more information about how everything will work, but all I can think about is the picture my future husband keeps hidden in his filing cabinet and the secret phone he has locked in his drawer.

But can I even be mad at him for keeping secrets when I'm carrying possibly the biggest one of all? That's an answer I don't currently have.

I can barely look at Grant the next few days because every time I do, I feel a confession bubble up in the back of my throat. So I do my best to avoid him by making up an urgent project at work and inventing birthday dinners with the girls. Anything to get me out of the house until I figure out what to do next.

On top of this, my father has been calling me. I guess he got the invitation to the wedding. To be completely honest, I regret sending it. I don't even know why Grant wants him at the wedding. The man is a convicted criminal. A liar. A manipulator. I shouldn't have gotten talked into inviting him. Right now, I don't have the strength to answer my father's calls. So I keep sending him to voicemail.

In my desperation for a distraction, I coax Kylie into coming to the Body Barre class again, since our first session ended so abruptly. An animal about to be hit by a car? Yeah, right. Not a single other person on that street seemed to have noticed anything. Something is *definitely* going on with her.

This time we make it all the way through the class and while we're at the barre, she's glorious. Graceful, poised. I can see she would have been a really incredible dancer. But the second we go back out to the studio's foyer to change our shoes, she's back to being distant and distracted again.

She doesn't say a word as we head outside, her eyes fixed on something in the distance. I notice her hands are trembling a little and she's chewing on her lip. I wonder for a moment if she's having some kind of withdrawal.

Or worse. Maybe booze alone isn't cutting it anymore.

'What's going on with you?' I ask as we walk down the street to the tram stop.

For a moment, it's like she doesn't even register that I've spoken to her. But when I reach a hand out and touch her arm, she jolts like I've yanked her out of somewhere deep and dark.

'Everything,' she says, her eyes eerily vacant. 'Everything is going on.'

'Tell me about one of the things.'

I used to do this with my mother when she was spiralling. In her stress, she tended to conflate problems.

She would take every single thing that was bothering her and mash them all together into one bloated, unmanageable mass. The only way to get out of that thinking was to slowly parse through things one at a time, looking at each problem in isolation until she felt able to tackle things.

'Beth is kicking me out.' Her gaze drops to her hands and her eyes grow wet. I hear the shame in her voice, ringing like church bells. 'She wants me gone by next month.'

'Okay.' I nod. 'You've been planning to get your own place for a while though, right?'

'Yeah.' She bobs her head. Her red hair is dry and frazzled, curly strands sticking out in every direction like she tossed and turned all night and then didn't have the energy to style it this morning. This theory is supported by the bags drooping under her eyes. Kylie is gorgeous with her pert nose, freckles, and big, curious, doll-like eyes. But today she looks haggard. Her nails are bitten down and I notice a small burn mark on the back of one of her hands. 'But there's a big difference between choosing to leave and being booted out.'

'Of course. What prompted the discussion about you moving out?'

A humourless smirk tugs at her lips. 'Calling it a discussion is a bit of a stretch.'

I want to comfort her. The pain in her voice tugs at me and there's a despondence to her posture – sagging shoulders, bowed head, fingers knotted together. I'm not a touchy-feely kind of person, though, and I don't

245

know how to infuse people with my warmth and care the way Isabel does. So I reach out and pat her on the back but it's a little stiff and awkward, as if I'm an alien trying my best to imitate human contact.

See, this is why I'm worried about being a mother.

'I got sacked from my job a while back, and uh . . . she found out.'

'That you were sacked?' It seems a harsh reaction, to kick a woman when she's down. Beth has always struck me as generous, from what Kylie has told me about her. She seems to really love her sister.

'That I lied and made out like I was still working.'

'Oh.' That makes more sense. 'Right.'

'I don't know what I was thinking.' She looks up at me as we walk, blinking through her tears. 'I put my stupid bloody blazer on every morning and left the house like everything was normal. I'd go to the library all day. Sometimes the pub. More often the pub, if I'm being honest. She's been covering rent all by herself because I told her payroll stuffed up my pay instead of telling her the truth.'

I try to hold myself back from sighing. Kylie and good decisions are like oil and water. She's the only person I know who can take an epic mess and make it steadily worse without even considering that there might be other options.

'Then I've been seeing this guy and . . .' Her eyes suddenly become vacant again, almost like she's mentally checking out. 'He gave me some money but I didn't know what to do with it and then Beth found it and—'

'Hang on, hang on.' I hold up my hands. 'Slow down. You've been seeing a guy and he gave you money . . . for what?'

She swallows. I can see the muscles in her neck working, almost like she wants to throw up and is trying to hold it back. This is the first time she's mentioned a boyfriend and she doesn't seem happy about it. Maybe they broke up. Maybe it was a casual thing. She's previously sworn off relationships after what her husband did to her.

'It was just there.' Her voice is distant.

'What do you mean?'

'When I woke up.' She refocuses on me, and her face is white as a sheet. 'There was money on the bedside table in an envelope.'

I have no idea what she's getting at but the expression on her face alone is enough to make me feel sick to my stomach. 'Did you ask him for money? Like, a loan or something?'

'No.' She shakes her head. 'Never. I would be too embarrassed, and besides, I've only seen him a few times. It's not like we're serious.'

'So this wasn't him trying to help you out of a bind?'

'He says he was but . . . something feels off.' Her bottom lip quivers. 'I think . . . I think something happened.'

The sick feeling intensifies. 'How so?'

'I think he did something to me. Something bad.'

For a moment I can't think of what to say, but a raw feeling grabs me and I grip the edge of my seat. 'What makes you think that?'

'Every time we're together I end up drinking too

much and passing out. That's not wildly unusual for me these days, I guess. But I can't remember anything the next morning but I'm always in a hotel room. The morning I found the money, I felt really sick and I threw up. When I had a shower, I found . . .' Her breath catches. 'I was bruised, on my inner thigh. And there were three champagne flutes in the hotel room but he says no one else was with us. I don't even remember how we got to the hotel.'

I press a hand to my stomach, wanting to throw up for a moment myself. Everything about this is ringing alarm bells in my head.

'I wish I could remember, but every time I try it's like my brain shuts down.' Her lip quivers. 'I know I shouldn't be drinking so much . . .'

'If he did something to you, that is *not* your fault, regardless of whether you've been drinking. Addiction is an illness, Kylie.' I want her to see that I'm not judging her. That she's loved and supported. 'It's not that you're weak or stupid or anything like that. But you *do* need help.'

'I've found an AA meeting close to my place. I mean Beth's place.' She sucks in a breath and shakes her head. 'I don't want to keep doing this to myself. I don't want to put myself in a position where I'm not safe and I definitely don't want to lose my sister over it. She . . . she's so disappointed in me.'

The catch in her voice strikes me hard in the chest.

'She's angry right now, but things will get better. Especially if you make strides to deal with the drinking.' I nod, wishing there was something more I could do

248

to help. But I have a feeling this is one demon she needs to battle for herself. 'And you're not seeing that guy anymore, right?'

She shakes her head. 'He tried to get me to come out the other night, and at first I said I would go . . . but I changed my mind at the last minute. He was really mad. Then he started calling me and calling me, so I blocked his number.'

'He sounds like bad news.'

'Yeah, I think he is.' She reaches into her pocket and pulls out a tissue to dab away her tears, a sense of resolve bringing colour back to her face. 'Part of me feels obsessed with wanting to know what happened that night. But I don't want to see him again.'

I'm uncertain how to help her tackle this issue. Addiction is outside of my experience and it's highly sensitive. I don't want to say the wrong thing and make her feel any more isolated than she already does.

We've reached the tram stop now. The one she needs to take through the city to the other side of town is still a few minutes away according to the electronic sign above our heads.

'The morning I left the hotel, one of the room-service workers was there and she was looking at me weird. It makes me wonder if she saw something.' Kylie keeps her voice low and she stands close to me, as if needing protection. 'I've been thinking about going back but I . . . I'm worried they'll think I'm a prostitute or something. What kind of woman goes to a hotel with a man and blacks out and then needs someone else to tell her what happened?'

I don't answer the question, because I know she's judging herself harshly right now. And she doesn't need answers from me. She needs a friend. An ear. Not judgement. 'Do you want me to come with you?'

Her eyes brighten. 'You would do that?'

'Of course. We're friends.' I nod. 'Whatever you need.'

'Thank you.' She lets out a breath, her shoulders lowering from her ears and the frown easing from her forehead. It whisks the years away from her face. 'That really means a lot.'

'We have to stick together, you, me, and Isabel.' I pause for a second, feeling guilty for leaving Hannah out. 'And Hannah. We have to support one another.'

'I'm going to be better.' Kylie nods, confidence strengthening her voice. I truly hope she can hang on to that feeling when things get tough, because something tells me she's headed towards the eye of the storm. We all are. 'I'm not drinking anymore.'

'One day at a time.' The road to sobriety isn't always one foot in front of another, that much I know. 'And we'll see if we can find you some answers.'

Chapter Twenty-Four

Isabel

Time at work resembles thick, sticky honey. The minutes tick down at an agonising speed and frustration makes me bounce in my seat. I'm eager to get back to digging into my boss's failed luxury apartment complex. The situation isn't so unusual – the buyers got screwed and my boss and his partners did some unethical things, but were ultimately protected by the fine print of the contract. Look at any building developer and you'll find a story of a project that went sideways and people who lost out.

Still, there is *one* thing niggling me.

A single email. I took a photo of it on my phone so I could refer back to it if I got a quiet moment to think, which I do now. It's quarter past four and the office is dead. A leadership offsite event has dragged the management team away, some 'trust-forming' bullshit and culture-strengthening activities and other such corporate horrors. Only the low-level worker bees like Gabby and me and the customer service team and IT

251

boffins are left behind, so I have plenty of time to stare at my phone without anyone bothering me.

I pull the email up. It was sent from someone named Peter Diakos.

What are we doing about the Foxworth thing? The sister left another screeching voicemail for me today. She's threatening to sue for manslaughter and psychological injury.

This is getting serious.

After looking through the sale records my boss meticulously saved on his laptop, I've managed to find a buyer named Stanford Tobias Archibald Foxworth III. What a name. I almost had to stop myself from rolling my eyes. Rich people, am I right?

My digging online produced little – no social profiles, no articles about what he did for work, nothing in the form of society gossip or announcements. The guy was a ghost. Yet this email feels important.

Manslaughter. Psychological injury.

Was someone grievously injured on the building site, perhaps? Surely that would have made it into the news. Or was it more sinister? A murder made to look like an accident?

A memory flashes of my night out with Gabby.

One guy turned up at the office screaming that he'd been scammed and that he was going to press criminal charges and blah blah blah . . . she'd said.

I wonder if that was him. Maybe he was making too much noise. Causing too much trouble. It wouldn't be

252

the first time someone had been silenced to protect corruption or criminal dealings. And there had always been links with construction and organised crime.

Glancing around, there's nobody coming in or out of the offices, and the reception calendar is completely free. There are no more external meetings scheduled for the day where I might need to greet someone and sign them in.

I push up from my chair and wander through the open-plan area, noting that Gabby's desk is empty. But I spot the bright yellow and orange print of her wrap dress in the staff room, so I head in her direction. She's hunched over, tapping away at her phone while she waits for the kettle to boil. Her hair is pulled back into a bun and several strands are coming loose, a bobby pin dangling precariously on one side.

'Hey,' I say as I walk up beside her, reaching for one of the mugs in the open cupboard in front of her. 'Enough water in that kettle for another cuppa?'

'Sure.' She tucks her phone away into one of the deep pockets of her dress. The colour combination is retina-searing. It's one of those dresses that was probably marketed as 'boho chic' but looks like a child's craft project gone wrong.

I catch the dark circles under her eyes and frown. 'What's going on?'

'It's the girls, they're . . . driving me up the wall.' She huffs in frustration. 'Do yourself a favour and never have children. Especially not girls.'

Too late.

'What happened?'

'I go through their internet search history from time to time, just to make sure they're not looking at anything terrible. We have one of those parental-lock web-blocker things so I know they can't stumble across porn or anything like that, but then I see that the youngest has been searching for things like boob jobs and lip fillers and eyelash extensions. She's thirteen years old, for Chrissakes.'

I make a sympathetic noise. 'The internet is making them grow up too fast.'

'At thirteen I thought it was scandalous to pinch a lipstick from my mum's handbag and wear it to school. We used to roll our uniform skirts up to make them shorter, but . . . cosmetic surgery?' She scrubs a hand over her face. 'I tried to talk to her about it last night, but she went apeshit at me for invading her privacy and told me I was a helicopter parent. Then do you know what she said to me?'

Gabby's voice is getting higher by the minute.

'Dare I ask?' I cringe.

'She said, "Okay, boomer." Okay fucking boomer! I'm forty-three, not sixty-three. What a little shit.'

I have to stifle a laugh. I suspect Gabby is as annoyed about the insult to her age as she is about her little girl looking up boob jobs. 'They parrot what they see online.'

'Like I said, never have girls.' She shakes her head ruefully. 'Anyway, enough about my stupid problems. How's your day going? God, I can't wait to get out of here.'

The kettle clicks off and she reaches for it, tipping the piping-hot water into both our mugs.

'You know, I can't get something out of my head. When we went for drinks you told me about the guy that turned up here screaming at the receptionist over that dodgy building project.'

Gabby's eyes dart back towards the kitchen door, but no one's there. 'Yeah?'

'It's the weirdest thing, I was reading an article about unethical practices in the building industry and they interviewed a few people, and it made me wonder if the guy ever went to the media.' I spit out the rehearsed lines I practised while sitting bored at my desk. Knowing Gabby, she'll be too worried about what she said while she was drunk to ask for the non-existent article I'm referencing. At least, that's what I'm hoping. 'You don't happen to remember his name, do you?'

'I shouldn't have told you any of that.' She shakes her head and jiggles her teabag aggressively in the hot water, turning it a darker shade of brown. 'I don't know what got into me. I *never* drink like that anymore.'

I set about making my cup of tea as well, not wanting to push too hard in case it causes her to clam up. But Gabby hates silence. It makes her uncomfortable. Anytime there's a pause in a conversation that goes on longer than a few heartbeats, she visibly sweats then fills the air with needless chatter.

The sound of my spoon clinking against the side of the mug breaks the quiet, and she glances at me, her hand still nervously jiggling her teabag. I don't say a word.

'You won't mention it to Mr Frenchman, will you?' Her eyes plead with me.

'Oh my gosh, of course not. We're friends, aren't we? I'd *never* do that.'

Her shoulders lower and some of the colour comes back into her face. She looks pleased. Gabby wants, above all else, to be noticed and liked, and I've presented her with a little trust hurdle to leap over. If we really *are* friends, like she wants to believe, then she has to answer my question.

It's manipulative, I know. But, as my mum always said, you have to crack a few eggs to make an omelette. Besides, I'll never actually let on that the information came from Gabby. There's no need to put her in hot water.

'Call it morbid curiosity.' I pass her the milk. Nonthreatening. Not too invested. Cool, calm, casual. 'You know the most interesting things.'

Suddenly the worry and guilt are replaced by the sparkle of superiority. 'Apparently the guy was from some well-to-do family. Old money. Probably one of those grammar-school boys.'

That seems to line up with someone whose name ends in 'the third'.

'He didn't come into the office straight away, though,' she says. 'He called first. Dozens of times, trying to get Mr Frenchman to talk to him. But I was told not to let the calls through. After all, it's not our business here. The company is completely separate from the boss's personal investments. But it seemed like he was sick of not being able to get through to the construction company's office, so he started going after the individual people involved in the project that he knew personally.'

Makes sense. If the guy felt like he was being stonewalled, he'd look for another way in.

'One time he said he was going to come here with a gun.' Gabby bites down on her lip. 'We had to increase security. There was a guard at the front door for months.'

'Then the guy showed up,' I prod.

She bobs her head. 'Yeah. He was in a state.'

'What do you mean?'

'Like, you could tell his suit was expensive but all the buttons on his shirt were done up wrong. He'd been drinking. Or taking drugs, maybe. Something. He was screaming like a banshee.' She shudders. 'It was scary. I thought he might do something.'

'What happened?'

'Security escorted him out and threatened to call the cops. He ended up leaving on his own, although I don't think he should have been driving.' She shakes her head. 'Honestly, I felt bad for him. He seemed desperate.'

She still hasn't told me if she remembers his name.

'Mr Frenchman was madder than a cut snake. Called the guy a lunatic. Said he was going to get a restraining order and everything.' She pulls her teabag out of the now milky brown liquid and drops it into the rubbish bin. '"It's not my fault the guy can't manage his money or think for himself," he said.'

Her imitation is pretty spot on, right down to the way he puffs out his chest when he talks.

'Between you and me, I think builders should be held responsible for delivering what they promise,' she says, frowning. 'Maybe it didn't start out as a scam or anything, but those people got screwed over. *Bad*. Mr Frenchman was meeting with lawyers for *ages* after it happened. He'd disappear in the middle of the day, tell me to change all his meetings and not put any calls through. I thought he was getting sued, but then all of a sudden it stopped and we never heard from him again.'

Gee, I wonder why the calls suddenly stopped . . .

Manslaughter? Psychological injury? A dead man can't make phone calls.

'What did you say his name was again?' I shake my head, like I'm enraptured by her story.

'Oh I can't quite remember.' She wrinkles her nose. 'It was something long. Foxley, perhaps? Foxbury? Fox-something, anyway.'

Bingo.

Chapter Twenty-Five

Kylie

Adriana and I meet at the hotel after work. I catch the tram down Collins Street, from the 'Paris end' all the way past Spencer Street Station. The shift in the city is stark – ornate heritage-listed buildings giving way to modern structures and the view of the Yarra River opening up to the left. The sound of the tram's bells mingles with honking horns and the hustle and bustle of the city. Suit-clad workers and backpack-carrying students flock to the train station from all sides, and the tram mostly empties before I make it to my destination.

The hotel is a bland affair, a silver and black rectangle with a glass turnstile at the front and a short queue of yellow taxis waiting to scoop up a fare. I exit the tram and cross the road, darting between cars and not bothering to wait for the lights, hoping there aren't any revenue-raising coppers around to book me for jay walking.

Adriana is already standing out front, wearing a tight grey pencil skirt, with a blue and white blouse in a windowpane check pattern and a pair of nude patent high heels. She has a laptop bag slung over one shoulder and her blond bob is secured on one side with a dainty mother-of-pearl clasp, which matches the heavy pearl studs in her ears.

As usual, she looks every inch the never-put-a-foot-wrong woman that she is.

I lift my hand in a wave as I approach. 'Thanks for coming.'

'Ready?'

Having her at my side is the only thing that could get me through this.

I nod. 'Ready as I'll ever be.'

We walk through the turnstile and into the hotel foyer. In daylight, it's especially obvious that this hotel is used for work travel. It's close to Southern Cross Station, which has the airport shuttle and all the regional transport like V/Line trains and coaches, and it's easily accessible by other types of city transport, with the Melbourne Convention and Exhibition Centre a short jaunt over the river.

A small group of men walk past, lanyards around their necks and satchels slung over their shoulders. They're relaxed, discussing where to go for a drink. One man's eyes linger on us as we pass, and I fold my arms across my chest.

We arrive at the front desk, where a young man smiles and stands up. 'Checking in?'

'No, uh . . .' My voice is wire-tight with nerves and I try to let my anxiety go. If we find something, great. If not . . . then I guess I'll figure out how to deal with it.

'This might be a weird request, but is it possible to speak with your cleaning staff?'

The young man looks confused. Then suspicious.

'My friend stayed here recently and she lost an important family heirloom.' Adriana steps in, speaking clearly and firmly with the authority of someone who knows that she should be in charge. The man immediately pulls his shoulders back, eyes focusing on her as he nods. 'It has a lot of sentimental value. We would be very appreciative if we might be able to speak with the person who cleaned the room to see if they found it.'

I shoot her a grateful look.

The concierge nods. 'Of course. I can have a look in our lost and found registry. When did you stay?'

'Eighteenth of May. The room was booked under Francis John,' I say.

'And what was the item?'

Ah, shit. What am I supposed to say now?

We didn't plan for this.

I clear my throat. 'A bracelet, uh, gold. With . . . pearls.'

I'm a terrible liar.

The man taps at his computer and he scans the screen in front of him. 'We don't have any jewellery items logged as found on that day. Let me check the rest of the week in case it wasn't logged until later.'

As he looks through his system, I scan the foyer. The lifts are set off to the side of the space, down the back, by a sign for the restrooms, and the bar is next to it. We can see into the bar from here and it looks a little sad – not dated, since this building appears fairly new, but it's totally devoid of personality. A few people sit, laptops open, pints of beer or glasses of wine beside them. It's a place where people come to work, not play.

I drag my eyes away from the people drinking, a familiar thread of desire tugging at my chest. I know I declared to Adriana that I wasn't going to have another drink, but I caved within the first twenty-four hours. Beth came home and things were tense and . . . I gave in. Yet another broken promise to myself.

Still, I'm going to get myself to a meeting soon. I will.

'I'm sorry. It doesn't look like we have any bracelets in our lost and found system.' The young man offers an apologetic shrug.

'Is there any way we could find out who cleaned the room that day and speak to them?' I ask.

'I'm afraid that's against our policy. All items that are found during the room turnover are brought to the management office and put into the system. If it's not listed here, then we don't have it.'

My shoulders deflate. It's obvious this guy isn't going to budge.

'Thanks anyway.' I muster a half-hearted smile.

You knew this might not work. Maybe you'll never know what happened.

'Let's go to the ladies' before we head off,' Adriana says. Then she glances at the man and offers a charming smile. 'It's a long commute home.'

He nods, his attention already drawn to the people waiting behind us.

I raise an eyebrow as she loops her arm through mine and drags me towards the sign for the toilets. Just as we get there, she turns back and I follow her gaze. The guy at reception is fully engaged with the next group of guests. Adriana changes direction and pulls me towards the lifts. We duck behind the wall that separates the lift bay from the foyer and she jabs at the call button.

'What are you doing?' I ask, eyes darting around to see if anyone has noticed us. But there's nobody around.

'Helping you find answers,' she says. A second later one of the lifts dings and the doors slide open. 'Come on, let's go and find that cleaner.'

Thank God Adriana is here. She's one of those people who can take charge of a situation and sound so confident that the only natural response is to do what she says. I've always admired that about her. Even with all the hardship she's faced, she still fronts the world with her chin up and her shoulders back, ready to speak up for herself.

I wish I could be more like her.

You're going to get control of your life back.

Like she said, one day at a time.

We step into the lift and Adriana presses the button for the top floor. 'We'll go level by level until we find someone who can help.'

I nod. 'Okay.'

She looks at me, her eyes holding me captive for a moment. 'You're strong, Kylie. I know you don't think it, but you are. It's in there.'

I don't feel it right now. Not truly. These days I'm

more like a shattered heart barely held together with duct tape, waterproof mascara, and motivational Instagram quotes. But pity never served anyone. I want answers. I want goals. I want more than to be disgusted with myself.

We exit at the top floor and see there's no one around. Usually the top floor of a hotel is the fancy part and while there *are* fewer rooms up here than I remember from the floor I was on last time, nothing about the decor indicates we're in a more prestigious area of the hotel. It's still brown and beige, with ugly swirling carpet and generic wall hangings and a general sense of blandness.

I turn right and walk along the corridor, checking to see if any of the rooms are open or being cleaned. They're not. We take the stairs down to the next floor and it's the same story. Then again, and again. There are twenty-five floors in this building and I'm glad I wore flat shoes. Adriana's heels make clicking echoes in the stairwell each time we descend.

Twenty-one, twenty, nineteen.

On the eighteenth floor, we finally encounter someone, but it's not the woman I remember. This woman is about fifty, short with brassy hair, a stubby nose, and the kind of lines around her mouth that tell me she's a smoker. She chews gum as she works, humming a song to herself as she carries a set of fresh towels into an open room, reappearing a moment later to dump some dirty towels into a linen basket on the cart.

'Excuse me,' I say, smiling. She looks up but doesn't return the expression. 'We're trying to find someone who was working here on the eighteenth of May. She's probably in her late fifties or early sixties, with dark hair and silver roots.'

'Most of the women who work here are that age and have grey hairs, love. That doesn't narrow it down.' The staff member doesn't even seem curious as to why we're asking. Not like the guy downstairs. 'If you've lost something, you need to see the concierge.'

'No, it's, uh . . . something else.' I try to think back to what the woman looked like in more detail to see if there are more distinguishing details I can provide. Then I remember something. 'She had a rather large mole on her chin, right here.' I point to my own face and the staff member nods.

'Oh, that's Caterina.'

'Is she working today, by any chance?' Adriana asks.

'Yeah. She should be doing towel service for the lower floors, but she might have finished already. I think her shift is ending soon.'

'Which floors are the lower floors?' I ask, my voice tight with desperation.

'One through ten.'

'Thank you.'

Adriana and I hurry to the lift and jab at the call button.

'Think she was working her way up or down?' Adriana asks me.

'No clue. But ten is my lucky number, so let's start there.'

The lift takes its time, but it would still be quicker

than trudging down eight flights. When it arrives, we pile in. There are three men and a woman already inside. The men wear suits and the woman wears a knee-length burgundy dress under a black tweed jacket. I catch one of the men looking closely at me, and something about him seems familiar but when I reach towards the back of my mind for a memory, there's nothing there.

You're being paranoid.

When the lift stops at level ten, Adriana and I pile out, and the other four people continue on to the ground floor. I spy an open room further along the hallway and we head towards it. There doesn't seem to be anyone coming or going, and at first I wonder if someone has forgotten to close their door. But then I notice that one of the towel trolleys is sitting against the wall, near the end, and a woman emerges from the room holding a large white sack. There's a slight waddle to the way she walks, as though she suffers with stiffness in her joints.

'It's her,' I say breathlessly. 'Excuse me. Caterina?'

The woman stops in her tracks and looks at us warily.

'I'm so sorry to interrupt you, but I was hoping you might be able to help me with something. I was here on the eighteenth of May and I think you might have seen me.' The words rush out like water over a waterfall, tumbling into the air and making the older woman's eyes widen. 'I, uh, can't remember what happened that night but you looked at me strangely the next morning and I was wondering if you knew anything about who I was with.'

For a moment, she says nothing. Then she bites down

on her lower lip, eyes dragging away from mine. 'Sorry. I no speak good English.'

I blink, totally stumped. Of all the issues I might have experienced today, this was not one I had anticipated.

I look at Adriana, my shoulders deflating.

'*Signora? Parli italiano?*' Adriana looks at the woman expectantly and she nods, eyes brightening. '*Mi dispiace disturbarla, ma . . .*'

What comes out of Adriana's mouth next is a melodic string of Italian words and Caterina responds, gesturing with her hands and looking to me and then back at Adriana. Her voice rises in pitch and I watch a frown appear between Adriana's brows. Eventually the flurry of words dies down.

'She says you were here with two men. It was around nine p.m. She had taken an extra shift and someone had asked for a turndown service while they were out at dinner. You looked drunk, and two of the men were helping you walk but your eyes were closed.' Adriana glances at the woman, whose hands are clasped together. 'She said she didn't like the way the men were looking at you. They were laughing, but she couldn't understand what they were saying.'

'Can she remember what they looked like?' I ask.

The flurry of Italian starts again.

'Both men were tall and had dark hair. One of them wore glasses. They were both wearing suits. She said it looked like they had money, so she wasn't sure exactly why they came here instead of one of the nicer hotels.'

'Did they . . . hurt me?' The words clog up in my throat and I catch a flash of concern in the older woman's face.

Adriana translates my question and this time

267

Caterina's response is less animated, her hands hanging limply her side. She doesn't take her eyes off me the entire time she speaks.

'She says she's not sure, but she didn't like the men. They seemed bad.' Adriana sighs. 'But she only saw them helping you walk to your room.'

'Thank you, Caterina.' I look the older woman in the eye. '*Grazie.*'

Adriana pulls her wallet out of her bag and retrieves two crisp fifty-dollar notes and hands them to the Caterina. The older woman looks uncertainly at me and I nod, even though I have no place encouraging her to take Adriana's money. She folds her fingers, with their short nails and dry, cracked skin, around the notes and pulls them back, nodding. Then she reaches for my hand and squeezes.

'*Grazie mille,*' Adriana says softly.

Caterina slides the money into the top of her shirt, presumably into her bra where no one else will see it, and then hefts the large linen sack. She walks towards the cart at the end of the hall, and Adriana and I turn back to the lifts.

'Do you think . . .?' She glances at me. 'Maybe you should speak to the police?'

'And say what?' I toss my hands in the air. 'That I have a drinking problem and I ended up at a hotel with money on the bedside table and a bruise on my thigh which leads me to believe I *might* have been assaulted? With not even my own memories as proof? Yeah, they'll *really* want to help me then.'

Admitting out loud that I think I was assaulted feels

both like unburdening myself and digging myself further into the hole that has become my life.

'What if it was just rough sex and I was too drunk to know exactly what I was doing? Who knows, maybe I wanted it.' But even as I offer this alternative, something inside me tells me I'm wrong. Whatever happened that night, I *didn't* want it. I know it in my gut. 'What are they going to do with this information? I don't know anything for sure and the one person who might know something only says they were helping me walk. She didn't see anything damning. The police will roll their eyes and tell me not to drink so much.'

'You don't know that,' she says softly.

But I do know it and so does she.

For a moment I want to sink down to the floor and cry. Everything feels so overwhelming right now – it's like I'm stuck in a whirlpool, being dragged around and around and around. I've been spun so many times I can't see straight anymore. I don't know which way is up. I don't know what to do next. I don't know how to dig myself out of this mess.

I'm desperate for a drink in this moment and that only makes me feel worse.

'There's nothing for them to investigate.' A lump lodges in the back of my throat. 'Maybe this whole thing was pointless. Maybe I'll never know what happened.'

We arrive at the lift and Adriana presses the call button with a perfectly manicured finger. Why can't I be more like her? She's strong and confident and would never be so self-destructive. I feel more despondent now than when I arrived at the hotel with her. I've put myself in a dangerous position and I know it's going to eat away at me. The lift doors slide open and I'm relieved to see that no one is inside. Hopefully we can go straight to the bottom and get the hell out of here. I stare at the floor as we descend.

'I'll support you however you want to handle it, Kylie.' Adriana stands close to me, but without touching. She's not the most affectionate person in a physical sense, but I feel her care in her tone and her words and the fact that she's here with me now.

'Thank you,' I whisper, tears filling my eyes. I blink them back.

'Promise me you *will* handle it, okay? If you need to scream and cry or talk to someone or write in a journal or punch something just . . . don't let it eat you alive.'

Knowing that I have her on my side – knowing that she believes me even when some days I'm not sure I believe myself – keeps me standing upright. It's a bolt in my knees to stop them from crumbling. It's a rod in my neck to keep my head up. It's a tiny little flame flaring to life in my belly.

I won't let it eat me alive. I won't. I won't.

Chapter Twenty-Six

The Watcher

Adriana walks out of the radiology clinic, head bowed and arms folded tightly across her chest. She's had a busy day. First it was a run at 7 a.m. through the leafy streets of Brighton, then a morning shower followed by work calls in the front room of her house. Usually she works upstairs in her office if she's working from home, but today she sat on the couch with a cup of tea and her hair wrapped in a towel. She must have left her camera turned off. I couldn't tell from where I was standing.

Then at noon she left the house again, this time driving to a café to pick up a takeaway coffee and a muffin, before getting back on the road and heading to a nondescript little psychology clinic about ten minutes from her house. After that, she came to the radiology clinic.

I wonder if her boss knows what's going on. Adriana is usually steadfast and reliable, but she's been taking a lot of time off work recently. They must have figured out she's pregnant. Not that you can tell from looking – there is no curve to her stomach at all. But it's early days yet.

How have I been able to keep such close tabs on her for months on end without anyone noticing? Easy. I blend in.

A cap or beanie to cover my hair, Oakley wraparound sunnies to hide my eyes, an outfit of jeans and a T-shirt with black Kathmandu jacket over the top if it's cold. I look like any of the other millions of people who live in Melbourne. I could be anyone. In fact, one time I actually walked up to her and tapped her on the shoulder.

'Excuse me, miss. You dropped this.'

It was her lanyard for work and I'd picked it up after it slipped out of a folder she was carrying – one of those leather kinds that makes a person look important. She'd smiled and said thank you, but it was like her eyes had glanced right off me. I bet the second she turned around she'd forgotten about the interaction all together.

I'm a ghost. A nobody.

And yes, I know it's creepy for me to be watching her. I get it.

But it's for her own good. I've been trying to keep her safe. Because Adriana is surrounded by people who are lying to her. People who are not who they say they are. People with ulterior motives for having her in their lives. People who do not have her best interests at heart.

I know their secrets. And I won't stay quiet forever.

Chapter Twenty-Seven

Kylie

KYLIE: *Hey, it's me. What are you doing tonight? I miss you.*

FRANCIS: *You haven't been responding to my messages or calls. Can't miss me that much.*

KYLIE: *I've had a rough few weeks. My sister kicked me out.*

FRANCIS: *. . .*

KYLIE: *Don't worry, I'm not looking for a place to stay. Just someone to help me forget.*

FRANCIS: *I can do that.*

KYLIE: *Same place we met last time? 10 p.m?*

FRANCIS: *I'll be there.*

I promised I would handle it, rather than letting it eat me alive. And I will. I am.

Beth can barely look at me as I get ready to head out. We haven't spoken much since she found the money and gifts from Francis, and I haven't tried to push the issue. I can only hope that we can repair things once I move out, and I know it starts with getting sober. But I can't be sober for tonight. I need courage.

I stand in the bathroom and blow-dry my hair, stretching out my red curls into a bouncy, shiny mane the way the hairdressers at the salon have been teaching me to do. Maybe in the future I'll have a career change and go to beauty school. I pause to sip from the single small glass of white wine I've allowed myself. Just enough to loosen me up. To give my confidence a boost. Working at the hair salon has been great and one of the girls who's currently in training asked if she could practise a new colouring technique on my hair, so my naturally ginger-red shade has been deepened to a rich reddish brown. It's stark against my fair skin and freckles, but I like it. Tonight I don't want to be me and the new hair helps me feel like I've put on a costume so I can be someone else.

I've got everything planned.

After I finish blow-drying my hair and applying a matte red lipstick and lots of winged liner, I slip into the dress I wore the night Francis and I met. The black shift dress has a panel of glossy faux leather down the side and the hem sits above my knees. The Louboutin shoes would look best, but there's a chance I'll need to make a run for it at some point tonight, so I opt for a pair of shoes with lower block heels. Not sexy, which he may notice, but I need to know that if the situation calls for me to run, I won't fall and break my ankle.

As I ride on the tram towards the city, my hands shake in my lap. I look like any of the other dressed-up women who are heading out for an evening of fun, but there is no fun in my future. At least not for the next few hours. I glance at a group of women in their early twenties who look like they're headed for a night of clubbing. They stand in the middle of the tram car, teetering on high heels, long hair flowing and giggles evaporating into the air like champagne bubbles. They're beautifully naïve, unafraid of the dangers that lurk in the shadows and in the minds of the men who watch them. They're vibrant prey. Easy targets. I want to call out and tell them to go home, to lock their doors, to be safe.

Of course I know not all men are predators. I loved my grandfather dearly and he was the kindest and most gentle man I ever knew. But I've had enough men in my life turn out to have some shade of monster inside them that I find it hard to tell the good from the bad. Sex used to be my revenge, after Marcus died. It was stupid, really. He was dead and didn't care who I opened my legs for. But it made me feel like I was getting back at him.

Now I see that it simply led me to more monsters.

After tonight, if I get out of this the way I hope I will, there will be no more men. I need time to work on me, to slay my own demons. To get control of my world.

The tram announces the next stop and slows to a halt. I merge into a small group of people exiting and

275

carefully step down onto the road. Buildings rise up around me, like fingers pointing to something beyond the reaches of my vision. People push past in both directions and I fight to get out of the way. For a moment, I feel impossibly small. Impossibly alone.

But I have a plan.

It's nine forty-five and when I walk through the door to the bar, I'm greeted by the woman I've seen a few times before – short, partially shaved dark hair, deep brown skin, burgundy lipstick, beautiful eyes. She lets me upstairs without issue. I head to the bar and scoot straight over to grab one of the last remaining empty seats. This place really gets busy after ten, so it will fill up soon.

And then I wait. I order a gin and tonic and sip, brushing off interested looks from other men and refusing some of them outright. Then Francis walks in. The first time I saw him – that I remember – I was shocked by how handsome he was. Fit figure, the smattering of grey in his thick, dark hair, the devastating smile. But now I see something else. The hard, uncompromising stare, the grey-flecked hair which shows his age and experience, the brutal line of his jaw and the will to have what he wants, no matter who it hurts.

My hand makes the tumbler shake and I have to put the glass down for fear I'm going to drop it.

'You've started without me,' he says smoothly, gliding into the seat I've been saving with my bag. I hang it on one of the cleverly concealed hooks under the bar.

'Traffic was surprisingly light,' I reply.

Usually at this point he would lean in for a kiss, but

he's still angry with me. It radiates off him like a scent, heated by the time that's passed. He's not a man who's used to being ghosted. I wonder if he's here to call things off, instead of what he usually comes for.

'Why did you change your tune?' He motions to someone behind the bar for a drink and I see one of the bartenders step in to make it. My heartbeat kicks up a notch.

But I don't look around. Instead, I keep Francis's eye contact. 'Honestly, I felt like things were moving too fast and . . . I got scared.'

He raises an eyebrow. Clearly that wasn't what he expected to hear. 'Too fast?'

'I was feeling things I wasn't ready to feel yet. I was getting too invested and . . .' I drop my gaze down to my hand and hopes he mistakes my nerves for contrition. 'We talked about not taking things seriously. I know you're not looking for anything permanent and neither am I.'

'But?'

'I worried that I was falling for you.'

Even if he doesn't want a woman to expect too much from him, I hope this answer appeals to his ego enough that he'll let his guard down tonight. I need him to act as he has before if I have any hope of pulling this off.

I'm not sure he buys my story, but his hand drifts to my knee and slides possessively up my thigh. It takes everything in me not to hurl. His touch makes me feel icy inside and I desperately want to brush his hand away.

You're strong. You can do this.

'And now you're not falling for me?' he asks, leaning forwards. His voice is deep and smooth, almost smoky. 'Have you got better control of your emotions, Kylie?'

'Yes. And I know that I'd rather have something of you, than none of you.'

This is what he wants to hear – me conceding. Being pliant. Being obedient. Putting his desires ahead of my own. I am nothing but putty to him, something to be shaped and moulded by his will.

'You're a smart woman,' he says in a way that tells me he very much thinks the opposite. But we'll see tonight if I'm smart or not. We'll see if I can best him. He brings his drink to his lips and knocks it back, downing the whole lot in one go. 'Shall we have one together?'

'Sure.' I push my half-finished G&T away, acting as though I'm eager to please. Then I slide off my stool. 'I'm going to powder my nose. I'll have whatever you're having. Be back in a minute.'

I turn and head towards the bathroom, without looking back. I can't seem like I'm anxious or it might scare him off. For this to work, I need him to believe that all is normal. As I reach the doorway that leads to the hallway containing the bathrooms, I duck around the corner and wait. After a few heartbeats, I chance a look around the edge.

Francis is at the bar, his back mostly to me. I see him reach for something inside his jacket pocket and my stomach clenches. It could be anything – most likely he's reaching for his phone. But I watch as he removes his hand, seemingly with nothing in it. In the dim

278

lighting, it's hard to tell, but then I catch the bartender sliding two glasses over the bar and Francis's hand waves over my drink.

He's spiking my drink, I'm sure of it.

A man approaches Francis. I can see the tension in his shoulders – they've hiked up around his ears and he white-knuckles his drink as the man starts talking, gesturing with his hand. I wonder what they're discussing. After a moment, the man leaves.

Now it's time for me to act. I head back toward the bar, fluffing out my hair and smiling broadly.

'What exciting thing did you order me?' I ask, sliding into my seat. I don't want to touch the drink, but I know I must. I must take that first sip, even though it terrifies me.

'It's called a Penicillin. Scotch, honey, ginger, lemon. You'll love it.'

It's an order. And tonight, I will. 'Sounds delicious.'

'Let's toast,' he says, raising his glass. 'To second chances.'

Not on your life, arsehole.

'Sure.' I raise my glass to his. 'To starting over.'

We clink crystal against crystal and I bring the glass to my lips, wanting to cry but managing to hold it all back. I take the tiniest sip, leaving the glass up at my lips longer than necessary to make it look like I took more in than I really did.

Now to distract him.

'I'm really sorry I went dark,' I say, putting my glass down and leaning forwards. This dress doesn't show much cleavage, so I place a hand on his thigh and slide it up his leg, bringing my lips to his. 'I want to make it up to you tonight.'

He doesn't resist. I press my mouth to his and coax his lips open, letting my tongue slide against his as my eyes flutter shut. His hand comes to my waist and my skin crawls at his touch. I kiss him deep and long, letting everyone see that I'm his.

At least, I let them think that.

Then I reach out for his drink and tip it over, the liquid rushing over the edge of the bar. It pours over him, darkening his light-grey suit pants.

'Oh my God, I am *so* sorry! I'm so bloody clumsy.' I let my eyes grow wide and I don't miss the hard flare of irritation that flashes across his face like lightning. 'I guess I must have had a bit too much to drink before you got here.'

'Kylie . . .' He shakes his head.

Does he suspect I'm up to something? I wave to the bartender for some towels and pass them to him. 'They've got driers in the bathroom. That will probably do a better job.'

Please go. Please go. Please go.

His eyes flick to mine, but before there's any suspicion I make a cringing face and reach for my poisoned drink, and pretend to take another sip. I can't let on that I know what he's done.

'Give me a minute.' He stands and presses the paper towels to his leg, swearing under his breath. Luckily – or unluckily – for me, the prospect of a drugged woman is too much temptation for him to abandon his plans for the night.

When he's across the room and rounding the corner into the men's, I turn to the bartender and say, 'Two more of those drinks please. Quickly – my boyfriend has a temper.'

My heart thunders in my chest as the tattooed man in suspenders sets about methodically remaking the drinks, moving at a snail's pace. I chant *Come on* over and over in my head, because I need these glasses on the bar before Francis returns. I need him to believe I'm drinking the drugs he's been feeding me, likely since the night we met.

Because I'm not going to be passive tonight.

I'm going to bring this asshole down.

I glance back toward the men's toilets and just as I see Francis emerge, I push the tainted drink towards the bartender. 'You can get rid of this one, please. It tasted off.'

Confusion splashes across the man's face, but my voice has the steely edge of someone who will not be deterred. Wordlessly, he takes the glass and pulls it behind the bar. I reach for the new drink and take a big swig with my back to Francis, hoping he didn't notice the switch.

Now I need to act the part.

I let myself get semi-drunk. What at one time felt like release now feels like a prison, and my blurred edges are terrifyingly grey. But I've got my wits about me. Mostly. Francis acts as though he has the upper hand, which is what I need for him to be lulled into a false sense of security, but now I get a terrifying glimpse into what has happened before.

We leave the bar and head to a hotel that's new, not the one at the casino or the one by Spencer Street Station. I stare out of the taxi window, pretending to be glazed over all while trying to keep track of where we're going. I'm a little dizzy and I hate feeling that I could be more in control. That I *should* be more in control.

I know, however, that my acting skills won't be enough to carry me through a performance of 'woman who had her drink spiked' all by themselves. I've chosen to let the alcohol help me and it's strange to feel, for the first time in forever, that I have to force each sip down. Maybe this will finally be the thing to make me give up drinking.

Now the alcohol sits uneasily in my stomach and the stop-start taxi ride isn't helping.

'We're going to meet a friend of mine,' Francis says to me, his fingers toying with the hem of my dress. I have to resist every urge in my body to swat his hand away.

'Hmm?' I loll my head back against the head rest and look at him, but keep my eyes on his ear instead so I appear unfocused. I blink sleepily. That isn't an act.

I'm exhausted. Exhausted of my life. Exhausted of putting myself in these positions.

This is the last time. As soon as you have what you need, you'll be free of this. It's a fresh start tomorrow.

'You're going to love him.' He squeezes me hard and I wince. But it only makes his smile grow. 'Are you going to be a good girl tonight, Kylie? Are you going to put on a show?'

I want out of this taxi. I want out of this dress and these shoes and this problem. I never want to see Francis again.

'Anything for you,' I slur.

For a second, I wonder if this is all pointless. Why do I need proof of what happened? Maybe ignorance is bliss, as they say. Maybe I'm better off staying in the dark. I've thought that about my husband, too. Some days I wish I'd never found his little black book so I could have mourned and moved on, instead of being stuck in this self-destructive purgatory.

The taxi pulls to a stop. We head outside and I lean on him. I'm feeling hot, a little sweaty, my stomach roiling. The blast of air-conditioning from the hotel's foyer is a shock, making me shiver, and goosebumps ripple across my arms and legs. Francis holds me closer, revelling in the appearance of being my protector while actually being my demise. We meet his friend in the bar and Francis introduces him as Dominic. One drink and then we head upstairs while I lean my head on Francis's shoulder as we walk – me closer to stumbling – to a hotel room.

This is what Caterina must have seen last time.

When we get into the room, Francis almost tosses me on the bed and I lie there, letting my eyes close, while clutching my handbag. They seem to think I've passed out.

'I'll wake her up in a minute,' Francis says. His voice is totally different now – there's no smoothness anymore. He's let his guard down. 'She's a bit unpredictable, this one.'

'Hot, though.' Dominic stands closer. There's a sound of a seal being broken, before liquid glugs and glasses clink. 'Those legs . . . mmm!'

'She's a real redhead, too. If you know what I mean.'

'You know how to pick 'em.' They both laugh.

Then they start talking about work and I get the impression they're in the same industry. It seems like Francis is trying to win Dominic's favour, trying to get him to agree to some kind of business arrangement. I must be part of the negotiation process.

I mumble something as if I'm stirring and slump over to my side, tucking the bag against my body. I can't tell if they're watching me and I don't want to open my eyes, just in case. Not yet, anyway. But they continue to talk and don't seem as if they've noticed anything.

A few minutes later, I hear a sliding door open and their voices fade a little – they've stepped outside onto the balcony. *This is my chance!* I crack my eyes open. The backs of the two men can be seen through the open glass door. The balcony is small and I know they won't stay out there long. I reach down into my bag and fumble for my phone. As quickly as I can, I turn on the recording app and then slide it into the outside pocket of my bag, speaker facing up, and lean over the bed to put it on the floor against the bedside table, out of the way.

Francis turns and I go limp, snapping my eyes shut again. The sliding door closes and cuts off the sound of the city.

'I'll have to think about it,' Dominic says. 'You know things are tight right now and we're locking into a contract with—'

'Think about it. That's all I ask.'

'You're not trying to butter me up with *her* now are you, mate?' There's a warning tone in his voice. 'You know I couldn't accept if that was the case.'

'Not at all. This is just a little fun between friends.'

'Good. So, how much do I owe you?'

'I usually charge two grand, but for you I'll do mate's rates. Fifteen hundred.'

I force myself not to move. Panic clogs the back of my throat and my head swims, like it's trying to disconnect. Footsteps get closer and there's a hand on my arm, jerking me up to sitting position. It's Francis. He has a drink in his hand and he grips my jaw, forcing it open. Instinct kicks in and I try to pull away, but he's too strong. He tips the liquid down my throat and I choke, not wanting to swallow, but he simply laughs.

'She's a little wild,' he says over his shoulder. 'Don't worry, this will help loosen her up.'

Tears well in my eyes, streaking out of the corners, and my edges begin to blur once more.

I wake some hours later and I'm alone. The pillow is damp, as if I've either been sweating profusely or crying in my sleep. Maybe both. I'm achy and sore, and my wrist is blooming with a nasty bruise. This feels worse than last time.

But then I remember why I came here and scramble to grab my bag, which has been knocked over, spilling some of the contents onto the floor. For once, my bag is devoid of the normal debris – the gum wrappers and crumpled receipts and lidless lipsticks. I couldn't risk not being able to find my phone in a hurry. *Shit. What if he took my phone? What if he saw it was recording?* I reach my hand into the outside pocket and almost cry in relief – my phone is there. There's a notification saying that my storage is full.

'Please, please, please . . .' Ignoring the epic pounding in my head, I hold the phone up to my face so it will unlock and then I look for the recording.

It's there. Four hours and thirty-six minutes. It must have cut out when I ran out of storage.

Do I want to play it? I sit there, debating how much I want to know, until I find the courage in me to open the file.

'*I'll have to think about it. You know things are tight right now and we're locking into a contract with—*'

'*Think about it. That's all I ask.*'

'*You're not trying to butter me up with her now are you, mate?*'

Thank God. Tears well in my eyes as the recording goes on and I skip parts because it hurts too much. I choke back a sob at the sound of myself, at the sound of them. I don't know that I will ever be able to un-hear my sluggish voice protesting weakly. Nor the men laughing at my expense. What they did to me . . .

I hang my head. But I have proof now.

After, the men are talking business again.

'*I won't let this influence my decision about the contract,*' Dominic says. '*But I'll address your proposal on merit.*'

'*That's all I can ask for.*'

'*I will say, if you run Brunswick Logistics like you do*

286

your personal life, then you would make a great business partner.'

Yes, I have a name! Brunswick Logistics. I'll look them up and—

'*How do you get away with it all?*' Dominic asks. There's rustling in the background. '*Surely the missus wonders where you are all the time.*'

'*Nah. She's one of the good ones. She doesn't harp on at me to come home.*'

'*You've done better than me.*' Dominic lets out a sound of exasperation. '*I swear to God I married a prison warden.*'

And then Francis says something that shocks me to my core.

Chapter Twenty-Eight

Adriana

I wake today with the raging urge to throw up and only just make it to the bathroom in time. As I heave, my knees pressing against the cold tiled floor and my stomach aggressively emptying itself, I know my time is up. I won't be able to put off telling Grant about the pregnancy for much longer. He's in Adelaide for the next three days, preparing for the opening of the new office. And while he's busy, he keeps checking on me. More than usual. *Much* more.

He knows something is up.

It feels like a chasm has opened between us. Some fissure I hadn't even known was there has been crowbarred apart to reveal a messy underbelly I've naively assumed didn't exist. But secrets are lurking, building. Multiplying.

My father has continued to ring me, almost daily, and I haven't picked up once. It feels like the walls are pressing in. The wedding is rushing closer and it weighs on my back like a sheet of slate. Time is running out.

Dr Phuong said I have 'options' and I understand what that means. In the past, I assumed my complicated feelings on motherhood would have meant I'd prefer to abort a pregnancy rather than bring a child into the world. I know several women who have done this, for a variety of reasons, and I strongly believe in a woman's right to choose. But right now, there's something in my heart that tells me to see this pregnancy through; that keeping the baby is the right choice for me; that I have an opportunity to give this child the kind of love and care I never received myself.

But it could tear Grant and me apart. It likely *will* tear us apart.

I have to tell him as soon as he gets back.

Putting my internal struggle to the back of my mind, I grab my phone and call in sick to work, feeling too weak to put on a front for my colleagues. This means I'll have to tell my boss about the pregnancy, too, once I'm further along.

I sit on the floor of the bathroom, throat burning from stomach acid and retching, my head pounding like a hammer against a nailhead. Mum told me once how her morning sickness was so bad it made her wish she'd never got pregnant. At the time it felt like a great insult, like I wasn't worth the discomfort, but now I understand what she meant – the feeling of losing control over your own body is terrifying.

My phone chirrups from somewhere in the bedroom, where I tossed it after calling my boss before running back to the bathroom to throw up again. I think I might be done . . . for now. I flush the toilet and stand, knees wobbling, almost gagging at the disgusting taste in my mouth. I turn on the tap and bend over to catch some water in my mouth, swishing it around and spitting, but not feeling like that helped much at all. What I really need is a couple of Panadol and a lie-down.

I slowly pad into the bedroom, making sure not to make any sudden or jerky movements, and grab my phone. There's a text from Isabel, checking in to see how I'm doing, and another from Hannah asking if Grant and I are having a gift registry for the wedding. I'll respond to them later.

I drop the phone onto the bed and cringe, clutching my head as the headache worsens. I know Grant keeps painkillers in his suit jackets, since he suffers with migraines. Early on in our relationship, I stayed here one night and found him the following morning huddled on the bathroom floor, clutching his head in pain and nauseous as hell.

Now I understand what it must feel like, because I can't even face the thought of going downstairs to the medicine cabinet.

I stagger into the bedroom, pressing the heel of one palm to my eye socket. The thumping makes it feel like there's a rave going on in my head and I can practically see the lights flashing. Grant's wardrobe is to the left – we have a walk-in each – and everything is as it normally is. His suits hang to one side, from plain black to navy, and then several shades of grey in order from dark to light. His shoes sit below, lined up like toy soldiers, and accessories – ties, cufflinks, and pocket squares – are all stored in flat, glass-topped display drawers. It looks like the men's section of a designer suit store.

I grope at his suit jackets, feeling for a lump that might indicate a sleeve of painkillers. After making it halfway down the rail, I get lucky and feel something hard.

'Thank God.' I breathe a sigh of relief and worm my hand in behind one of the lapels, reaching for the interior pocket. My fingers brush something plastic. It's not quite what I was expecting.

I pull out what looks like one of those small fish-shaped vials that are usually filled with soy sauce and come with your sushi order. Only, the liquid in this vial is clear. I stare at it, lying innocently in my palm, the little red cap tight on its nose and its plastic fishy eye staring back at me. I trace the top of it with my fingertip, feeling the scale indentations and a rough edge of one of the tail fins.

It's a drug of some kind.

At least, I assume so. I've never come into contact with any illicit substances myself. I'm a good girl from way back – never smoked, only ever drank socially and in reasonable amounts. Never tried weed or party pills. So I have no earthly idea *what* type of drug it might be . . . But I know it can't be anything good.

Nothing legal comes in a plastic fish, unless it's soy sauce.

My mind scrambles for an alternative. Maybe it's eye drops? Maybe it's some medicinal cannabis oil that he obtained illegally? Maybe it's something to help him relax? He'd come home pretty hammered recently – a big night out with some mates he hadn't seen for years,

291

and I'd chuckled at him, saying he stank like a university student during orientation week.

But what if it wasn't just beer? What if he was high?

Is that why he keeps a secret phone locked away in his desk drawer, so he can contact his drug dealer without me knowing?

I suddenly feel sick for an entirely new reason. The lies and secrets are mounting and I'm starting to wonder if the man I'm marrying is a complete stranger. Fury bubbles up inside me, hot and sticky, and I find myself heading towards the stairs, despite my pounding head and swishing stomach. Gripping the handrail, I thud downstairs and turn into the kitchen. But instead of going to our medicine cabinet, I open the junk drawer and pull out the screwdriver we keep there. Then I head to Grant's office.

If he wants to keep things from me, fine. But he can't expect me not to go in search of answers.

For a moment the hypocrisy of my thinking stops me in my tracks. I am *also* part of the secret-keeping – there's no denying that. But not telling him about the baby isn't about hiding it from him, not really. It's because I don't know how to process what's happening and I'm scared of what it will do to our relationship.

That's not the same as drugs. That's not the same as a secret phone.

What about the email? The baby shoe with the note tucked inside?

I shove those inconvenient questions away and charge into his office, my teeth clenched and my headache worsening by the second. I drop in front of his desk, knees sinking into the plush pile of the carpet, as I try to jimmy the lock with the screwdriver. When that doesn't work, I slam my fist against the drawer, yelping as my bones take the impact.

'What are you hiding from me?'

I stare at the drawer, anger building inside me.

My frustration reaches boiling point and I do something from which there's no going back. I jam the screwdriver between the edge of the drawer and the frame of the desk and I leverage it with all my might. The wood splinters and I feel the skinny screwdriver protest, bending under my brute force. This is a screwdriver for tightening the backs of the handles on our kitchen cupboards, not for breaking and entering. And I am no criminal mastermind.

I try again, pushing my weight into it and then I hear a *crack*. The wood splinters further but the drawer remains locked in place, keeping the answers out of reach. I throw the screwdriver down in anger and it bounces on the carpet.

But then an idea strikes me.

I could call a locksmith and have them open the drawer. After all, there would be nothing suspicious about that, would there? I live here, so I have a right to access every drawer in the house . . . or so they would think. Grant is gone for three days, so it's not like I need to worry about him coming home in the middle of things.

I stand, and suddenly a wave of morning sickness comes over me, sending me stumbling towards the powder room.

* * *

The locksmith arrives by mid-afternoon. I have been throwing up for the better part of the day and have managed to stomach little more than a slice of plain toast with butter and a mug of green tea. I try to make myself look presentable because the wild hair, bathrobe, and family holiday's worth of baggage under my eyes does not present a good look. I want to seem calm, like nothing more serious is going on than that I've been a ditz and accidentally misplaced my key, rather than that I'm some crazed woman trying to get into her husband's things.

I've thrown on a slouchy pair of jeans and a simple Breton striped T-shirt. I've also brushed out my hair so it sits neatly in place, skimming the nape of my neck. My eyes are too raw for contacts today, so I perch a pair of tortoiseshell glasses on my nose, which I think makes me look more trustworthy.

'Thank you so much for coming,' I gush as I welcome the man into my home. 'I know it's such a small job.'

He's attractive – tall and athletic, with a mop of reddish-brown hair and warm olive-green eyes. He smiles easily. 'No worries. It's a desk lock, you said?'

'That's right.' I nod. 'My husband has gone away and he accidentally picked up my keys instead of his and I need something important out of the drawer.'

The man nods. The booking agent told me his name was Steven, though he hasn't introduced himself. I lead him through the house toward Grant's office. It occurs to me, as we step through the doorway, that this office doesn't look like it belongs to a woman –

it's all heavy dark-wood, big furniture, and other masculine touches like a dark-green leather mat on the desk and a bronze statue of a rearing stallion on one of the bookshelves.

If Steven notices anything, he doesn't say it. Perhaps he's been called out to unlock things in far more unusual circumstances than an office that doesn't look like it fits – perhaps some bondage play gone wrong? Or maybe he simply doesn't care about anything other than getting his service fee.

'Just there.' I point to the drawer and he gets to work.

It takes less than two minutes for him to insert a metal contraption into the lock and jiggle it around until the lock pops. Not exactly high security then. Just enough to keep out someone who can't think of anything more creative than a screwdriver. And for that I'm charged the seventy-dollar minimum call-out fee.

He slides the drawer open and looks at me with a curious expression. It's empty. Well, nearly empty. There's a single notebook sitting in the drawer and nothing else. The phone is gone.

'Thank you so much,' I say tightly, my face feeling like it's going to crack from the force of having to smile while feeling such intense frustration.

Since I've already paid the minimum call-out when I booked the locksmith, there's nothing else for me to do except usher Steven out of my house and race back to the drawer. It stares at me, like an open mouth. Mocking. Its secrets maintained.

How am I going to explain this to Grant when he gets home?

'What the fuck?' I say in frustration. I kneel down and pull out the notebook.

It's empty. An empty bloody notebook and nothing more. I want to scream but it's pointless. Whatever my fiancé is up to, he's far more of an expert at hiding things than I have ever given him credit for.

And now I have to figure out how to cover up the fact that I've been snooping, or else it's going to make him work harder to keep things from me. Tears prick at my eyes. I'm a fool, about to marry a man I clearly don't know and bring a baby he doesn't want into the world. I press a hand to my stomach and close my eyes for a moment as I sink back on my heels.

I feel like I understand my mother now more than ever.

She never wanted to be in this position either – married to a liar, ill-equipped to be a mother, trapped in a beautiful home with every corner darkened by secrets. I have tried so hard not to become her and yet here I am, a perfect living image of her.

I look down at the notebook in my hands and fan through it to see if there's anything important inside. The pages are mostly blank. But then something falls onto the floor. A business card.

My breath catches in the back of my throat and I stare, my eyes welling with tears as something horrible flares to life in my imagination. The anonymous email was right – Grant is *not* the man I thought he was. The secrets he's been keeping from me are vast. I pull my phone out of my pocket and dig through the emails I've deleted until I find the one from the anonymous sender.

I reply with shaking hands.

If you really want to help me, then tell me what you know.

Chapter Twenty-Nine

Isabel

I've spent days trying to find more information about Stanford Foxworth, but I've come up mostly empty-handed. I couldn't even find an obituary or funeral information online. I assume he's dead, based on the emails I've lifted from my boss's computer. But I haven't been able to confirm it. I suspect the threat of a manslaughter suit didn't go anywhere, because I couldn't find any court records about that, either. I've spent every spare moment—before work, during morning tea and lunch, quiet time between checking visitors in and out, during dinner and before bed—searching for answers.

Still, nothing.

The second it hits five o'clock, I gather my things and burst out of the office, like I'm a prisoner tasting freedom for the first time. As I walk to my car, my mind whirrs. I'm close to something and I can practically taste the honeyed satisfaction of revenge on my tongue.

Part of my bitter brain tells me that this won't be enough. That my arsehole boss can withstand a public-relations shitstorm, even if it does involve something as awful as a potential manslaughter suit. But how did Stanford die? Surely not on the D'Or Prime property, because *something* would have come up in the news about it. At least, I would think so.

Does my boss have underworld connections? Maybe he had someone rough him up? Keep him quiet? Cut his brakes? And if there was anything that pointed to murder, that would have to be reported, right?

But I'd found no articles about a homicide mentioning Stanford Foxworth III despite spending all afternoon Googling on my phone.

I turn the car keys in the ignition and Jonathan's poor battered car grumbles begrudgingly to life. As I reverse out of my parking spot, I turn the volume up on the radio.

'It's going to be a warm one tomorrow – an unseasonable high of twenty-eight with a low of just nineteen overnight. Brace yourself for temperatures to remain steadily in the high twenties for the next few days, making this autumn week feel a whole lot more like summer. But you might want to pull out those winter woollies anyway, because we've got storms and temperatures in the mid-teens on the horizon for the weekend.

'Now, in Melbourne's north-western suburbs, police caution people to watch out for a man in a blue tracksuit and red cap who's been seen in Brimbank Park . . .'

I jab at the buttons on my dashboard to change the station until I find one that's playing music instead of the top-of-the-hour news and traffic report. My car falls into a line trailing out of the staff car park, behind a red Toyota with a dent in the back bumper. Behind me, Gabby sits in her silver four-wheel drive and when she catches me looking in the rear-view mirror, she waves.

Brimbank Park . . .

The name sticks in my head and I try to think about why it sounds familiar. Then it comes to me – the park was one of the selling features for the area around the D'Or Prime Residences project. The building is walking distance to the park and the Maribyrnong River.

I drum my fingers on the steering wheel, waiting for my turn to exit the car park and merge into the steady, trudging stream of traffic. At the last minute, I change my indicator from right to left, and head off in the direction of the ill-fated building.

I'm not exactly sure what I'm hoping to get out of a visit to the D'Or Prime Residences building. Maybe I want to see it for myself, to understand the aching disappointment the buyers must have felt when their new luxury home dreams turned out to be a nightmare.

The entire drive there, I'm trying to think about what I'm going to say and do when I get there.

'At the roundabout, take the second exit.' I follow the instructions of the robotic voice on my GPS. 'In two hundred metres, you will arrive at your destination.'

I slow down to let someone backing out of their driveway pull out in front of me. At first glance, the street doesn't look too bad. Some of the houses are a little dated, sure, but it's still better than the area of Springvale where I live. There's a smattering of peeling weatherboard places – which ambitious real estate agents will label as 'trendy mid-century' – and single-storey brick homes with a car port instead of a proper garage. A few corners are capped with Sixties style triple-fronted brick homes and dated brick-and-iron fences, but there are also larger and more modern pavilion-style homes as well.

Like many Melbourne suburbs, it's a real mixed bag. And in reality, even the older homes here would fetch a pretty penny because the land is where the money lies. But I guess that's the difference between a house and an apartment: with the latter you don't own the land.

Given what I can see on my GPS, the advertised 'walking distance' to the park is overstated, as we're definitely more than a stone's throw away like it said in the marketing materials. I spot the homeless shelter, which is actually far more modern than I expected. In my research, I found out that it's a 'super centre' with short-term crisis accommodation and extended-stay housing, as well as other services and amenities like a café, business centre, and a space where professionals like doctors, counsellors, and recruiters cycle through to help the residents.

Honestly, it seems like a wonderful idea.

As I drive past, I see a cluster of people standing on the street. Some of them look bedraggled and others are well put-together, but it hardly seems worthy of the fear-mongering the development company had been spouting in the emails in my boss's files. Still, I can imagine that the clientele of a luxury residence complex probably wouldn't want a homeless super centre on their doorstep.

And it practically is.

D'Or Prime Residences looms two blocks down the street. It's a shadow of what the artistically rendered design images promised potential buyers, with the drab grey colour looking like an angular storm cloud. The grand entry features a garden that looks barely tended, with patchy brown grass and a couple of large trees shading a few concrete benches and a murky pond. It's a huge plot of land, and I can see the vision that should have come to life.

It could have been an oasis in the middle of the suburbs, but instead of feeling modern and glamorous, there's something brutal about it. Something barren.

I park my car on the side of the road and step out into the early-evening air. It's hot and my car's air-conditioning has been on the fritz, so I'm already sweating. My polyester blouse clings to my skin and the back of my neck itches from where the damp underside of my hair sticks to it. But I forge on.

Two big glass doors are protected by an electronic lock, most likely activated by a fob key. There's a small screen, however, to activate the intercom. I peer through the glass doors and see a security desk in the foyer, but it's empty. In fact, the entire space has the feeling of an abandoned building. Nobody seems to be coming or going, and since I exited my car, I haven't seen a single sign of life in the property. There's no noise, no music. Nothing.

I tap the screen and it comes to life, showing a pin pad and asking for a buzzer code for the desired apartment. There's no point randomly buzzing people to see if someone will let me in – that will only draw attention if someone happens to see me trying a bunch of numbers.

I glance up and there is definitely a security camera staring down at me. Looking back at the screen, I find an option to navigate to a directory and this brings up a list of surnames with initials next to them. The number of names in the directory seems *far* less than the number of apartments I know to be in the building, based on the blueprints I've seen. I wonder if that's indicative of the actual occupancy level or not.

One name immediately jumps out at me: Foxworth, S.

Is the apartment just listed under his name or is there someone living there who knows him? My finger hovers over the screen. What am I even going to say?

Hi, I'm inquiring about a possible dead person.

I squeeze my eyes shut and jab at the name before I can talk myself out of it. Perhaps no one will answer, anyway. There's a trilling sound coming from the speaker on the side of the screen and for a moment I'm sure it's going to ring out.

'Hello?' a voice of indeterminate gender and age crackles through the speaker.

'Uh, hello . . .' I shake my head, flustered. 'I'm looking for someone who knows Stanford Foxworth.'

The speaker crackles and pops. The equipment isn't good quality, or perhaps it's damaged. I notice a large scratch on the metal casing that holds the screen, and a dent as though someone has slammed a fist into it.

'Who are you?'

'My name is . . .' I falter, not wanting to give out my real name just in case. 'Susanna. I'm doing some research on this building and I know you've all been lied to and—'

There's a loud buzz and the lock releases on the door. *Shit. This is really happening.* I glance at the screen to get the apartment number: PH4. A penthouse.

'Thank you,' I say to the speaker, but the connection has already been cut.

I head through the front doors and toward the lift, wondering what on earth I'm walking into. This person could be furious that I'm prying into their business. They might not even be related to Stanford Foxworth III at all.

Nobody knows I'm here. Nobody is looking out for me. If I went missing, nobody would have any clue where I went after work.

Fear clutches at my heart as I step into the lift. But I'm too curious to turn back now.

The door slides shut in front of me, cutting off the view of the foyer which has an open panel in the ceiling and a bucket on the floor to catch drips of condensation from pipes above. The front desk doesn't even have a sign indicating if someone is supposed to be there. The lift, strangely, feels much closer to the vision promised in the brochure, with its gilt touches and a high-gloss finish on the wall where the buttons are. I push the one that says *PH* and glance around. My face is reflected back at me multiple times in the slim panels of glass, distorting me and making it look like a thousand eyes are watching.

It has a vaguely Art Deco look, but with clean modern touches and an air of glamour, and for a moment I see what this place could have been. The wasted potential.

When we reach the top, the door slides open and I step into a hallway. The walls are covered with wallpaper that has a slight texture to it, in a shade of light pearly grey. The carpet is lightly spongey beneath my feet and the light fixtures overhead look nice, although a bulb appears to have blown which makes a shadow right outside the door to PH4. The little patch of darkness feels like a bad omen.

Holding my breath, I raise a hand and knock.

I hear shuffling inside and the sound of a cupboard being closed aggressively or perhaps something being dropped. My heart thuds in my ears as I wait.

A few seconds later, the door swings open and a woman stands in the gap, a cigarette dangling from her thin lips. She's wrapped in a silky robe that's a rich shade of emerald green and patterned with lush tropical flowers – it's a beautiful piece. Real silk, I would bet. Fine black lace trims the sleeves and hem, and the fabric has an incredible lustre to it. The luxurious robe seems at odds with the ten centimetres of salt-and-pepper regrowth in her orange-blond hair and the smudges of black eye-makeup that have settled into the lines around her eyes, aging her. Her lips are dry and cracked, and as a shaking hand comes up to hold the cigarette, I see that her cuticles are similarly damaged. One finger has some dried blood crusted at the corner, possibly where a hangnail was torn.

'Are you a reporter, or something?' She squints at me. 'Funny how none of you lot gave a shit about us here when the building was finished. A tiny little article in the paper was all we got. Barely a mention. Why come now?'

'Do you know Stanford Foxworth the Third?' I ask, ignoring her question. I doubt any reason would satisfy her, especially if she's been fobbed off before.

'He was my little brother.' Her eyes glimmer and she puffs on the cigarette – three quick huffs – and blows the smoke out the side of her mouth.

'Can I come in?' I ask. 'It sounds like people have ignored your story before. But I want to listen. I think other people might want to listen, too. And I can help make that happen.'

On the drive over, I tried to come up with a plan. I don't think I could fake being a proper reporter, but I could certainly pretend to be a podcaster. Isn't that how old news stories gain new life these days, anyway?

'Do you know the people who built this place *told* him to off himself?' Her lip trembles and the cigarette bobs precariously, shaking ash onto the floor, narrowly missing her bare feet. She doesn't seem to notice.

For a moment it feels as though time has slowed down. Come to a standstill. He wasn't pushed off a building or had his brakes cut. It was almost worse than that. The ultimate manipulation.

I understand now, why there was no mention of Stanford's death in the papers. Suicide isn't inherently newsworthy. I think back to the email in my boss's files. Manslaughter was mentioned, although I don't actually know if that would be the correct charge for inciting someone to commit suicide.

But still, it *is* a criminal offence. One that would result in jail time if convicted.

'Stanford – he hated that name, you know – was always a sensitive one. He cared a lot. Too much. And he went off the rails when . . .' She closes her eyes a moment, the tears further smudging the black eyeliner. Her hand shakes as she pulls the cigarette out of her mouth and blows more smoke into the air. 'Those fuckers *put* that idea in his head. He would never have left us if not for being pushed to the edge like that. They told him . . . they told him to do it. Not in writing, of course. They were too smart to leave evidence.'

'Let me help get his story out,' I say. A sick feeling gathers in my stomach. *What kind of person encourages another to do something like that?*

The same person who would assault a woman in a dark alley.

Because someone who is capable of such violence has no conscience. Of that, I'm sure.

'What's the point?' the woman says, shaking her head. 'Everything's ruined now. None of it will bring my little brother back. None of it will stop us missing him.'

'Because the person who put that idea in his head deserves to pay for their actions.' I swallow, anger making my throat feel thick. 'Let me listen to your story, at least. Doesn't your brother deserve for people to know the truth?'

She looks up at me with watery eyes. A smell wafts off her – body odour and nicotine and something boozy. It's the smell of sadness. Of grief. I know it well. I smelled like that for months after my husband died and I have nothing but compassion for this poor woman.

'Fine,' she says with a resigned shrug. I get the impression she's drifting through life at the moment, without purpose. Without direction. Maybe I can help us both.

She steps back and motions for me to come inside. The apartment is a mess. Piles of books fill almost every corner, most of them in some stage of toppling over, with no thought given to size or structural integrity as they've been stacked. There's a sink full of dishes in the open-plan kitchen, and the smell of something sour, like rotting fruit, emanating from that direction. Wrappers and bottles litter the floor, and a washing basket with a pile of clothes spilling out sits on the couch – laundry duties abandoned halfway through. There's a cat huddled in the corner of the room, hunched down low and staring at me with almost glowing yellow-green eyes.

On the coffee table there's an open book of poetry and several half-drunk cups of tea, with milk curdling on top. But as I continue to let my eyes roam around the room, it's the view that captures my attention. The glorious, expansive view of Melbourne through the floor-to-ceiling windows, filled with gold-tinted light and a swath of green cutting through the urban sprawl where the park is. It's spectacular.

'Take a seat,' she says, gesturing to the couch. 'I was actually looking through this earlier today.'

I push the laundry basket to one side and she makes no apologies for the mess. On a small side table next to the couch is a pile of scrapbooks, which are the only thing in the place that look in pristine condition. They're neatly stacked, away from any of the abandoned drinks or food, with each one being covered in a different material. She picks one up and hands it to me.

'I started making these after . . .' She doesn't meet my eye as she settles into a sofa chair opposite, the hem of her robe pooling on the floor around her feet. The cat immediately comes over and seeks out her lap, eyes still lingering warily on me. 'I thought it was a nice way to remember him. I have a hard drive with all his old photos and I print them out and make these books.'

I open the first one and see a picture of three kids, each one with hair that's so blond it borders on white dressed in adorable Seventies clothing.

'That's us and our big brother, Jake.' She points. 'Jake hasn't been the same since we lost Stanny. I can only thank God that our parents were already gone before it happened. Mum wouldn't have been strong enough for that.'

I flip the page, and there are more photos lovingly labelled with a neat, swirling script and little flourishes like decorative tape, pleated paper, and beautiful pieces of watercolour art.

'Did you paint these?' I ask, pointing to an image of a peacock in shades of blue, turquoise, purple and teal.

'I used to be an artist.' Her eyes are glazed now, fixed on something I cannot see. 'Stanny loved my work. He even had one of my paintings hanging in his home office. It was of the beach we used to visit as kids.'

I flip another page and then another and another. More photos and pieces of art, more love. More memories. I reach for another book and this time I'm stopped in my tracks by more recent photos of Stanford. In one, his sister stands next to him, smiling brightly. She looks decades younger than she does now, although I can tell this photo cannot be more than five years old at most because of the bus stop in the background, which displays a movie poster for a film that came out only a few years ago.

But it's the other photo I can't take my eyes off. A woman stands next to Stanford, a happy smile on her face as she holds her hand up to the camera, a diamond glittering on her ring finger. The caption reads:

Stanny and his future-wife . . .

Oh my God. It's Adriana.

PART TWO

Chapter Thirty

Present day

Isabel

I've been waiting all day for this moment. And what a long day it has been. Adriana's wedding is everything you would expect – elegant, expensive, with a guest list populated by notable and newsworthy people. A local politician, a news presenter, someone I'm pretty sure is part of Melbourne's 'Underbelly.' Why am I not surprised there are criminal connections here?

Adriana, of course, looks exquisite. A long, silky gown, artfully applied makeup, and a bouquet of trailing white flowers. She is a vision of serenity. Of poise.

I don't know how she's done it.

I've spent the day chewing on my nails, anxious energy swirling up a storm in my stomach, anticipation burning me from the inside out. Today is the day I confront my attacker. Today is the day I let him know that I have won.

It's later in the evening, the mains have been served and the cake has been cut. Dessert is supposed to be coming out shortly. But I don't have the stomach for flame-torched French vanilla crème brulée or red-wine-poached pears with champagne-infused ice cream.

I'm hungry for something else.

'Sir?'

I catch my attacker's attention as he comes out of the men's room. We're standing in a hallway off to the side of the winery's reception area and it's just the two of us. Alone. My nerves jangle like bells and every sensor in my body is firing off warnings. Stop. Danger. Go back.

But I have to do this. It's my moment.

My time to shine.

'Yes?' he responds tersely. 'If this is a work matter—'

'It's not.'

In the office, I speak like a mouse, squeaking and chittering and scuttling out of his way when he gets near me. I've been doing my best to fly under his radar, to stay outside of his gaze. To fade into the background.

Yet in this moment, I can finally meet his eye. 'Can I have a moment, please? It's important.'

Irritation flashes across his face like lightning. 'I don't have time—'

'Yes, you do. Or at least, you should.' My voice is like flint. I tuck back the curtain of my blond hair that usually hides my shame from the world, to reveal my scars to him. He shakes his head as if trying to dislodge something from his mind. From his memory. 'Do you remember me?'

314

Unease flickers in his dark eyes. 'I'm your boss.'

'Before that.' Despite being much shorter than him, I feel tall all of a sudden, like I'm looking down my nose at him. Like I'm the one who holds the power. I *do* hold the power. 'Quite a few years before that, in fact.'

'I don't have time for these games,' he snaps. 'What's so important that you've bailed me up here?'

'I know your dirty little secrets. Every last one of them.' I am bright. I am fury. 'I *am* one of them.'

His eyes narrow. 'What are you talking about?'

I shake my head. I guess I'm going to have to hold his hand. Metaphorically speaking, of course.

'I was Susanna, back then. We met in a bar near Melbourne University and you tried to chat me up. You wanted to buy me a drink. But I had an exam the next day, so I was planning to go home early and I said no. I thought you took it well. But you didn't. You followed me out of the bar with an empty beer bottle in your jacket pocket.'

It comes back in a rush – the dampness in the air, the smell of cigarette smoke and Chinese food from the dumpling place on the corner of the street. The neon lights from the seedy bar tucked into the alley. The feeling of his strong hands as he grabbed me from behind, clamping one hand over my mouth and dragging me into the shadows. Drunk people had stumbled out of the bar, not noticing us. Further down it was darker, behind the big rubbish skips. I'd struggled against him and he smashed a bottle over the side of my head, changing everything.

'You fucking bastard.' I shove him, hard. The action seems to take him by surprise and he steps back further into the hallway. 'You ruined my life and now I'm going to ruin yours, Grant Frenchman. It's over for you.'

Watching the blood drain out of his face is priceless. I've imagined this moment for so many years – long bloody years during which I've ridden the rollercoaster of recovery. I'm a survivor, or so they say.

I'd rather be a vigilante. I'd rather be a hunter. A taker. A nightmare.

I want to savour this moment. Treasure it. Let it fill me with a sense of satisfaction and closure. Here, I know he won't risk hurting me. Not with Adriana in her wedding dress in the other room. Not with people from work who know I'm here. People who would notice if I went missing.

For the first time ever around him, I feel strong.

'What . . . ?' He shakes his head, dumbfounded.

'I know you're a rapist, a liar, and a criminal.' I count the items on my fingers. 'I know you call yourself Francis when you pick up women behind your wife's back. The name Francis actually means Frenchman, doesn't it? I bet you thought that was clever.'

His eyes grow wider with every accusation I make.

'Have you seen Kylie yet? She's here. We sat at the back of the chapel while the ceremony was taking place, because we didn't want to spoil the surprise. Couldn't risk you seeing us before it was too late.' I smile. 'She's a lot smarter than you give her credit for. That last time you were together, she recorded everything that happened. I don't know that I would *ever* be brave

316

enough to do that. Knowing you're capable of driving people to death, I would have been worried that you'd take the next step into actually murdering someone.'

His mouth opens and closes like a fish, and his usually tanned olive skin is white as a ream of paper.

'She got the one thing I never had: proof. All the times she asked you to stop and you ignored her? We've got it. All the times she said you were hurting her and you laughed? We got it. Oh, and that extra voice on the recording that identified Brunswick Logistics by name when you thought she was passed out from the drugs you forced her to take . . . we've got that, too.'

He looks like he's about to vomit.

'And we've got copies of it all over the place. In fact, there's one sitting in Adriana's inbox right now in case you think you can keep us quiet.'

'What do you want?' Grant's voice is hoarse. 'Money? I can give you money.'

Money can't fix my problems. The egotistical arsehole probably thinks the scars on my face are the thing I'm worried about fixing – that maybe if he pays for a plastic surgeon, I'll go away. Wrong. 'I don't care about money.'

'Then what? Shares? How about property? I can give you an apartment.' Panic flares across his face like a firework. 'I own a building—'

'D'Or Prime Residences? I'm familiar.' I nod. 'Actually, now that you bring it up, does Adriana know that her first husband invested heavily in your real estate project? That you screwed him over to the point that he felt the only solution was to kill himself? That you *told* him to go and kill himself.'

'You can't prove that.' His voice is barely a whisper.

'Oh, I can. You've kept a lot of "insurance" in case your old partners turned on you, huh? I guess you were too busy trying to keep your laptop out of Adriana's hands that you didn't think to worry about anyone else looking too closely.'

He's looking at me like I'm a ghost. It's a glorious mix of horror and disbelief, of wide eyes and a subtle but constant shaking of his head. *Believe me, buddy, I'm real.*

'I'm not sure if you can be charged for inciting suicide, but a recording of you arranging for your business associate to assault Kylie will certainly do the trick. The courts don't look too fondly on sex trafficking.'

He takes one step back and then another. Honestly, I expected him to put up a fight. But he's cowering. Preparing to run.

'This is the beginning of the end,' I tell him. 'You're done.'

'What do you want?' he asks again. Desperation clings to the air around him.

'I want you to disappear.'

Chapter Thirty-One

Grant

He jogs up the stairs, looking back over his shoulder every few steps to see if she's following. She isn't. He pulls his room key out of his pocket and hurries towards the door to his suite. When he taps the key against the black pad, a mechanism whirrs before making a soft *click*. Glancing behind him, the hallway remains deserted. Thank God. He pushes the door open and stalks inside, heart pounding. Sweat beads along his brow and it's starting to gather in other places too – under his arms and in the small of his back, where it slides down below the waistband of his suit pants.

He has to get out of here. Now.

Yanking his suitcase out of the wardrobe, he rolls it to the bed and hoists it up. The sound of the zipper being pulled open cuts through the quiet air and he tosses the lid open. It gapes at him like an open mouth. Or maybe it's an open eye, unblinking and judgemental.

It knows what he's done.

He grabs everything he brought with him as fast as he can, shoving his clothes and toiletries into the suitcase. He'll go straight to the airport where a private jet will be waiting – his ripcord. The plan has always been here, a backup should he need it. A Greek passport – the only good thing his mother ever gave him – and a secluded villa north of Kalabaka where he can lie low and formulate a plan.

He never thought he would need it.

He's become arrogant in his success. Overconfident. But now he's fucked up.

How did he not see what was happening? How did he find himself one step behind?

Then he hears footsteps. The click of high heels against wood is like a pickaxe in his brain. A sound which once filled his body with lust, now renders him paralyzed.

He holds his breath as the footsteps draw closer. The sound is silenced now. She must have reached the carpet runner. Closing his eyes, he prays. He hasn't prayed in a long time.

For a moment, he consoles himself that the footsteps might belong to a guest going to their room. Perhaps the wearer of the heels needs to change into some flat shoes, her ankles tired from dancing and wobbly from too much wine. Outside the window, the vineyard looks like a painting, bathed in rich golden light. The neat rows of vines are perfectly drawn lines over the cresting hills. But the clouds are gathering.

The rasp of knuckles against wood sends a shiver down his spine. It echoes off the high ceilings and wood floors. He doesn't move.

Fuck, he thinks. *This is it. I'm done.*

There's another knock. 'It's me.'

Adriana. His wife.

He pulls the door open and he's met with a concerned expression. She's so beautiful when she looks at him like that – like he's the most important man in the whole world. The *only* man in the whole world.

It makes him feel powerful. Like he might be able to get out of this mess.

Her expression grows more concerned when her gaze slips past him to the open suitcase on the bed. She walks into the room and the door closes behind her. 'Wh . . . what's going on?'

'I have to go.' He rubs his hands up and down her arms. She's cold. Goosebumps ripple across her skin, her silk dress leaving her shoulders and décolletage exposed to the elements. It's extremely elegant. It was mild earlier in the day, but as the sun goes down and the storm approaches, the air has developed a chill. 'You should put a wrap around your shoulders or something.'

'Don't change the subject.' She marches over to the bed and looks down. 'Why are you leaving? This isn't . . . What the hell is going on?'

There's a shrillness to her voice and he knows this is a make-or-break moment. He has to contain this or else it's game over.

'It's work, darling,' he says, offering her a warm, confident smile.

Darling? He never calls her that. It's a word he saves for the *other* women, the ones he needs to subdue. But not her; he never needed to do that to her. He's panicking.

321

Her eyes dart across his face, looking for the lie. The tell. He has to take control of this situation.

'I didn't want to tell you about it, because I didn't want you to worry,' he says smoothly. 'Especially not today. But I *have* to deal with this issue. There's— It's urgent.'

She shakes her head. There's a small bag slung over her shoulder and the strap is made of gold chain that glitters in the evening light. She fiddles with the clasp, also gold, snapping it open and closed. It's a nervous habit that he's only seen once or twice before – on both occasions it was because she had something to confess.

For some reason, he can't drag his eyes away from the action.

Does she know what's going on? Has his receptionist filled her head with falsehoods and poison? Has she listened to the recording in her inbox? There's so much he hasn't told her. But maybe there's a chance she'll see his side of things – that he has compulsions he can't control, but that he would *never* hurt her. Never ever.

'It can't wait until Monday?' she asks, looking up at him with her luminous brown eyes. 'Grant . . . this is our wedding day. We don't get a do-over for this kind of thing.'

'I know.' He reaches for her and she comes to him. 'But it can't wait. I need to go now.'

Then he has a thought.

'Actually, could you ask the concierge to have a car ready for me? You could come with me if you want.' There's a hopeful note in his voice, like sunshine peeking between clouds. 'I want you with me today, even if we're not here.'

322

If she asks for the car, then he can keep packing and they can be out of here soon. He just needs to get into the safe and grab his passport. Thank God they were supposed to be leaving for the airport first thing tomorrow, because driving all the way back to Melbourne to get it would have made things far riskier.

He won't tell her that they're leaving the country until they're on the road.

Surprise! I couldn't wait to get you all to myself, so I decided we should go on our honeymoon right now. There's no work problem after all.

Will she buy it? He has no idea. She's started to ask a lot of questions lately and he's had a harder time convincing her.

'If that's what you want . . .' There's an uncertainty to her voice. He's going to have to play his cards carefully – really act the part.

'It is.'

She walks over to a phone – fashioned to look like one of those black and gold vintage corded types, but it's a replica with modern functions – and lifts the receiver. With one dainty finger she reaches for the speed-dial number for the concierge desk. Grant turns back to the room and heads for the safe, dropping to his knees to punch in the combination he set only the afternoon before.

'Hello? Yes, thank you. Is it possible to have a car ready downstairs? We, uh . . .' There's a break and he looks over his shoulder. She's glancing back at him, brow furrowed and lips pinched as she cradles the phone by her face. 'There's been an emergency back in Melbourne. Grant and I need to leave shortly.'

The breath whooshes out of him as the safe lock whirrs and the door pops open. She's going to come with him. She hasn't been tainted yet. If he can get her out and make sure she hears his side of the story first, then maybe everything can be saved. He can turn her against them, rather than the other way around.

'Twenty minutes?'

He snaps his head around, about to ask if they can get a car ready any quicker, but she's nodding. 'Okay, I understand. No problem. We'll wait up here. Can you call us when it's ready? Thank you so much.'

The receiver is returned to the cradle.

'Twenty minutes?' he asks, pulling his documents out of the safe. 'Why so long?'

'The driver isn't on site since they weren't expecting us to leave until tomorrow morning.' Adriana glances toward the large window that frames the view.

Outside, the weather has turned. What was previously a day bathed in crisp sunlight is now festering with blackened clouds. Rain spots the glass, softly at first, then harder in bursts. It's like an angry child, beating its fists against the window. The wind picks up, howling, crying.

It feels like an omen. Like a visual representation of how the tides have turned against him.

'You should pack,' he says.

'You seem more anxious than if this was simply a work issue.' She comes over to him, brows creased. He's got to be careful with her – she's a woman who sees too much, who notices things. The hoops he had to jump through to keep her out of his entanglements . . .

Separate codes to the house so he could track her movements. A private phone. Keeping his devices locked and near him at all times. Never inviting her to his work or introducing her to his industry associates. Never telling her about his daughter.

The daughter who was never actually aborted and who is very much still alive.

It was necessary.

But as he looks into her beautiful face, her full lips parted in worry, he knows it's all been worth it. She was supposed to be a trophy. A collectable. Instead, she has become so much more. He cares for her – more than he's been able to care for anyone in a long time.

He loves her.

'It's a serious work issue,' he replies. 'I'm so sorry. I tried everything to stop it interfering with today.'

She nods. 'Well, we're not going anywhere in a hurry. The driver won't be speeding over in weather like this, especially not on these muddy country roads so there's no point scrambling. I'll fix us a drink.'

There's a bar set up on the other side of the room, one of those fancy touches that was the reason he wanted this venue for such an important occasion. She grabs two glasses and reaches for the decanter of smoky whisky sitting on a vintage silver tray along with its companions – XO cognac and a single-barrel bourbon. There was a handwritten note sitting there when they arrived yesterday.

Enjoy. Marriage deserves the finer things in life.

He grabs the passport and his other personal effects and takes them to the bed, where his suitcase is half-packed. He hears the clink of a single oversized ice cube in each glass, sourced from the mini fridge and freezer, then the gentle *thunk* of the decanter's stopper being placed down followed by a glug of liquid. Waiting up here with her is better. At least here he can keep her away from those women. But he knows it's better to be cautious. To protect her from them.

He goes to the door and reaches for the pin dangling from a chain, sliding the lock into place. If she notices, she doesn't say anything, and when he turns she is holding two glasses.

'Sit,' she says. 'Have a drink and relax. Everything will be okay.'

He isn't one for taking orders – he's the boss, the head of the house, the father, the husband, the string-puller – but in this moment he finds her quiet authority soothing. She has the qualities of a good wife. She's able to anticipate his needs, be quietly reassuring, put him first. So he does what she says, dropping down into a velvet chair by the window. There's a door that leads out to the balcony and it rattles in its hinges, shuddering in the wind. She presses a glass into his hand.

'I'm glad we got all the important bits out of the way before the weather turned nasty.' She brings her own glass up to her lips, the amber liquid catching the lamp light. It reflects on her fair skin, casting her in a warm glow. 'It's awful out there now.'

No kidding, Grant thinks to himself, although he isn't thinking about the weather.

He takes a sip of his drink and the liquid slides down the back of his throat, warm and familiar.

'Lucky I have you to be the sunshine,' he says. 'You light up the room in that dress.'

His gaze glances over her tight, wiry frame. The liquid silk skims her body, the barest shadow of her nipples showing through the fabric, breasts braless and her body firm. Her blond hair brushes her shoulders, heavy pearl earrings dangling from her ears.

Seeing her walk down the aisle took his breath away.

He never meant to fall in love with her. The only reason he was at her first husband's funeral was to see if people were talking. You might not think people gossip at funerals, but they do. They gossip everywhere. He and his business partners all attended. It was a risk, sure. Someone might have known they were the building developers of that failed luxury apartment complex, but Grant was the kind of man who would rather know what he was up against. If there was speculation about his involvement in Stanford's – or Toby, as he preferred to be called – death, he wanted to know.

That's when he saw her, the young widow. She was beautiful beyond comprehension, her sadness muted like a watercolour painting. Did she know what her husband was involved in? A few days after the funeral, Grant reached out to her to offer his condolences again. Then he made sure to bump into her at the café she frequented, striking up conversation to see how she reacted. She didn't seem to hate him. Even better, she didn't seem to have any idea who he was at all.

He pursued her at first for information, but it became clear she knew nothing and wasn't involved in her husband's finances. She didn't even know about the building. The initial plan was to assess whether she had connected her husband's death to his building and then ghost her.

But he couldn't.

She was captivating, totally lacking in vulnerability like one might expect from a young widow. There was a glass-like strength to her – not the kind of glass that shatters on impact, but the kind they use in high-rise buildings, which appears transparent but is actually shiny and impenetrable. He liked the challenge of her. The unexpected nature of her.

He became obsessed with having her. She was a rare treasure, a priceless painting, an objective. The kind of woman who would complete his life picture, a stunning figure on his arm and a warm embrace waiting for him at home.

'What are you thinking?' she asks.

She sips her drink and he follows suit, taking a long gulp of the whisky in the hopes it might ease the panic fluttering behind his sternum. They stay there, quietly drinking, and when she offers to top up his glass, he refuses. A little will take the edge off, but he needs to keep his wits about him.

'Just how happy I am that I married you,' he replies. 'How beautiful you look today and every day.'

'Is it everything you hoped for?'

'Marriage?' He nods. 'This is only the beginning.'

Time slows to a snail's pace as they wait for the call

328

from downstairs. Grant finds himself blinking more sluggishly than normal, his head suddenly stuffed with cotton balls. Is it the stress? Maybe he's coming down with something? There is a bit of a draught in this old building.

He tries to push up from his chair and the world tilts suddenly, the ground turning to liquid beneath his feet and the walls becoming crashing waves. The crystal tumbler slips from his hand and clatters to the floor, tipping over and letting the last few sips of his drink slide out and pool on the floorboards.

'Adriana? Something's . . .'

She blurs for a second, her figure wavering in front of him. Something is wrong. He's ill. He needs help. Now.

His wife's eyes narrow and at first he thinks that it's concern. But then he sees the corner of her mouth tilt up in satisfaction.

Chapter Thirty-Two

Adriana

I walk over to the phone, my plan firmly in place. I wasn't sure how Grant would act when this all came to a head. Would he lash out or flee? Personally, I thought the former, but once again he has proved to be a self-serving coward, all bravado on the outside and totally lacking a spine on the inside.

It's difficult to hold my disgust in. Difficult not to let it show on my face like I want it to.

This is not the time for instant gratification.

But make no mistake, gratification is coming.

I might have been too naïve to predict any of this, but that's no excuse not to do something now. For Toby. For Kylie. For Isabel. For the life growing in my belly. For the other women he likely hurt, because a man like that doesn't stop until he's forced to stop.

And I *will* force him to stop.

I reach for the phone's receiver and press my finger to the speed-dial button, but I don't push down. My heart thunders like galloping horses in my chest.

330

Can he see what I'm doing? What if he catches me?

He'll overpower me like he overpowered Kylie and Isabel.

But then I hear the *whoosh* of the sliding mirrored door opening behind me. He's gone to open the safe.

'Hello?' I pause to make it seem like there's someone else on the line. 'Yes, thank you. Is it possible to have a car ready downstairs? We, uh . . .' My voice is wobbling, so I take a breath to centre myself. 'There's been an emergency back in Melbourne. Grant and I need to leave shortly.'

There's a *beep-beep-beep-beep* as Grant punches in the code to the safe and then a whirr of the locking mechanism opening. How long should I make him sweat? Too short and he might be eager to leave the room before we get through what I have planned. Too long and he'll be likely to snatch the phone out of my hand to complain.

I can't have that.

'Twenty minutes?' I say, nodding my head in case he's watching me in the mirror. 'Okay, I understand. No problem. We'll wait up here. Can you call us when it's ready? Thank you so much.'

The receiver is returned to the cradle. I've bought myself some time. No one is coming for him.

Over the next few minutes I play my role well – doting wife concerned about her new husband's workaholic ways, while also being resentful that her big day is being mucked up. If I don't protest at all, it will raise red flags but I don't want to push too hard in case it causes an argument. I need him to be calm around me.

Now comes the important part: making drinks.

My hand trembles as I grab two crystal tumblers from the bar cart and reach for a decanter of whisky. I move slowly, so as not to encourage his eyes to linger, and I hear the rustle of him packing behind me. As I bend down to open the small refrigerator, I draw my evening bag between me and the bar cart, shielding it from view. I've opened and closed the clasp so many times that it has loosened on its hinges and now it opens easily and silently. While I'm pouring the Scotch with one hand, I slip the other into my bag and feel for the little plastic fish.

Gamma hydroxybutyric acid. GHB. Liquid X. Fantasy.

When I was in university, my friends and I used to carry drink-spiking test kits around, because we knew a girl from the year above us who'd been slipped something at a party. We were fastidious about testing our drinks after that, and I still had a couple of the kits in the back of my wardrobe. I wasn't even sure if they would still work.

But they did.

A quick test told me that the substance in my husband's pocket was a popular date-rape and party drug. Combined with the business card that slipped out of Grant's notebook for the hotel where Kylie thought she'd been assaulted was too much of a coincidence to ignore. Luckily – or unluckily, depending on how you look at it – more proof came rolling in . . . like a firehose to the face.

I unscrew the cap and drop the clear liquid into his drink, and then slip the now empty fish container back into my bag for later disposal. I'll wipe it off and flush it down the toilet when I'm done. Out of the corner of my eye, I catch movement near the door and hear the gentle clink of the security chain being slid into place.

He's locking me in.

My heart feels like it's going to explode. I'm holding my breath. *Does he know? Did he see? Is he going to catch me in the act?* I try not to retch. Instead, I reach for the glasses and make sure I keep track of them so I don't accidentally serve him the wrong one.

'Sit,' I say. 'Have a drink and relax. Everything will be okay.'

I barely hear him as he tries to make conversation and it takes everything in my power not to stare him down as he sips his drink. Normally, Grant likes to savour his alcohol, so I expect this to be slow. But he's clearly more rattled than he wants to let on, because he downs it quickly in big glugs. I can relax a little. He has no idea.

I pretend to sip my own drink, only letting the alcohol dance across my lips, but not pass between them. I don't think he's noticed. I'm not a big drinker anyway, so my slow progress won't seem suspicious.

Outside, the weather continues to blacken and my joints ache from being bunched against the chill. Or maybe that's simply my stress about what I'm planning to do. But then I think of all the people Grant has hurt. My gut tells me there are others I don't know about. Other women like Kylie who didn't see his evil coming. Other women like Isabel who sadly did.

Other people like my husband, who were robbed of everything.

I've never thought of myself as a violent woman. I've certainly never thought about murdering someone. But as we sit here making small talk and I feel his eyes on me – on my body – it makes my skin crawl. This man is a stranger to me now.

In reality, he's always been a stranger.

For a second, I swear his face shifts and becomes that of my father. But when I blink, he's Grant again. Rage burns quietly in my stomach, a fire not yet allowed to grow out of control.

It's going to happen soon. Just wait.

He tries to stand and sways, his eyes widening as his near-empty crystal tumbler slips from his hand and clatters to the wood floor. I draw in a sharp breath. *Can anyone hear us downstairs?* But there's still a faint pulse of music coming through the floorboards at my feet. Everyone down there is getting drunk on the open bar stocked with top-shelf booze. They're not worried about what we're doing up here.

'Adriana? Something's . . .'

He's starting to figure it out now. *Good.* I watch the drugs take hold of him, slowing him down. He steadies himself with one hand on the chair, but his large body moves back and forth like he can't find his centre of gravity. I stand and place my own glass down on the table.

'Something isn't right.' His words are beginning to slur. 'I don't feel good.'

'Let's get you some fresh air, shall we.' I walk over to the balcony, where rain beats against the window like a thousand angry fists. 'Fresh air always makes you feel better.'

When I flick the latch on the gold-rimmed glass doors, the wind pushes them open so furiously that I take a step back. What started as a beautiful day is ending with Mother Nature's wrath. Grant grips the edge of the chair, his eyelids drooping. He looks pathetic.

I think about Kylie being dragged down the hotel hallway by my husband and another man – a man whose name I undoubtedly will find in the second phone tucked away in Grant's luggage – and I want to scream. I think of her blaming herself for a drinking problem getting out of control and I wonder if that's why he chose her. If he saw that flaw and exploited it for his own gain.

Maybe that was exactly what he was looking for.

'Come on.' I walk over to him and drag his arm over my shoulder. He's heavy, but thankfully I don't have to carry him. He can still shuffle and he comes with me, compliant and confused.

'It's rainy,' he says dumbly as we step outside.

'Yes, it is.'

Below us, the pool ripples in the wind, a miniature ocean storm. The loose strands of my hair whip around my face as water soaks me through. I release Grant in front of me so he's standing with his back to the balcony railing. The lush accommodation grounds – with neat rows of grapevines and rolling hills in the background – have turned to mud. The weather has driven everyone inside and our balcony is private, closed in by frosted glass walls and tall plants on either side. A true romantic retreat for the happy couple.

335

We are alone.

'I'm cold.' He's like a little boy now, reduced to shivering and snivelling.

'It will all be over soon and you'll feel much, much better,' I say. He sways again, taking a step back and bumping against the railing. His hands press back, but the stonework is slick and I watch as his palms slide, fingers catching on nothing. 'But before we get to that, I think you owe me an explanation.'

His gaze is fixed on mine but I can see he's struggling to maintain concentration.

Some people take GHB for pleasure. I never knew that. Apparently it's popular in the nightclub scene. Even more popular, I suspect, with swingers' parties and other types of group sex activities. In smaller doses, it lowers inhibitions, boosts sex drive, and incites feelings of euphoria. Sounds good, right? Some people even mix it with other drugs, like ketamine or MDMA.

At least, this is what I found out while researching it on Google with specific search phrases like:

Why would someone take GHB?

Is GHB addictive?

How do you help someone with drug addiction?

Drug treatment centres Melbourne, Australia.

I spent several hours last week doing these searches and laying the foundations with my internet history in case anyone comes looking. But I know, deep down, that Grant never took the GHB himself.

He uses it on other people. People like Kylie.

You see, when taken in larger doses, GHB makes people ultra relaxed, drowsy, and eventually knocks them out. It also causes loss of short-term memory. Convenient, if you want to assault someone. It's also known for making people vomit and sweat, and elicits feelings of dizziness and nausea, which to someone with a drinking problem might not seem so out of the ordinary.

After all, how would they know the next morning that their drink was spiked when they're used to being blackout drunk?

'How do you know Kylie?' I ask him and his eyes widen, head shaking back and forth. There's a slackness to his mouth now. 'You know her. Red hair, beautiful figure, likes a drink. She's a party girl. Not your type, you led me to believe when we first started dating. You liked that I was quiet and well-behaved.'

'Adriana, I . . .' His head hangs forward, like he doesn't have the energy to lift it up.

'And what about Isabel, huh? Did you even know who she was when you raped her?' My lips pull back and the facade of the loving wife is shattered like a champagne flute being hurled against concrete. 'When you disfigured her? She was working for you this whole fucking time and you had no idea.'

The worry in his eyes hardens into pure panic.

'And what about my husband?' The word catches in the back of my throat and tears fill my eyes. 'My poor, sweet Toby. He might not have been the smartest man alive but he was kind and generous and sensitive. You reeled him in like a fish and then left him high and dry. How could you ever tell someone to kill themselves? It's abhorrent.'

Grant shakes his head but it seems like a response to everything that's happening rather than to the question itself.

'And your daughter?' A tear slips out of my eye. 'The one you told me your girlfriend miscarried?'

Oh yes, I know about that, too. I know everything.

'What about her and her mother?' I ask. 'Did you kill her, Grant? Are you a murderer as well?'

The last week has been one blow after another. The anonymous email turned up with information about Grant's involvement in my first husband's death, and it wasn't long before Isabel cracked and told me she'd sent it. Then Kylie turned up on my doorstep with a recording. I couldn't listen to it all the way through, but I would know his voice anywhere.

Then maybe the biggest shock of all . . . Someone had been following me. Trying to warn me. Grant's own flesh and blood.

His daughter.

She broke into our house and left her own baby shoe. A gift from the mother who died while she was still young enough to be taking the bottle. A drowning, made to look accidental. But her family have always been convinced he was behind it. That he lied to the police. He'd killed one woman over a baby and she feared it would happen again if he knew about my pregnancy.

'You . . . you drugged me,' he slurs.

Intense disappointment washes through me. Even when faced with a litany of heinous acts, he's only focused on himself. Whatever man I once thought he was, it's clear there's no shred of that person inside him.

That man is a fantasy. In reality, Grant is everything I've discovered him to be.

An abuser. A liar. A criminal.

'Yes,' I say, knowing now that I'm not going to get the apology I want. Monsters are always the hero of their own stories. 'I drugged you.'

'Why?'

'Because you deserve it.'

I take a step forward, tears filling my eyes and mixing with the rain pelting my skin. I can barely see. Barely breathe. I'm soaked through and trembling in the cold, but inside I am black smoke and red flame and so filled with hatred that I want to scream. There's no saving this man.

'This is for everyone you've hurt,' I say. 'For all of us.'

And with that, I thrust both hands into his chest with all my might and watch him tumble over the edge.

Chapter Thirty-Three

Isabel

I want to see it happen. I want to make sure he dies.

Kylie and I exit the main room, giggling and making a show of ourselves so everyone notices us together. Ahead, Adriana is walking up the grand sweeping staircase to the floor where all the accommodation is situated. She's going after Grant. Kylie and I stand guard. Nobody comes into the hallway from the main room. Around the corner, I hear two of the venue staff talking and laughing, not really paying attention to the wedding.

Dessert is currently being served and most people are returning to their seats for something sweet to soak up the alcohol.

'Are you coming?' Kylie asks, keeping her voice low. We're supposed to wait upstairs in our room, providing Adriana with an alibi where we'll claim to have been fixing her makeup and hair before she finishes the night off with a bouquet toss.

At least, that's what we'll say if the police question us.

But I need to make sure for myself that Grant Frenchman takes his last breath.

'You go ahead,' I say. 'I'll wait by the pool.'

Kylie's eyes go wide and her cherry-tinted lips part in surprise. 'But that's not part of the plan.'

Adriana's plan is to let Grant fall over the edge of the balcony and into the pool, leaving him to drown. She underestimates the resilience of the human body, however. Even when drugged, if he manages to make his way out . . .

It's a risk I cannot take.

'I'm going to make sure he never hurts anyone again,' I say, gripping her shoulders. 'We can't leave anything to chance.'

'But if you're the one to find the body and people make the connection . . .' She shakes her head. 'Don't they always suspect the person who finds the body?'

Maybe they do. Frankly, I'm not sure I even care anymore. If someone has to take the fall for this – no pun intended – then I'd rather it be me. I have nothing else going for me. The baby I birthed belongs to another family, the career I wanted was abandoned years ago, and I'll be resigning from my dead-end job in a few months once all this has blown over. Unless the company is shut down before that. I hope it will be.

Even the Young Widows Club won't have meaning for me anymore.

Guilt is bitter on the back of my tongue. These women think of me as a friend, a sister. But in some ways I'm no better than Grant – I'm a liar, a cheat, a manipulator.

'I started this group on purpose,' I confess. Whatever happens next, I have to unburden myself.

'What do you mean?' Kylie asks, her brows knitting together. She's beautifully naïve. It's her best quality, though I know she will disagree.

'The Young Widows Club.' There's a lump in the back of my throat and my eyes dart to the clock on the hallway wall. 'Our group. I started it.'

'I know you started it,' she says, shifting her weight from one foot to another, her hand smoothing nervously over the front of her pretty floral dress. 'You were the one to suggest we meet up.'

'I mean . . .' I hang my head, shame filtering up into my cheeks. The repercussions of my actions have snowballed and in my need for revenge, I've hurt people. I've betrayed people. I've betrayed Kylie and Adriana. 'I found Adriana on purpose and started the group to get close to her.'

Kylie blinks. Her innocent mind can't comprehend how low others might stoop.

'I was stalking Grant while I figured out how I was going to get back at him after my husband died,' I say. 'I followed him everywhere – from his home to his work to his gym . . . to anywhere he met up with people. I followed him while he went on dates with Adriana. And so I started following her, too.'

Kylie's mouth pops open and she covers it with a shaking hand.

'I found out everything I could about Adriana because I figured getting close to her was my best bet in fucking up Grant's life. I wasn't content with simply getting a job at his company and digging up dirt there. I wanted to ruin *everything* in his life, including his relationships.' I feel sick even saying the words out loud. 'I found out that Adriana was a widow when I followed her to the cemetery one day. Then I sat in a café where she was using their unsecured Wi-Fi and I accessed her internet session. I saw that she was browsing a support forum.'

It's a little technique called sidejacking. Most people think hackers are weedy, pimple-faced incels living in darkened rooms and, to be fair, some of them are. But others are people who've developed those skills with a mission, people who blend in at the local café and at whom you wouldn't look twice.

It's amazing what you can learn online.

'I got her username and password, and I read through everything she posted there. Then I made an account and befriended her. I wanted to infiltrate every aspect of his life,' I say. 'And I invited you because you were a random person whose account I happened to find when looking for people in Melbourne. I felt it would be less suspicious if it wasn't only me and her. If anything came out, I could claim it was a weird coincidence. But I unintentionally put you in his path . . .'

A tear slips out of my eye and rolls down my cheek.

Kylie looks on in horror, like I'm no longer a person standing in front of her but a monster myself. And she's right. *I'm* the reason she met Grant. It was me who pulled her into my plans by inviting her to join our group. It was *me* she saw at the bar that night when she decided to stay for a drink. It was me who knew what he was capable of and yet I didn't warn either one of them.

Well, I tried to warn Adriana. The anonymous email . . . not my finest moment. The closer I got to her, the guiltier I felt about her being collateral damage. But with Kylie, I didn't know she'd been lured in by him. The night we met at the bar, I had been watching him from afar and she happened to see me follow him inside. So she came in after me and we had a drink. I didn't tell her why I was there and after I left, he must have come onto her. The next day she was late for our meeting and turned up in those expensive heels . . . I should have known it was him. But I was so focused on my revenge plan that I didn't see what was going on.

If I had stayed with her that night, then maybe . . .

'I never intended to become friends with either of you,' I admit. 'That wasn't part of my plan.'

'And Hannah?'

By the time I met Hannah, part of me had started to think my life could be different. That I *could* have friends, sisters-in-arms. That maybe I wasn't alone in the world. Maybe I could rebuild some semblance of a life. But what kind of life would it be if I kept this secret? I'd live in fear of it coming out; of slipping up.

'I thought we could help her,' I say. 'She wanted to be my friend.'

Kylie's hand falls away and I see her lip trembling. 'So Adriana and I, we were your pawns.'

'Yes.' I don't shrink away from her accusation.

'You knew all along that he hurt people.' She takes a step back. 'And you didn't say anything.'

I deserve her disgust. I deserve her hate, although I'm not sure Kylie is capable of feeling that emotion the way Adriana and I are. She's the softest of the group, the most vulnerable. The look of utter betrayal on her face almost paralyzes me.

'That's why I have to make sure he doesn't hurt anyone else *now*.' I implore her to believe in me one last time. 'I have to make sure this works. If I end up going to jail . . . so what? So long as he's dead, that's all that matters.'

We're speaking low, keeping our voices down, our eyes roaming the hallway for anyone coming or going.

'I'm going up to Adriana,' she says, taking another step away from me. 'I'm going to follow the plan. You . . . I don't care what you do.'

She turns and hurries upstairs. For a moment, I'm stuck there, wondering if the expensive champagne I've been drinking will come rushing back up. But I manage to hold it down. I can't let all this pain go to waste.

At the sound of tipsy giggling coming from near the entrance to the ballroom, I press my back against the wall, hiding myself behind a large potted plant. But the woman and man who stumble out of the room, faces flushed and eyes glazed, head towards the bathrooms on the other side of the foyer. Probably running off to have a quickie. Shaking my head, I slip further into the hallway and, when I'm sure no one is watching, I open the side door that leads out to the accommodation grounds and slip outside, confident I haven't been noticed.

The rain beats down, lashing at my skin and the screaming wind claws at my hair, which – for the first time in a long time – is pulled away from my face, leaving my scars on show. My dress flaps round my legs and I walk with a hand pressed to the side of the building. The pool is around the corner, surrounded by a fence which also encloses some banana lounges and chairs, the cushions of which shudder in the wind, testing the strength of the ties that keep them attached.

If anyone finds me out here . . .

It will look suspicious as hell. I know that and yet it's a risk I'm willing to take. Because everyone knows the final boss in a video game gets up when you think they've gone down for good. The monsters in horror movies always have a final surprise attack. I won't make that mistake.

I press on, my heels slipping on the sleek tiles underfoot and the rain stinging my skin like a thrown handful of sewing pins. I inch my way forwards, head bowed, determination fuelling every step. When I reach the pool area, I look up, using the back of my hand to swipe the loosened strands of hair from my face. It's hard to see. I focus on the balcony I'm sure is Adriana's and see nothing. No movement. No life.

What if she chickens out? What if something goes wrong and the drugs don't work? What if he manages to overpower her?

My heart thuds like a bass drum and I shiver as the rain runs in rivulets down my face and neck and arms and back. I look around. The umbrellas have been wrapped up but the ends of them fight against their restraints, the wind trying to force the fabric free. The pool is overflowing and the water ripples violently, sending it gushing over the edge. Above, thunder echoes like a whip cracking.

Come on. Please.

I stare and stare and stare. Nothing.

But then a shadow flickers behind the glass and the doors burst open. I see Adriana standing there, her wedding dress gleaming in the light that pours out of her room. She hauls Grant outside. *Yes!* What happens next occurs in slow motion. They're still for a moment, frozen and suspended in time, and then she pushes him, the shove so forceful she almost topples after him. But she catches herself on the railing.

Grant goes over.

He twists as he falls, arms outstretched and suit pants flapping. I expect him to scream or cry out, but it's soundless until he hits the edge of the pool. The crack sends a jolt through me. It's an awful, ungodly sound and my stomach heaves in response, but to anyone inside, it might have sounded like the storm.

He rolls into the pool, the splash displacing even more water and it rushes over the edge like a mini tidal wave, lapping at my feet. His dark form drifts down into the blue-tinted depths. There are lights on underwater and it makes murky shadows, but I see him moving. I rush over to the edge, dropping down onto my knees and feeling the sharp edge of a tile scrape against my skin. There's blood on the side of the pool, but it washes away as the water laps over the edge again and the rain dilutes it further, turning it pink and then clear.

Grant is a shapeless blob in the water, but he's getting closer to the surface. I almost shriek when his hand breaks free, grasping for the edge of the pool. He's alive.

'No.' I shove my hand into the water and feel for his head. My fingertips wade through nothing,

347

nothing, nothing and then I feel something hard. 'Stay down.'

I shove my other hand under the water and press with all my strength. His head pushes against me and I struggle to keep him in place, the water lapping at my knees. Tears roll down my cheeks and I heave deep, painful breaths. This is it. The moment I wanted.

Payback. Restitution. Justice.

'You've done enough,' I cry into the wind.

I don't know how long I kneel there – maybe seconds, maybe minutes. Longer? Eventually he stops pressing upwards, and his hand stops thrashing. He slides back into the water as the weather howls all around me. I'm sobbing at the edge of the pool, bent over on all fours and heaving like I'm about to throw up. Each one wracks my body as I let it out. Years of nightmares and despair and looking over my shoulder. Years of jumping whenever I'm alone and I hear an unexpected sound. Years of looking at myself in the mirror and wondering when I won't see his face staring back at me.

I wait for his hand to burst through the surface of the water again, one final swipe to prove what a strong villain he is. But nothing comes. He's gone. For good.

'Daddy!' The shriek that cuts through the air makes me whip my head to the side where I see a woman in red running barefoot towards the pool, her hair fluttering in wet ribbons around her face.

Oh my God.

It's Hannah.

Chapter Thirty-Four

Hannah

Isabel looks like she's about to faint.

She had no idea, all this time, that I wasn't simply some random chick she bumped into at yoga class. I don't actually have a dead husband. Dale is dead, yes, but he was my half-brother and Grant Frenchman is my father.

'People have already noticed he's gone,' I say as I rush over, dropping to my knees. 'Come on! Help me pull him out.'

Her brows slam together and she opens her mouth, but no words come out. Her skin is pale and slick from the rain. She's trembling and probably on her way to hypothermia.

'We have to act like we're trying to save him,' I hiss. 'Why else would you be out here, huh? Unless you want people to know you were holding his head under the water or something?'

The sharp intake of breath makes her cough, and her slender shoulders wrack so hard I'm worried she's going to dislocate something. 'Wha—?'

'I know what you did and I'm happy for it.' I shake her, trying to bring her out of the daze. 'But if we're going to get you out of this, then we need to work together.'

Not far away, I hear voices. The slam of a door. Shouting.

'Help us!' I bellow at the top of my lungs. 'My dad! He's fallen in!'

I plunge my arms into the water and feel for him, but he's already started to sink and my hands have nothing to grab. The guests that have tumbled outside seem reluctant to come forward. They're drunk . . . or high. They stumble on the wet tiles and won't be of any use to my father.

Good.

Isabel is next to me, also reaching in but she comes up empty. Her eyes dart to mine, wide and wild. Black mascara is smeared all around her eyes and it trails down her cheeks like devil's tears, the colour settling in the indentations of her scars, highlighting them to gruesome effect.

'Someone call triple 0, please!' I shout, knowing from my experience living in the countryside that an ambulance out here could be a good fifteen to twenty minutes away in regular conditions. In a storm like this, who knows how long it could take.

There will be car accidents on the highway, downed powerlines, and trees . . .

Staff members pile out of the building, one of them a young man with broad shoulders and dark hair who dashes towards the pool and jumps in, fully clothed. He locates my father and drags him back up to the surface. Two further staff members surround Isabel and me with towels, wrapping them around our shoulders and begging us to come back inside.

My father has been underwater for probably close to three or four minutes. Maybe five.

More staff members herd the crowd back into the building and we stand around, waiting as the young pseudo-lifeguard brings my father's limp body into the building, dripping water everywhere. It soaks into the carpet in dark patches and the young man attempts CPR, but he's shuddering from the cold. Nobody else steps in.

He must be the resident first aid guy.

'The ambulance is on its way.' A woman dressed in a black suit with a white shirt looks on, her skin pale and clammy. A fine gold pin at her breast tells me she's the manager on duty. 'I don't know how long . . .'

I can't take my eyes off my father. His skin is an ashen white, his lips tinged with blue, and there's a deep gash above his brow. The water seems to have washed the blood away and the cold is keeping it from gushing back out, but the cut looks deep and there's a lump beginning to form on his forehead. He doesn't move.

'Everyone, please stand back and give us space.' The manager and her staff begin herding people towards the ballroom, where the music has stopped playing. More people are looking on, trying to figure out what's happening.

Then a terrible crack of thunder rips through the sky and lightning flashes before we're all plunged into

351

darkness. I freeze. An alarmed shriek pierces the air and a worried murmur rises from the crowd. I hear the manager swear under her breath. She's standing only a few feet away from me.

'Please remain calm everyone,' she calls out. 'Try not to move. Storms here sometimes knock the electricity out but we have a backup generator that should kick in momentarily.'

'What's going on?' someone calls from further away.

'Someone fell in the pool.'

'Where's Grant?'

'Where's Adriana?'

'It was Grant!'

The room erupts as voices rise. There's a loud *thunk* as someone knocks into a piece of furniture and yelps, then there's the sound of smashing glass and another shriek. The event manager tries to calm the crowd but it's chaos and I'm jostled hard to the side as someone pushes past me. I blink, trying to get my eyes to adjust. A crack of lightning makes light flare for a moment and I see a crowd of scared faces before we're plunged back into darkness. Then I feel someone beside me and a hand slips into mine.

Isabel.

'Are you okay?' I ask, leaning in. I can smell her perfume – the same one she always wears, which smells like freshly cut grass and sunshine and water-drenched lilacs. We huddle together and move back until we feel solid wall behind us.

Both of us are shaking from the cold and we cling together, trying to generate some warmth.

'No,' she says. 'I'm not sure I'll ever be okay.'

'You will.' I squeeze her hand. 'I promise you will.'

'What if someone figures out . . .' She lets out a breath.

'They won't,' I reassure her.

Because I know, more than anyone, how easily a drowning death can be ruled an accident.

After all, that's what happened to my mother.

Chapter Thirty-Five

Three months later . . .

Adriana

I know who's knocking at the door before I even get a peek out the front window. I can picture him – starched shirt, shiny black shoes, buzz cut, an attempt at an intimidating stare. He doesn't look like the detectives you see on television, who always have a diamond-in-the-rough look about them – shirt not quite tucked in, dishevelled, bags under their eyes, but with some redeeming feature like a twinkle in their eye or really nice teeth.

Detective Sergeant Kirk Perry is neither the affable, underestimated expert nor the tortured-genius archetype. He's cold and hard and driven, much like my late husband was. My *second* late husband. And he's been sniffing around for the past few months, certain that I am a murderer.

I arrive at the door and pull it open, offering a warm smile I'm confident will grate on him. 'What a surprise,'

I say with a hint of irony. It's never a surprise when he turns up on my doorstep. 'What can I do for you today, Officer?'

His eye twitches. Another thing that grates on him is how I call him *Officer* instead of *Detective* because he sees it as me not respecting his rank. Luckily for me, one can't get arrested for minor needling of an officer of the law and, technically, he *is* an officer.

'I wanted to ask you a few more questions,' he says stiffly, his blue eyes piercing in the late-afternoon light. The sun beats down and I catch a hint of pink across his nose and cheeks. Has he been outside for a while? Watching the house? Watching me?

'Of course.' I step back and welcome him into my home.

Yes, it's my home now. It's *all* mine. At least it will be once probate is officially cleared.

Grant's properties – *plural* – his cars, the 50 per cent share of his business, the money in his bank accounts – again, *plural* – money I didn't even know was there, money he'd clearly been hiding from me, it's all mine. But of course, we were married when he died, even if the ring had been slipped onto my finger only a few hours before.

Not that it matters *too* much, since I'd been living here long enough to be classified as a de facto spouse anyway, and his will named me as his sole beneficiary.

'Have a seat, Officer.' I gesture to the couch.

He doesn't stop to remove his shoes before stepping onto the white carpet. No doubt it's a way to get back at me for the perceived slight about his title. I watch little bits of dirt and natural debris track across the plush white pile, marking the path he has taken. But I don't let it bother me. I could have this place deep cleaned several thousand times over and not even make a dent in what I have in the bank now.

Kirk lowers himself across from me and spreads his legs wide in a show of power. At least, his thinks it is. I suspect whatever he's hiding underneath his neatly pressed slacks isn't worthy of quite that much breathing room. Then he leans forward and braces himself against his thighs, his eyes locked onto me like lasers.

'What questions do you have for me today?' I ask, lowering myself into a chair across from him, taking my time, slipping one leg over the top of the other and making myself comfortable.

Inside there's a hard knot developing in my stomach, because this man is like a dog with a bone. *What if he's found something that he can use to pin Grant's murder on me? Or worse, what if he tries to pin it on Isabel or Kylie or Hannah?*

Turns out *she* was the little girl in the photo I found, the baby that was never aborted. Oh, and her name is actually Camille. Not Hannah. Hannah was her mother's name.

Over the last three months, we've grown close and she's told me everything. About how her mother randomly drowned in the bathtub in their home without any explanation for how it happened. About how Grant was questioned a few times and the detective was sure he did it – but they could never make any charges stick. About how her grandmother devoted her entire life to trying to prove he did it.

356

She died several years back without any justice for her daughter.

I wonder if there was a brief moment when Grant and his fiancée had tried to make it work. They'd taken that photo, hoping for good things to come. Thinking of it, I press a hand to my stomach, cradling the bump that's only just starting to show now. I see Kirk's eyes flick down to my hand and his lips tighten. My pregnancy is inconvenient for him, because why would a newlywed who's carrying her husband's child want to murder him?

'There's a couple of details I want to go over with you,' he says. 'Starting with Grant's alleged drug use. You claimed in an earlier interview that he was regularly taking drugs, and yet this isn't something I've been able to corroborate with any of his friends or family members, even after all this time.'

'Grant was good at hiding his addiction,' I reply, lifting one shoulder into a shrug. 'A lot of addicts are. He was still a functioning adult with a business to run, so he never let it get to the point where it impacted his work. But he liked to party. Hard.'

I guess I'm technically not lying, although we're talking about two different types of addictions. Grant was addicted to using drugs . . . *on other people*. Women, specifically. From what I understand now, by going through Grant's secret emails and text messages, Kylie was far from the first.

'I find it strange that none of the people who supposedly partied with Grant ever noticed him take the drugs. Nor did he offer them around.'

'Do you think a man of his standing is looking to get himself a possession charge? Or worse, get labelled as a dealer?' I snort. 'My husband wasn't an idiot.'

'You still think of him as your husband, even though you were only married a few hours?' he replies testily.

'Of course. He was the love of my life.' I smile, but Kirk doesn't flinch. He continues to stare at me stonily.

'How did you come to learn about his drug use?'

We've been over this before. I retell the tale about finding the strange liquid in his suit-jacket pocket, only I fudge the dates. In this new version of the story it happened a few months before his death and we argued about it. A big fiery blow-up. Then I tell the detective I started monitoring him, and that I saw him take the drugs one night; that I knew he had a second phone to make calls to his dealer. A phone which 'frustratingly' no one has been able to find.

After I pushed Grant over the balcony, I went through his luggage and found the phone. It was filled with hundreds of photos of unconscious women, spread eagled, bruised, some lying in a pool of their own vomit. I downloaded all of the images – including screenshots of the text messages that Grant hadn't yet deleted – to a hard drive I brought with me to the wedding. Then I turned the phone off. The last place it pinged would have been the closest mobile phone tower to the winery where our wedding was held. Then I hid the phone in my own luggage and brought it home with me.

On the way to my lawyer's office in the city one morning, I wrapped the phone up in some napkins and stuffed it into a McDonald's takeaway bag filled with wrappers for a McChicken and some fries and an apple pie, and disposed of it all in a public rubbish bin. If the cops had been tracking my movements, then I wasn't going to risk driving out anywhere remote or strange, and unless they wanted to search every rubbish receptacle I passed in my day-to-day life, then they had no hope of finding that phone.

As for the hard drive, it's buried in the back yard. It's my insurance policy – because Grant isn't the only man who appears in the photos, standing over those poor women. There are at least ten different men featured. One is Tom, Grant's business partner at the freight company. Another I remember seeing at the wedding – one of his old university buddies. It seems Grant had a side hustle going, meeting business contacts in hotel rooms whenever they were in town and supplying a woman for them to assault.

My husband was a sex trafficker.

I don't think I'll ever be able to scrub those images from my mind. I didn't show them to Kylie. In fact, I never even told her there were images. The way she sobbed in my arms when she told me what he'd done . . .

I suspect it will haunt me for a long time. Probably forever.

As for justice, I haven't contacted Tom yet, but I'm putting a plan in place. There are several photos of him without Grant and without Kylie. When the time is right, I'll make sure he knows I'm watching.

'So you claim he was using regularly, then? GHB, specifically?' Kirk asks.

'I think so, but I don't use drugs myself so I'm not exactly sure. All I know is that any time he used, he wanted to have sex. Lots of it.' I look Kirk right in the eye to see if he squirms. He doesn't. 'Whatever he was taking, it increased his libido.'

'Did you know that GHB is commonly used as a date-rape drug?'

'I thought that was Rohypnol,' I reply innocently.

'There's more than one kind of drug that can be used for that purpose,' he says. His fingers are interlaced in front of him, the knuckles whiter than they should be.

'What are you getting at?'

'Are you aware that your husband was engaging in sexual relationships with other women?' He ignores my question and forges on.

Interesting. I was wondering when he might start down this line of questioning. It was only a matter of time before he came across some CCTV footage or a witness account that placed him with another woman.

'Yes, I was.'

'Really?' Kirk looks surprised but covers it quickly.

'We made an agreement to have a less . . . traditional style of relationship,' I lie. 'Frankly, Grant's sex drive was more than I could personally handle, especially once I found out I was pregnant and the morning sickness was making me feel nauseous all the time.'

'So you were happy to let him have sex with other women?'

'Yes,' I reply, swallowing back a wave of disgust. 'So long as he didn't form an ongoing relationship with anyone else. I loved him and I trusted him.'

The lies come easily because I've practised them over and over in the mirror. I cannot let my true feelings show. I cannot let my rage show. Because my whole defence hinges on me *not* having a motive to kill him . . . and that includes me not denying he was visiting hotels with other women.

Kirk is perplexed. He really thought digging up Grant's activity would be the key to solving his case. *Better luck next time, arsehole.*

'The amount of GHB found in Grant's system was well above what would be considered recreational use,' he says, switching tactics again.

I know this. We've been over this ad nauseum ever since the autopsy report came in.

'Okay . . .'

'Why do you think that would be?'

'How am I supposed to know? Like I've told you *many* times, Officer, I don't take drugs. I don't condone taking drugs either, which is why we argued about it. I didn't think it was safe to take something when you didn't know where it was made or what was truly in it.' I frown. 'He'd also been drinking a lot that night. Maybe he made a mistake.'

'He made a mistake in the dose he took and then he decided to go onto the balcony in the middle of a thunderstorm and then he magically fell over the edge into a pool?'

He's said this to me now more times than I can count. And I always have the same response. 'Inebriated people don't act with the same logic as sober people. Nor the same level of coordination.'

And he can't argue that.

'We never found the vial that the drugs came in.'

This was a problem with my plan. Since I slipped Grant the drugs, my fingerprints were on the fish-shaped vial. And since my not-so-darling husband went over the edge of the railing, I couldn't exactly wipe mine off and then press it to his fingers to reapply his. So I'd cleaned the container and flushed it down the toilet.

'Don't you find that odd?' Kirk says, watching me to see how I react.

'Perhaps it was in his pocket when he fell?' I suggested. 'It could have fallen into the pool or somewhere outside and then been washed away in the storm. Everything about that night is quite extraordinary, so I'm sure there are dozens of things that could have happened.'

'You don't seem greatly upset about the loss of your husband.'

But that's where he's wrong. I *am*.

Instead of mourning Grant Frenchman, however, I am mourning Toby.

Because we could have stuck out the financial difficulties.

We could have rebuilt things.

We could have survived.

He could have lived.

'Just because I don't allow you access to my private grief, Officer, doesn't mean that I'm not experiencing it.' It's my turn to be stony now. 'Because I am *very* sad for what I have lost. For what my child has lost.'

I cup my stomach again.

'One last question before I let you get back to your

362

day,' he says, unmoved. 'You recently withdrew a sum of thirty thousand dollars from Grant's bank account.'

'*My* bank account,' I correct him. 'It's a joint account, so that money was mine before the wedding.'

Kirk's nostrils flare. 'What did you do with the money?'

'I'm not sure it's any of your business what I do with my money, Officer.' I lean back in my chair and stare him down. 'But if you must know, I made a donation to an advocacy group for victims of sexual assault.'

'That's a generous donation.'

It's the first of many.

'I'm a generous person. And I believe Grant would want me to continue using my money to do good in the world.'

He would fucking not, but I'm no longer bound to care about what my second husband wanted.

Kirk makes a grunting sound and I'm not exactly sure what it's supposed to mean.

'If you like, I can show you the receipt,' I offer. 'I made the donation in his memory. He was extremely charitable, my husband. When his father died a few years back, the family asked that donations be made to a Parkinson's research centre. Grant himself made a donation so large they have his name on one of the rooms there.'

Kirk's eyes flick back and forth.

Maybe I should have waited longer to make the donation, but Grant *had* done enough fundraising for various charities that it shouldn't look too suspicious. Of course, when Grant was alive any charitable work was about making business contacts rather than actually helping anyone, but the police don't know that.

And thirty thousand dollars doesn't even come close to taking the edge off my guilt. Nor my shame. How had I lived with a monster for *so* long and not seen what he was? Not known the harm he was causing others? I existed in ignorant bliss because he never laid a hand on me. I guess I never did anything that made him want to.

For a moment I swear I feel the baby shift inside me, even though I know it's only a trick of the mind. It's too early for that.

If I'd told him I was pregnant, then . . .

Maybe I would be the one who had an accident.

'You have an answer for everything, Mrs Frenchman,' Kirk says.

'It's Ms Gallo,' I remind him, standing up to indicate the interview is over. I'll keep my calm with the overzealous detective but I won't allow myself to be led into any traps.

My days of being kept in the dark are over.

Epilogue

Five months later . . .

Camille

We sit, hands linked, in the waiting room at the hospital, anticipating an update. Adriana has been in labour for more than seven hours now. Isabel has been staying at her place and drove her here as soon as the contractions started. Then she called us – Kylie and me – and we came as soon as we could. I'm itching to go outside for a smoke, but I want to be here as soon as the doctor calls us in. So I sit with the women, waiting. Excited.

The group is almost unrecognizable from the night of the wedding.

Isabel has cut her hair into a blond pixie cut, leaving her scars free for the world to see. She doesn't try to hide them anymore. They're evidence of what she has survived. She's enrolled in university now, too, as a mature student, and wants to become a lawyer for non-profit groups, helping those in a vulnerable position in society.

Kylie is currently two months clean, after a relapse.

But in general she's doing well and we're all so proud of her for getting back on the horse. She sees a therapist who has a long history of working with victims of sexual assault, and has started taking adult ballet classes. Oh, and she's got her own place now. Adriana helped her out with a loan and the place is small, but it's only a block from Beth's apartment. They're in the process of repairing their relationship and it's going slow but well.

As for Adriana . . . well, she's about to take on the one role she never envisaged: mother. It's a word that's hard for us all, in many ways. I miss my mum like nothing else, even though I was just a baby when she died. What I've missed is the presence of a mother figure. My grandmother did her best, but she was so broken by losing her daughter that she was never able to nurture me the way I needed. She poured her hate for my father into me for years. I think she would be happy with how things turned out.

As for Dale . . . God. My dear, sweet Dale.

We shared our mother and her surname, but had different fathers. So he had none of Grant Frenchman's darkness inside him. He was, in many ways, my soulmate – if a soulmate can be a platonic familial relationship and not a romantic one. If not a soulmate, then he was my guardian angel. He understood me and he took me in when my grandmother passed away the day before my seventeenth birthday, even though we hadn't grown up together.

He barely knew me and yet as soon as he knew I was alone, he made us a family. He loved me.

I still visit his grave every week and play that last voicemail message whenever I feel lonely. I'm not over the fact that he left those words for me ten minutes before a drunk driver ran a red light and ploughed into his car. I don't think I'll ever get over it.

But at least now, however, I am one of the Young Widows, even if only an honorary member. So I have sisters, instead of a mother and brother.

It doesn't matter that I'm not actually a widow. It doesn't matter that I lurked around these women, at one time unseen, while I tried to piece together what was going on. I'd been watching Adriana for months before I figured out that Isabel was both part of the widows' group *and* my father's receptionist.

That seemed like *way* too much of a coincidence not to mean something. So I found a way in. I saw her real name on her licence one day when she left her bag at the café table to use the bathroom. When I searched her name online, I found a little article about a sexual assault that had occurred at her university and the pieces all clicked into place.

At the sight of the doctor coming into the waiting room, we all shoot to our feet.

'Mum and baby are ready to see you now,' she says with a smile.

We hurry down the hallway, chittering eagerly, and pile into Adriana's room. This is no ordinary hospital room. It's comfortable and luxurious, with art on the wall and a vase of flowers on a table in the corner. Adriana is propped up in bed, with a tiny little jellybean of a human in her arms. The swaddled baby has a shock of dark hair, like my dad.

This is my half-sister. I swallow and fight the tears that want to rush forth.

'How are you doing?' Isabel's brows crease as she squeezes Adriana's arm.

For one, she looks spent. Her hair is damp, her cheeks are flushed, and there's a sheen of sweat on her skin. Exhaustion is etched into her face, but there's also a smile. Relief. I can feel it in the air.

'I'd like you all to meet Hannah.' Adriana's eyes catch mine and my knees almost buckle.

It's my mum's name. The name I used to befriend these women. A name that, to me at least, represents the triumph of sisterhood. Of how strong we can be when we work together.

I brush away the tears that escape my eyes and look down at the sleepy little baby. 'She would be so happy knowing her name lives on.'

'It's a beautiful name.' Adriana reaches her free hand for mine. 'I hope it's okay?'

'It's more than okay.'

None of us mentions the dark hair, the clear imprint Grant has left on this child.

None of us mentions that Isabel started this group to use Adriana as a weapon.

None of us mentions that I was stalking the lot of them, trying to get close to my dad, in order to find out if he really was a monster. It all goes onto the pile of things we don't talk about, chief amongst them being the fact that we murdered a man in cold blood.

My only regret is that I didn't get to hold his head under myself.

Acknowledgements

I'm not sure what it says about me if I tell you this is the book of my heart, but in many ways it is. My husband and I came up with the idea for *The Young Widows* (at least, its first iteration) over dinner after I declared that instead of writing a happy book, I wanted to write a dark, angry, vengeful, cathartic book. We were almost the last people in the restaurant because we had talked for literal hours about this idea, tweaking it and coming up with other story ideas. It was a night of pure joy and creativity.

So, my first thank you must go to my husband, Justin. We've faced some dark times ourselves in the last few years, and I am constantly in awe of your resilience and ambition. I wouldn't be able to do this without you helping me back up every time I stumble. Thank you for always believing I can take the next step.

A huge thank you to my agent, Jill Marsal, who not only supported me in writing something totally different from my previous books but also provided multiple rounds of valuable feedback to help shape this story into what it is now. I can't overstate how wonderful it is to work with an agent who always pushes you to be your best and who is always up for the challenge of trying something new.

Thank you to the Harper Collins UK and Avon team, particularly Sarah Bauer and Helen Huthwaite, for taking a chance on *The Young Widows* and understanding what I was hoping to achieve with this story. Thank you for giving it a wonderful home and for all your clever insights during the editing process.

Thank you to my family for always asking *how's the writing going?* knowing you could get literally any kind of response. And a big thanks especially for letting me commandeer your office so I could work on revisions when I was visiting, and to Cici and Zorro for keeping my lap warm while I was working.

There are so many other people I could thank and I hate to leave anyone out. But I want to say a blanket thank you to all the people who've ever supported my writing in any way, big or small. It truly means the world. This job is not for the faint of heart, but I can't think of anything I could possibly love as much as dreaming up stories, and I couldn't do it without readers, reviewers, librarians, booksellers and everyone else who touches the publishing industry. You're all amazing.

Look out for S. J. Short's next book, coming soon!